WELCOME to PECULIAR

WITCHES of PECULIAR

WELCOME to PECULIAR

* ✴ DOUBLE, DOUBLE, TWINS AND TROUBLE
* ✴ THRILLER NIGHT
* ✴ MONSTROUS MATCHMAKERS
* ✴ GLIMPSE THE FUTURE

LUNA GRAVES

ALADDIN
NEW YORK   LONDON   TORONTO   SYDNEY   NEW DELHI

This book is a work of fiction. Any references to historical events, real people, or real places are used fictitiously. Other names, characters, places, and events are products of the author's imagination, and any resemblance to actual events or places or persons, living or dead, is entirely coincidental.

ALADDIN
An imprint of Simon & Schuster Children's Publishing Division
1230 Avenue of the Americas, New York, New York 10020
This Aladdin paperback edition May 2023
Double, Double, Twins and Trouble; Thriller Night; Monstrous Matchmakers
copyright © 2022 by Simon & Schuster, Inc.
Glimpse the Future copyright © 2023 by Simon & Schuster, Inc.
Cover illustration copyright © 2023 by Laura Catrinella
Interior illustrations copyright © 2022–2023 by Laura Catrinella
All rights reserved, including the right of reproduction in whole or in part in any form.
ALADDIN and related logo are registered trademarks of Simon & Schuster, Inc.
For information about special discounts for bulk purchases, please contact Simon & Schuster Special Sales at 1-866-506-1949 or business@simonandschuster.com.
The Simon & Schuster Speakers Bureau can bring authors to your live event. For more information or to book an event contact the Simon & Schuster Speakers Bureau at 1-866-248-3049 or visit our website at www.simonspeakers.com.
Designed by Heather Palisi
The text of this book was set in Really No. 2.
Manufactured in the United States of America 0423 OFF
2 4 6 8 10 9 7 5 3 1
Library of Congress Control Number 2023932016
ISBN 9781665933612
ISBN 9781665906241 (*Double, Double, Twins and Trouble* ebook)
ISBN 9781665906265 (*Thriller Night* ebook)
ISBN 9781665906289 (*Monstrous Matchmakers* ebook)
ISBN 9781665906302 (*Glimpse the Future* ebook)
These titles were previously published individually in hardcover and paperback by Aladdin.

CONTENTS

DOUBLE, DOUBLE, TWINS AND TROUBLE

CHAPTER 1

Since its founding in 1692 as a safe haven during the witch trials, Yvette I. Koffin's Exceptional School for Supernatural Students has seen its fair share of catastrophe and tomfoolery. Take, for instance, the year 1906, when Gertie the ghoul got stuck inside the faculty gramophone for three days. Or that unfortunate morning in 1844, when a mischievous warlock put sleeping elixir in the potion master's tea to get out of a test and ended up exploding the entire east wing. (Nightshade and caffeine do *not* mix well, it turns out.) It's even rumored that there was a week, in 1717, when the dormitories inexplicably disappeared. Most suspect that particular incident was not a prank but instead had something to do with the veil of protection that hangs over the school grounds, making all magical goings-on invisible to any human that might be passing by.

And yet, despite all the chaos the school has endured over the years, never in the history of YIKESSS has any student caused such widespread destruction as Bella and Donna Maleficent—and on their first day of sixth grade, no less!

It's a dreary Monday in Peculiar, Pennsylvania, when their story begins. An hour ago, before the Maleficent twins set foot in Spell Casting class, the window in Yvette

Koffin's tower framed a view of birds chirping beneath clear, sunny skies. Now, however, a steady rain rattles against the glass, and gusts of wind shriek as they roll through the hemlock trees in the courtyard below.

Unlike the rest of the school, Principal Koffin's office is mostly dry, save for two young witches, soaking wet and sulking on a bench in the center of the room. While the principal is nowhere to be found, a four-eyed crow sits on its perch behind her desk, silent but alert. It has two dark, beady eyes locked on each of the Maleficent twins.

"This is all your fault," Donna says quietly. Her arms are crossed, her gaze fixed straight ahead. A tiny raindrop falls from her chin onto her emerald-green blazer, right in the center of the YIKESSS school crest. It doesn't matter. The blazer, like the rest of her uniform, is already drenched.

"*My* fault?" Bella is wringing the rain out of her long black hair and letting it pool around her feet. There's so much water on the floor already, she figures a little more won't make a difference. "No way, Dee. I was only cleaning up *your* mess."

Dee squeezes her eyes shut. Conjuring those huge, desk-devouring flames in Spell Casting and nearly burning down the school was definitely *not* how her first day as a Real and Powerful Witch was supposed to go. After she'd spent five years trying and failing to blend in at the human school, YIKESSS was supposed to be a fresh start. Her chance to finally be a normal witch.

Bella, on the other hand, has never been satisfied with normal. When the twins came into their powers over the summer and they received their official welcome letter from YIKESSS, Bella assured Dee that sixth grade was going to be *their* year. It didn't matter that nobody liked them at the human school. Now that they had full access to their powers, all the supernatural kids would want to be their friends.

And then Spell Casting happened.

After a lesson on conjuring, Bella and Dee's teacher, Professor Belinda, had the class practicing simple sparks, a spell so easy that even a human could do it. At least that's what Bella said when Dee wasn't getting it right.

"Turn your wrists to a hundred and thirty degrees, Dee," Bella explained, repeating Professor Belinda's words in that annoying, know-it-all tone of hers that made Dee want to zap her own ears off. "No, not like that. Spread your fingers apart, like you're turning a really big doorknob. Here, watch me."

Bella is the older by five minutes and is always telling Dee how things should and should not be done. Or how *she* believes things should and should not be done, anyway.

"But I didn't *need* your help," Dee says now, opening her eyes and slouching farther into the bench. A stray black curl, sopping wet and heavy, falls over her face. She tucks it behind her ear with a huff.

"Oh, you did too," Bella says. "You *always* do."

Dee's jaw drops in outrage. "Do not!"

"Do too!"

Dee fixes Bella with a glare. "I would never even have conjured those flames in the first place if you hadn't distracted me. You're so pushy."

"Pushy?" When the desk they shared caught fire, Bella didn't hesitate. She did what any brave witch would have done in her situation: she *acted*. That wasn't pushy. It was heroic. Besides, she only meant to summon a little rain. It wasn't her fault her magic was so strong that she summoned a storm cloud all the way from Seattle instead.

"A good witch always listens to their instincts," Bella says matter-of-factly. It was one of the first things she learned in *A Beginner's Guide to Witchcraft*, the Level 1 Spell Casting handbook she's already read cover to cover. "And my instincts were telling me I *had* to summon the storm cloud to stop the fire."

"You could've summoned a fire extinguisher," Dee mumbles. "That would have been way less messy."

Bella frowns at Dee, frustrated and a little hurt. Why can't her sister see that she was only trying to help? She looks out the window and starts fiddling with her necklace, a silver crescent moon on a thin chain. It was a first-day-of-school gift from the girls' dads. Dee got one too, except instead of a moon her charm is a gold star. *The moon and stars work together to light up the night,* their dad Antony—or Dad—explained, presenting the twins with two dark jewelry boxes. *Stronger together,* their dad Ron—whom the girls call Pop—added. *Just like the two of you.*

Bella thinks about that crucial moment in Spell Casting, the one when Dee's sloppy wristwork—she looked more like she was swatting a fly than opening a door—made their desk catch fire. Bella remembers staring at the flames, so tall that they grazed the ceiling, and imagining, for one terrifying moment, those flames reaching out like tentacles and snatching Dee away.

So Bella curled her hands into fists, let the fire turn her green eyes red, and thought, *Make it rain.* And rain it did, all over the classrooms, the hallways, and the rest of the school grounds, inside and out. She'd had no idea such a simple spell could be so powerful. By the time Professor Belinda managed to banish the storm outside, the entire first floor of the school was flooded.

On the dark side, at least the fire was out.

"I don't care what you think." Bella flips her wet hair over her shoulder with a flick of her wrist. She's been waiting her whole life to grow into her powers, and now that she has, Dee wants her to feel bad about using them? No way. "I stopped the fire, and I'm not sorry."

Dee rolls her eyes, the same shade of radioactive green as her sister's. Dee knows getting Bella to admit she's wrong is like pulling vampire fangs. Most of the time it's pointless to even try.

Dee sighs and looks down at her black Mary Janes, a brand-new pair for the new school year. When she put them on at breakfast, she imagined all the different places the shoes would take her. To the courtyard, where she could listen to music by the mermaid fountain. To the flyball field for her first broom-flying lesson. To a lunch table in the center of the cafeteria, surrounded by friends. She had not imagined they would bring her here, to the principal's office. She should probably pay extra attention in Clairvoyance class this year.

"When Principal Koffin comes, let me do the talking, okay?" Dee looks at Bella. "We're going to be in enough trouble as it is."

For the first time since they arrived, Bella's brow creases with concern. "You think we'll get in trouble?"

"Duh," Dee says. She looks up at the four-eyed crow, quiet on its perch. Two of its eyes are still watching her, unblinking.

Bella stands up quickly and starts pacing in

small circles. "But it was an accident," she says. Her black boots squeak with every step she takes. The crow uses its other pair of eyes to follow her movements. "We can't be punished for an *accident*."

"We're in the principal's office, Bella," Dee says, shaking her head. "And Principal Koffin is a *harpy*. Haven't you heard what harpy principals do to kids who break the rules?"

Bella stops pacing. "What do they do?"

Dee glances back at the crow, a mischievous look in her eye. Then she sits up straighter and reaches her hands out toward Bella, hooking her fingers like talons. "They snatch them up with their big, birdy claws, fly them back to their nest, and *peck out* their eyes."

Bella's face is skeptical. "Really?"

"No, doofus," Dee says, relaxing into her seat again. "We'll probably just get detention."

Bella's eyes grow wide. "I *can't* get detention," she cries. "It will ruin my chances of getting on Horror Roll!"

Dee shakes her head in disbelief. She's pretty sure Bella loves school more than Dee loves anything. Well, except maybe strawberry milkshakes. And cats. "So you don't get on Horror Roll," Dee says. "Big deal."

"It *is* a big deal!" Bella stomps her foot, and red sparks fly out from beneath her heel. Suddenly the bookcase behind her starts to tremble.

"What's going on?" Dee jumps up. "What did you do?"

"I don't know!" Bella replies, and the trembling intensifies. A stack of books falls from the top shelf and lands with a heavy *thud* just inches from where she stands. Bella lets out a scream of surprise. Around her more furniture starts to shake.

"What does the handbook say about stopping earthquakes?" Dee yells.

"It doesn't!" Bella shouts back. "Natural disasters are Level Two!"

A thick, leather-bound book falls from the middle shelf and grazes Bella's shoulder. She jumps to the side, screams again. That's when Dee realizes: the more Bella panics, the worse the earthquake gets.

"You have to stop freaking out!" Dee says. She extends a hand toward her sister. "Seriously, Bella! *Stop!*"

Blue sparks fly from Dee's fingertips, and a moment later the room goes still and silent. Bella and Dee let out synchronized sighs of relief.

"Wow," Dee says, more to herself than Bella. She pulls her hand back, examines it. Did *she* do that? Fascinated by her fingers, Dee takes a careless step backward and collides with an antique lamp on Principal Koffin's desk. It starts to tip forward.

"Watch out!" Bella calls, pointing over Dee's shoulder.

Dee lunges for the lamp and catches it just before it crashes to the floor, but in her haste she accidentally fires off a giggle charm that hits the four-eyed crow. The bird lets out a string of low, even snickers.

Bella smacks a hand to her forehead. The girls still do not have complete control over their powers and, as such, are no strangers to occasional magical mishaps. "Jeepers creepers, Dee."

Unsure how to reverse the spell, Dee tries the same one that worked on the earthquake. "Stop!" she says, one hand clutching the lamp and the other pointing at the crow. "Stop laughing!"

It doesn't work this time. The bird continues to snicker.

Bella crouches over the fallen books. "Quick, put the lamp back and help me pick these up before—"

The door swings open, and the sisters look up. The rest of Bella's sentence dies in her throat.

Standing ominously in the doorway, her dark red wings filling up the mahogany frame behind her, is Principal Yvette Koffin.

CHAPTER 2

Principal Koffin is tall, even for a harpy. Measuring just over seven feet from the bottom of her taloned toes to the top of her blond head, and with a wingspan nearly double that, she's a perpetually looming presence. She's older than the school, though no one knows exactly how old, and has lived in Peculiar since long before it was even given that name. For centuries she has been walking the halls of YIKESSS with her sharp chin in the air, her hands clasped tightly in front of her, and her dark red wings tucked behind her—resembling a cape. Only those unlucky enough to get on her bad side know how the red goes from dark to bright on the undersides.

Inside her office, wet and frowning, Principal Koffin closes the door behind her. She stretches her wings out wide, casting a shadow over Bella and Dee. A crack of thunder booms outside the window. The four-eyed crow stops its snickering at once.

"Bella and Donna Maleficent." Principal Koffin's voice is stern. "I wish I could say I am surprised to see the two of you here."

The twins exchange a glance. Unfortunately, their reputation as mischief-makers preceded their arrival at YIKESSS. There were a few "incidents" at their human school, magical flare-ups that sometimes occur when a young witch is growing into their powers. Most witches generate little inconveniences—for instance, a disappearing doorknob, or a sneeze that turns their hand blue—but Bella's and Dee's flares were bigger, and much harder to cover up. The humans didn't know exactly how the twins managed to zap their cranky teacher's hair hot pink, or turn the whole school's chalk supply into worms, but everyone suspected that they were involved.

Principal Koffin flaps her wings once, twice, until she's hovering a few feet off the floor. Dee puts the lamp back on the desk and hurries to Bella's side. Bella shrinks back, leaning into her sister for comfort.

"It was an accident, I swear!" Bella covers her face with her hands. "Please, *please* don't give us detention or peck out our eyes!"

Principal Koffin gives Bella a disapproving look. Instead of responding, she flutters her wings quickly, sending tiny droplets of water flying across the room. When she lands on the floor again, she tucks her wings behind her back and smooths down her long red skirt.

Dee puts on a nervous smile. "Um, about the books, and the lamp? We can explain—" she starts, but Principal Koffin interrupts her.

"I saw everything that happened." The principal gives the four-eyed crow a pointed look. "Argus and I have a special connection."

"You mean, like, you can see into his mind?" Bella drops her hands, a look of wonderment on her face.

Principal Koffin, crossing the room to sit behind her desk, nods once. Her movements are so swift and silent that it almost looks like she's floating.

"Creepy!" Bella moves to get a closer look at Argus. "I want one!"

Argus squawks, then flaps his wings and perches on Principal Koffin's shoulder.

"Sit down, girls," Principal Koffin says, and then does so herself. The sisters do as they're told, with Bella perching anxiously on the edge of the bench and Dee slouching into it, more relaxed.

Principal Koffin glances from one twin to the other. "I assume you know why you're here?"

"We do," Bella said. "But like I said before, it was a total *accident*—"

Principal Koffin holds up a hand to silence her. "You do not have to explain it to me. As I said before, I know *everything* that happened. I know about the fire, the storm cloud, and the earthquake."

Dee grimaces. "You do?"

Principal Koffin looks at Argus. She reaches out one long, slender finger and scratches him under the chin. "There are many crows that call YIKESSS home." She looks back at Dee. "And crows love to talk."

"Really?" Bella examines Argus curiously. "Well, what'd they say?"

"They believe that you two did not mean to cause the school any harm. It was, as you said—" Here Principal Koffin raises one sharp eyebrow at Bella. "An accident."

"So does that mean you're not mad?" Bella asks hopefully. Dee looks into two of Argus's eyes and gives him a small smile.

"No," Principal Koffin says. "In fact, I think your display in Spell Casting was quite impressive."

The sisters drop their jaws in unison.

"It has been many years since I have seen such powerful spellwork from witches as young as yourselves," Principal Koffin says. The corner of her mouth turns up into what could *almost* be considered a smile. "Indeed, Bella and Donna Maleficent, I think you will do quite well here."

"Really?" Dee sits up a little straighter. She thinks, again, about that lunch table at the center of the cafeteria. She imagines herself zapping milkshakes from Scary Good Shakes into the hands of all her new friends. She bites her bottom lip to hide her smile.

"So does that mean we won't get detention?" Bella asks.

Principal Koffin nods again. "You will not be receiving any detention today."

Bella breathes out a heavy sigh of relief.

"*But*," Principal Koffin continues, "while your spellwork was impressive, it was also very dangerous. You put your classmates in harm's way, almost destroyed the academy, and risked exposing us to the entire town."

Bella fidgets in her seat. "But it was an—"

"Accidents still have consequences, I'm afraid," Principal Koffin says. "As a result, you two are prohibited from practicing hands-on magic on school grounds for two weeks." As if to emphasize the principal's point, Argus lets out a squawk.

"What?" Bella and Dee say at the same time.

"Two weeks? But that's not fair!" Bella says, jumping out of her seat. Principal Koffin gives her a stern look of warning, and she quickly sits back down. "Can't we have detention instead?"

"Try to understand, girls." Principal Koffin picks up a pair of spectacles and places them on her nose. "Peculiar is a safe haven for the supernatural community, but only because we have gotten so good at hiding in plain sight. What do you think the humans would do if they found out there were monsters living among them?"

Dee shrugs. Despite failing to fit in with her classmates at her last school, she has always had a soft spot for humans. It must be nice not to have to worry that you're going to accidentally destroy the whole town.

"They would cast us out," Principal Koffin continues. A dark look crosses over her face, but she quickly blinks it away.

"But we don't know that for sure," Dee argues. She thinks of one time last year, when a boy in her math class, Peter, watched her sneeze and turn the chalk in her hand into a worm. He was surprised, but as far as she knew, he never told anyone what he saw. That had to count for something. "Things have changed. Humans are more accepting than they used to be."

"Some of them, perhaps, but not all," Principal Koffin says. "So we must be careful."

"We *promise* to be careful," Bella says, her green eyes wide and pleading. "If you just let us do magic, I promise we will *never* risk the safety of the monsters in Peculiar again!"

Principal Koffin fixes her gaze on Bella. Her eyes are magnified behind her spectacles, making them look like dark orbs.

"After the accident today, Professor Belinda had to fly to the news station and bewitch the weatherman so he could explain the storm cloud to the human community. No harm done, really. But what if your next accident is not so easily concealed?"

"But—" Bella whines.

"Do I need to remind you about the council's warning after your last . . . *incident* at your human school?"

"No," Dee says quickly. Bella shakes her head. They're both thinking about the yell-o-gram the Creepy Council sent to their house after the chalk-worm incident. Though Peter never told anyone what happened, the council has spies everywhere. They made it clear that the twins were being watched at school. It wasn't something anyone in the Maleficent family would soon forget.

"*Two* weeks," Principal Koffin says. "And not a word more shall be said on the matter. Take this time to think about the mistakes that were made and consider how they can be avoided in the future."

Bella crosses her arms. "Hmph." She slumps back in her seat like Dee.

Principal Koffin stands up, and Argus returns to his perch. She walks to the small stack of books that fell during the earthquake and gathers them in her arms. Then she flaps her wings and flies to the top of the tall bookcase, returning them to their rightful place.

"Patience is a skill, girls," Principal Koffin says from above, her focus no longer on the twins but on organizing the books alphabetically.

"One you would do well to acquaint yourselves with."

The sisters leave Principal Koffin's office feeling defeated. Bella stomps down the spiral staircase back to the main corridor, while Dee trails behind her, quiet except for her growling stomach.

"This is so unfair," Bella grumbles.

"At least it's just two weeks," Dee says. "Hey, when's lunch again?"

"Two weeks is *plenty* of time for us to fall behind," Bella says, snapping her head around. "Don't you want to be the best?"

Dee shrugs. She mainly wants to get through the rest of the day without embarrassing herself. Still, she can't help but replay Principal Koffin's words of encouragement in her mind: *Bella and Donna Maleficent, I think you will do quite well here.*

Bella pushes open the door to the main corridor, and the sisters are met with a wave of clapping and chatter. Bella steps through the doorway and stops in her tracks. Dee, lost in her thoughts of what could be, bumps into Bella's back.

In the middle of the hallway, surrounded by a crowd of students cheering her on, their classmate Crypta Cauldronson is conjuring an arc of perfect blue sparks.

"Oh, for the love of all that's unholy," Bella says with a scowl. "Does she have to show off like that?"

~~~~~• CHAPTER 3 •~~~~~

In the cafeteria the Maleficent twins are positively glum. While the incident in Spell Casting has made them the subject of many curious
glances and whispered remarks, it hasn't done
much to give them any actual friends. As a
result, Bella and Dee sit at a table by themselves
at the edge of the room, close to one of the big

bay windows that face the courtyard gardens. The glass in all the windows at YIKESSS filters out UV rays that would be considered harmful to ghosts, ghouls, and vampires. Outside, the storm still rages on. Dee watches absently as a handful of garden gnomes tend to the flowers, protected from the rain by their little mushroom umbrellas.

"Crypta Cauldronson," Bella says, glaring into her lunch box. "She thinks she's *so* amazing because her mom is president of the Creepy Council." Bella pulls out a banana and slams it down onto the table.

Every monster in Peculiar knows Crypta Cauldronson's mother, Gretchen. Or at least they know her voice. As president of the Creepy Council, she sends out monthly memos detailing the latest community events and supernatural goings-on. There are a variety of ways in which monsters can choose to receive these memos, but in the Maleficent household memos are delivered to the shrunken skull that sits on the living room mantel. Ms. Cauldronson also sends yell-o-grams: warnings delivered right to the ears of monsters who act in ways that threaten to expose the supernatural community to the humans. Rumor has it that the yell-o-grams are usually the secretary's responsibility but Gretchen Cauldronson likes yelling so much that she volunteers to do them herself.

Thanks to Bella's and Dee's flare-ups, the twins have been on the receiving end of three yell-o-grams, each more threatening than the one before. In the yell-o-gram after the chalkworm incident, Ms. Cauldronson warned that if they put the supernatural community at risk one more time, their family would have to leave Peculiar. That means it isn't just Bella's and Dee's futures on the line but their dads' futures as well.

Dee unzips her lunch box, then pulls out a square piece of paper and unfolds it. When she recognizes the handwriting, she grins. "It's a note from Dad and Pop."

Dearest Deedee, we hope you have an
amazing first day! Knock 'em dead! But
not literally!
We love you,
Dad & Pop
P.S. The green stuff on your sandwich is
pesto sauce. It's Ant's new recipe! Try it,
you'll like it.

Dee's smile fades. "They're going to be so disappointed." She folds up the note and puts it back inside her lunch box. "They told us to make friends, not natural disasters."

She clutches her star necklace and recalls her dads waving from the doorway that morning as she and Bella walked to the bus stop. Antony is a ghost, so he's translucent, but his smile was so big that she could see it from all the way down the block. And Ron, a werewolf whose human form resembles a huggable lumberjack, was actually wiping away tears. They had never looked so proud.

Bella digs through her lunch box and finds her own note. Instead of reading it, she crumples it up and throws it.

"Really nice," Dee says, frowning at her sister. "Throwing tantrums is a *great* way to make new friends."

The note lands on the floor several feet away, and bounces off the sneaker of a student with light brown skin and dark hair. They're standing in the middle of the aisle, tightly clutching their lunch tray.

"Um." The student looks down at the paper, and then up at Bella and Dee. That's when the twins notice their eyes, the telltale bright red of a vampire. "Did—did you drop this?"

"'Drop' is one way of putting it," Dee says, perking up at the chance to meet someone new. She gets out of her chair and walks over to pick up the paper. "Wow, I love your shoes!"

"Hey," Bella says, studying the vampire as Dee puts the note in front of her again and sits back down. "You okay? You look a little sick."

The vampire shuffles their feet. "My friends on the flyball team are sitting over there," they say, and then look left, toward a table in the center of the room. "And my friends from choir are sitting all the way over there." The vampire looks right, toward the tables by the kitchen. "And I can't decide who I should sit with." They look back at Bella and Dee. "What if I choose wrong and I hurt someone's feelings?"

"Well, you've got to decide sometime," Bella says. She takes the sandwich out of her lunch box and unwraps it. "Or are you going to eat your lunch standing up?" She brings the sandwich closer to her face, studies the bread. "Ew, what's this green stuff?"

"Or you could sit with us?" Dee offers, giving Bella a disapproving look before smiling up at the vampire. "That's what she meant to say."

"Really?" The vampire's bright red eyes dart from Dee to Bella, looking unsure. "You're not saving these for your friends?"

"Jeepers creepers, it's the first day of school,"

Bella says, looking around the room. "How does everybody else have friends already?"

"Probably because they didn't spend their morning in the principal's office," Dee mutters.

The vampire clears their throat. "So, should I . . ."

"Oh!" Bella snaps her head up and scoots her chair over. "Right, sorry. Sit next to me!"

"Okay." The vampire smiles, revealing two pointy white fangs. "Thanks." They put their tray down next to Bella.

"What's your name?" Dee asks, picking up Bella's banana.

"Charlie," they say, and then take a bite of pepperoni pizza. "And by the way, my pronouns are 'they, them.' How about you?"

"Donna," she says. "But call me 'Dee.'"

"And I'm Bella. Our pronouns are 'she, her.'" Bella leans a little closer to Charlie. "We're witches."

"Bella and Donna Maleficent?" A goblin with

light green skin, pointy ears, and orange hair appears, seemingly out of nowhere. His clothes and hair are damp, and he's bouncing in place at the end of their table. "*The* Bella and Donna Maleficent?"

"She prefers 'Dee,'" Charlie says, and Dee smiles into her lap.

"Spooktacular!" the goblin says. "I'm Eugene, and I just wanna say that I think you witches are absolute *legends*. You've gotta tell me all about what went down in Spell Casting."

Dee's smile fades. "You heard about that?"

"Of course! The whole school knows." Eugene sits in the empty seat next to Dee, who sinks farther into her chair with embarrassment. He pulls his green eyephone out of his pocket. The eye opens, and the screen lights up.

"Check this out," he says, and then hands the phone to Dee. It's a video of a classroom caught in the midst of a torrential downpour. Students are scrambling for cover, running into the hallway and ducking under desks.

Above all the screaming, Dee can hear Eugene's commentary from behind the phone. *"Totally crazy! I mean, this rain just came out of nowhere and it's already flooding the room. I wonder if I could turn one of these desks into a rowboat? Oh, snap! Was that thunder? Or was it my stomach? Ha! Man, I'm hungry—"*

Dee puts the eyephone down on the table, groaning. "Great. Who's going to want to be friends with us now?"

"Uh, hello? Me!" Eugene says as Bella snatches up the phone. "Tell me everything. Were the flames really as big as everyone says? Did the desk *just* catch fire, or was there more cool destruction? And what was with all that rain?"

"That was me. *I* summoned a storm cloud all the way from Seattle," Bella chimes in, sliding Eugene's phone back to him. "I'm the one who put the fire out."

Dee shakes her head. Leave it to Bella to brag about their accident now that they aren't in any serious trouble.

"You put it out?" Eugene says, his excitement fading. "Bummer."

"*You're* the one who flooded the school?" Charlie says, shocked at Bella. "My socks are soaked because of you!"

Bella crosses her arms, scowling at them both, and Dee feels a wicked sort of satisfaction.

"Hey, you're witches," Eugene says. "Can you zap us dry?"

Bella snorts. "Don't you think that if we could zap ourselves dry, we would've done it by now?"

Dee meets Bella's eyes and frowns. Dee mouths, *Be nice.* In response Bella sticks out her tongue.

"What Bella means to say," Dee chimes in, "is that we aren't allowed. We got banned from doing magic on school grounds for two weeks." Not to mention, she doubts whether they even have enough control over their powers to successfully pull off a spell like that. But she decides to keep that part to herself.

"That's totally unfair!" Eugene says.

"I don't know," Charlie says nervously. "Maybe it's for the best. I mean, no offense, but I don't think I can handle any more surprises. My stomach is *way* too sensitive for that."

"BOO!"

A translucent ghost in a suit and top hat pops up in the middle of the table, making Charlie and Dee scream and jump in their seats. The ghost, whom the students now recognize as their vice principal, Augustus "Gus" Archaic, keels over in a fit of laughter.

"Oh!" he says between giggles. "Oh! I got you!"

"A ghost who says 'boo'?" Bella asks, looking unimpressed. "Kind of unoriginal, don't you think?"

Vice Principal Archaic twiddles his handlebar mustache. "Perhaps. But still a highly effective form of scaring." He points at Charlie, who looks a little green. "I mean, just look how scared they are!"

Dee gives Charlie a sympathetic look. She is not a fan of being scared either. If Vice Principal Archaic were a spider, or a creepy doll, Dee would be halfway across the cafeteria by now.

"Vice Principal Archaic," Bella says. She points at a table near the center of the cafeteria, where Crypta Cauldronson is seated. "I think that table could use a good scare, don't you?"

"Excellent idea, Miss Maleficent." Vice Principal Archaic rubs his hands together. "Oh, I do love keeping you students on your gnarly toes!"

He disappears. A moment later Crypta's scream cuts through the cafeteria chatter. Bella grins, then takes a big bite of her sandwich.

"Does he always do that?" Dee asks, looking warily after the vice principal.

"Unfortunately," Charlie says. They push their tray into the center of the table, their appetite gone. "This morning I saw him jump out of a water fountain in the crypts. He scared Trixie Fae half to death." They glance from Dee to Bella. "There was pixie dust *everywhere*."

"I heard he's been scaring since the beginning of time," Eugene adds. "You know that one painting of the screaming man?" He puts his hands on his cheeks and drops his jaw, mimicking someone about to let out a bloodcurdling scream. "Apparently, Archaic is the one who scared the man."

"Well, he's not going to scare me," Bella says, still munching on her sandwich. As it turns out, she quite likes the green stuff on the bread. "I'm unscareable. I'm going to be the next Bloody Mary."

"No way," Eugene says. Every monster knows the legend of Bloody Mary, but few have been lucky enough to meet her in person. She's quite elusive and can only be summoned by great power or extreme fear. "Have you ever met her?"

"Not yet," Bella admits. She thinks about all the hours she has spent in front of the bathroom mirror with the lights off, holding a candle and chanting Mary's name. It has never worked. "But I will one day."

"Don't beat yourself up." Eugene shrugs. "Wanting to be the next Bloody Mary, though? That's, like, the toughest gig to get."

Bella glares at him. "You don't think I'm scary enough?" She puts her long black hair in front of her face and tilts her head down, giving Eugene a menacing look. "How about now?"

"You're terrifying!" Charlie says, and then puts their head in their hands.

"So, Eugene," Dee says, changing the subject before Charlie passes out. "You're really into fire, huh?"

"Not just fire," he says, smirking. "I'm into mischief of *all* kinds."

"Like what?" Bella asks, fixing her hair.

"Like experiments, and explosions." Eugene gives them a proud smile. "Last month I built a waterslide in my bedroom." His smile dims a little. "That one didn't work out the way I'd hoped."

"An indoor waterslide?" Bella is skeptical. "You made that all by yourself?"

"Oh, yeah," he says. "Hey, you ghouls wanna come to my house after school and see what I'm working on now?" He leans in eagerly, lowers his voice. "Think 'jetpack,' but with whoopie cushions."

"Creepy," Dee says, smiling wide. She and Bella have never been invited to a friend's house before. That boy Peter, from the human school, once invited their entire class to the community pool for a birthday party, but Bella and Dee's dads said they couldn't go. Apparently, budding witches were supposed to avoid chlorine. Then someone started a rumor that the twins were afraid of the water, and nobody invited them to any more pool parties. Or parties of any kind.

"Yeah," Bella agrees. "It sounds like something I'll have to see for myself."

"Me too," Charlie adds. "As long as nothing is going to jump out at me."

"Wicked!" Eugene springs up. "This is gonna be awesome!"

Bella and Dee look at each other, exchanging a small smile. Each sister knows what the other is thinking. Their morning might have gotten off to a rough start, but now look at them, making new friends! Just like they promised their dads they would.

The sisters finish their lunches, feeling hopeful again. Maybe their first day as Real and Powerful Witches isn't completely ruined, after all.

❦〰〰 CHAPTER 4 〰〰❦

While some YIKESSS students, like Charlie, live on campus, others, such as the twins and Eugene, commute from home. And where is *home* if you're a monster in the suburbs, trying to hide in plain sight?

Welcome to Eerie Estates.

For generations most of the supernatural community in Peculiar has lived in a gated housing development called Eerie Estates. The matching two-story homes, painted in the most cheerful shades of boysenberry and black, were built in the 1800s in the Gothic style, and then renovated with modern appliances in the 1960s. The original architect was a centaur who greatly valued his privacy, so his final, most important touch was to enclose the estates in layers of tall, dense shrubbery. Not even the nosiest joggers or dog walkers passing by have been able to glimpse what goes on inside.

Of course, most might think: *Eerie Estates— could they* be *any more obvious?* But supernatural creatures are not, nor have they ever been, known for their subtlety. Why else would there be so many legends and myths about them? And too many of them wholly unflattering! Why do humans never talk about the venerable and lifesaving zombie doctor who studied for his degree by practicing on himself?

But truly, when it comes to Eerie Estates, there's no need to worry. Most humans in Peculiar assume that the name of the estates is simply a misspelling of "Erie," a nearby town, and residents don't bother correcting them.

Now, back to the young witches.

After school Bella, Dee, and Charlie follow Eugene back to his house in Eerie Estates. The Seattle storm has passed, but gray skies still hang overhead.

"I'm gonna call Dad and Pop and tell them where we're going," Dee says to Bella. She pulls her blueteeth out of their pouch in her backpack and sticks them into her mouth. The device, which resembles a retainer from human dentistry and features the latest supernatural technology, allows Dee to communicate with her dads through her thoughts. It also makes her look like she has blue teeth.

She thinks about calling her dad Ron. A

moment later she hears his voice inside her mind.

Deedee?

Hi, Pop!

Is everything okay?

Everything is great! I just wanted to tell you that Bella and I are going to a friend's house for a little while.

A friend? That's wonderful, hon! Who's the lucky monster?

They arrive at Eugene's house. A sign that reads STUFF & FLUFF TAXIDERMY in fancy cursive is staked into the grass in the front yard.

His name is Eugene, Dee thinks. *His house is just a couple of streets over from ours. And we made another friend, Charlie. They're here too.*

Dee glances over at Charlie, who's keeping a comfortable distance from the wooden stake.

Oh, Dee. Dad and I are so happy you and Bells are making friends.

Me too. Tell you about it later, okay?

Absolutely. Love you.

Love you, too.

"Taxidermy?" Bella studies the sign, eyes widening. "As in, stuffing dead animals?"

"You got it," Eugene says, leading them up the driveway. "The family business." His smile dims a little when he says it.

Dee puts the blueteeth away and looks at Eugene. "You don't want to be a taxidermist?"

Eugene shakes his head. "It's more my parents' thing. They're zombies, so it's kind of a perfect job for them. You know, because they like to pickle the brains and save them for later."

"Gross," Charlie moans. "I think I'm going to be sick."

"Hey, no need to be rude." Eugene glances back at them as he opens the front door. "I don't judge your bloodsucking habits, do I?"

"Oh, of course," Charlie says, throwing up their hands. "You assume that just because I'm a vampire, I like to drink blood?"

"Well," Bella says, raising an eyebrow. "Don't you?"

"Excuse me?"

The twins turn their heads in unison. Standing in front of them is the mayor's son, holding the issue of *Haunted Housekeeping* and looking right at Dee.

The image shows the magazine cover reading: "Haunted Housekeeping", "MONSTER'S CHOICE!"

CHAPTER 2

Do you work here?" the mayor's son asks. "I'm just some random human," he jokes, "looking for help."

Dee quickly removes the rainbow sunglasses. She searches his face for clues that he heard too much, but she doesn't see anything that suggests he's offended by their phrasing.

She gives her sister a discreet pinch that hopefully says, *Do not perform any magic on this boy in our dads' store!*

"Um, yeah, I do." She glances down at her black pharmacy coat. "I mean, sort of. Our dads own the place." She gestures to Bella, who purses her lips.

"I thought so." He smiles at Dee, the corners of his eyes crinkling behind glasses with black frames. "I mean, I've seen you here before."

"You have?" She feels the fluttering bats in her stomach again. "I mean, totally. You probably have."

"Did you need help with something?" Bella interjects.

"Oh yeah," Dee says, a little too eagerly, in Bella's opinion. "How can we help you?"

"Do you guys have the new *Howler* comic?" he asks. "I was looking over there, but I didn't see it with the rest of them. I did find this, though." He holds up the issue of *Haunted Housekeeping* he's been looking at. "There's some pretty weird stuff in here. Who knew there were over thirty-five different ways to hang cobwebs?"

"Everyone?" Bella mutters.

"Everyone except spiders," Dee jokes. "Their webs all look the same."

The boy laughs. "Maybe I should buy this for the spiders in my basement, then. They could definitely use some decorating tips."

Bella snatches the magazine out of the boy's hand. "It's not for sale." She looks pointedly at Dee. "There must have been a mix-up. *Someone* put this here in place of the new *Howler* comic, which means the new *Howler* comic is in the back, where this is supposed to be." She holds the magazine out to Dee, and Dee takes it from her.

"Right." Dee looks from Bella back to the boy. "I'll go check."

"Thanks," he says. "I'll wait by the register." He meets her eye and smiles, making her blush.

Dee hurries to the back with the issue of *Haunted Housekeeping*. A few moments later Bella follows behind, carrying the rest of the copies that had accidentally been put in the front room. Cornelius meows a greeting from his perch on the top shelf.

"Jeepers creepers, Dee. Count your lucky skulls that Dad didn't find these magazines in the front room." Bella drops the stack by Dee's feet. "He would've freaked."

Dee searches through their inventory of supernatural magazines until she finds the new *Howler* comic, shelved in the spot for *Haunted Housekeeping*, right where Bella guessed it would be. Dee pulls it out and examines it.

"These covers look exactly the same," Dee complains. She picks up a copy of *Haunted Housekeeping*, then shows them both to Bella. "It didn't seem like he cared, though," she thinks out loud, flipping through the comic. It's got spaceships with laser beams and aliens with purple skin. "It *seems* like he's into creepy stuff, just like us."

"So?" Bella furrows her brow, bored by the human reading materials and confused about her sister's interest. She looks at Dee curiously. "What was that out there, anyway? Why were you being so weird with him?"

Dee feels her face get hot. She quickly closes the comic. "I wasn't being *weird*," she says, avoiding Bella's intense gaze. "I was being nice."

"You were fraternizing with the enemy!" Bella shakes her head. If she didn't know any better, she'd think her sister has a crush on that boy. But that's just silly. Dee would never risk exposing the truth about their powers for a human . . . would she?

"Oh, give me a break," Dee says, moving toward the door. "If he knew about Cornelius, he would have said something by now. There's nothing to worry about."

Bella crosses her arms. "There's *always* something to worry about when humans are involved."

Comic in hand, Dee walks out of the room and away from her sister, slamming the door closed.

Cornelius jumps down from the top shelf and walks over to where Dee just exited. When he gets to the door, he meows and paws at it twice. Bella scoops him up, then puts his face to her nose and looks into his wide yellow eyes.

"She'll be back," Bella says, her words of assurance as much for herself as they are for Cornelius. "Don't you worry."

In the front room Dee hurries to the register, where the boy is already waiting. "You found it!" he says. "That's awesome."

She bites the inside of her cheek to keep from grinning like a big goof at having pleased him. "No big deal," she says, and puts the comic book on the counter. She tries typing in the code to unlock the register, but she fumbles over the keys twice.

Focus, she tells herself. Ron only just taught her how to use the register last week. She has never checked anyone out before, let alone a cute boy.

Moving very carefully, she types in the

correct code, then picks up the magazine and takes a deep breath before she scans it. When she presses enter, and the total pops up on the screen the way it's supposed to, she lets the breath out and smiles to herself. "That will be three ninety-nine," she tells him, feeling very sophisticated.

"Here you go." The boy gives her a five-dollar bill, and her heart skips a beat when his hand grazes hers. She's struck by its warmth—not hot like a werewolf, but balmy and just right. For a moment she forgets where she is and what she's supposed to be doing. It's only when she notices the digital numbers flashing $3.99 and feels the five-dollar bill in her hand that she returns to earth.

Dee quickly enters the bill amount in the register, and the drawer pops open. "One dollar and one cent is your change," she recites in her best customer-service voice. She hands him the money the way she's practiced with her dads.

"Thanks." He picks up the comic, seemingly

oblivious to what just occurred. "I'm Sebastian, by the way."

"Dee," she says. "It's short for 'Donna,' but everybody calls me 'Dee.'"

"Dee," Sebastian repeats. "Cool name. Like Dee Dualla from *Battlestar Galactica*."

Dee blinks. "Battlestar . . . what?"

Sebastian grins. "*Battlestar Galactica*. It's a sci-fi comic. One of my favorites. It's all about the Colonial Fleet and their enemies, the Cylons." He glances at her from under the brim of his cap. "I, um, love books about space."

Dee smiles. "Creepy." She doesn't know much about space, and she isn't really a reader, either, but Sebastian doesn't need to know that yet.

"Creepy?" he repeats, a small smile forming.

Dee's eyes go wide. "I meant, like, cool."

"Creepy." Sebastian is still smiling. "I like that." He looks past her, toward the bulletin board on the back wall, and points to something hanging there. "By the way, are you going on Friday?"

She turns around to see a bright orange flyer with a pumpkin border advertising the Peculiar Public School's sixth-grade fall dance. "Oh," she says, blushing. "No. I actually go to YIKESSS."

Dee has never been to a real dance before but has always wanted to go. The human elementary school didn't have dances, and the closest thing YIKESSS kids get to a dance is the Creepy Carnival in the spring. The rides are fun, and the blueberry cotton cobwebs are *so* yummy, but there's no dance floor. Or humans.

"Whoa." Sebastian looks impressed. "A YIKESSS kid. Hey, I have to ask. Do you really have to take all your tests blindfolded?"

"What?" Dee says, trying her best to sound amused. "No."

As a matter of fact, according to the Spell Casting syllabus, blindfolds *are* going to be required during the Nocturnal Spells unit, but she decides to keep that bit of information to herself.

"Right," Sebastian says, laughing off his question. "Sorry. I'm sure you get questions like that all the time. There are a lot of rumors floating around about that place, you know."

Dee laughs nervously. She heard plenty of those rumors at the human elementary school. Fortunately, none of them came close to the truth. "People have really wild imaginations," she says, and then adds in a moment of bravery, "You can ask me anything you want to know."

"Really?" Sebastian smiles. "Well, maybe you can tell me more at the dance. YIKESSS kids are invited too. Didn't you see?" He gestures to the flyer again, and Dee takes a closer look. Printed at the bottom of the page, in small but bold type, is *YIKESSS STUDENTS WELCOME!*

Dee has hardly had time to process Sebastian's words when Bella appears out of nowhere with an eager look on her face. She was listening, Dee realizes, probably with the snooping spell she's been practicing.

"Jeepers creepers, we're really invited to the PPS sixth-grade dance?" she says, glancing from Sebastian to Dee. Like Dee, Bella has never been to a dance before, and her curiosity outweighs her general distrust of humans. Not to mention that she would never miss an opportunity to get all dressed up with her friends. "*Really* really?"

Dee takes the flyer off the bulletin board, her head spinning. Given that most PPS business doesn't apply to them, neither sister paid much attention to the flyer when it first went up. Now it seems that not only is Dee invited to a PPS dance but Sebastian *wants* her there too. Maybe he will even dance with her?

Dee's heart nearly skips a beat. She has to start practicing her human dance moves *immediately*.

Dee hands the flyer to Bella, who reads it quickly and then hugs the piece of paper to her chest. "I can't believe it!" Then she drops the flyer and looks at Dee. "But what are we going to *wear*?"

Sebastian laughs. "So maybe I'll see you there?"

Dee looks at the ground and smiles. "Maybe."

Sebastian leaves the store, and Bella and Dee exchange a look. After a beat of silence, they both scream.

Less than a second later, Ant is there, a look of terror on his face. He was so panicked by his daughters' screams that he didn't even bother to use the door, opting instead to float straight through the wall. "WHAT IS IT?"

"We're invited to a dance, Dad!" Bella tells him. "A human dance!"

Relief washes over Ant's face, and he puts his hand to where his beating heart used to be, recovering from the shock. "Girls."

"PPS is having their sixth-grade fall dance this Friday, and kids from YIKESSS are invited," Dee continues. "Can we please go, Dad?"

"*Please?*" Bella says.

"Girls, you *cannot* scream like that in the store. I thought something dreadful was happening!" Ant rubs at his temples like he has a headache.

"We're sorry," Bella says quickly.

"Really sorry," Dee echoes. "Can we please go?"

When Ant drops his hands, he has two translucent spots on the sides of his head where he smudged his makeup. "I don't know, girls. It seems like it could be dangerous. What if you can't control your magic and someone gets hurt?" Bella's and Dee's expressions morph into identical frowns, and Ant sighs. "All right, all right. You can go to the dance—"

Bella's and Dee's faces light up.

"—as long as Principal Koffin allows it."

Bella and Dee exchange a glance. *Would* Yvette Koffin, their strict harpy principal, allow her supernatural students to risk exposure by attending the human dance? It doesn't seem very likely. Add in the fact that Principal Koffin never told them about the event, and their chances seem even *less* likely.

The front door chimes again. Bella, Dee, and

Ant all look up to see a big purple troll duck through the entryway. "Afternoon', Antony," says the troll as he takes off his hat. "The wife sent me for some Dead Sea salt. Got any in stock?"

⊱•⊰ CHAPTER 3 ⊱•⊰

The next morning the dark halls of YIKESSS are alight with chatter and excitement at the possibility of attending the PPS fall dance. Never before have the two schools mingled together for a function, and all anyone can talk about is whether or not Principal Koffin will agree to it.

On the bus Bella showed the dance flyer to Crypta Cauldronson, who promptly zapped it into a stack of flyers and began handing them out to the other students. By the time the bus got to school and the ravens squawked to signal the start of homeroom half an hour later, the entire school knew about the dance.

"I hope Principal Koffin lets us go," Charlie says in homeroom, their red eyes bright with excitement. They're sitting behind Bella, next to Dee, and diagonally across from Eugene at a desk carved from iron. All the desks in Professor Belinda's Spell Casting classroom were replaced with less flammable materials after Bella and Dee's accident on the first day of school. "I've been waiting for the chance to bust out my moonwalk."

"You can moonwalk?" Dee asks, looking up from the *Howler* comic on her desk. "That's impressive!"

"There's no way Koffin lets us go to the dance." Eugene leans back in his chair so it's balancing on two legs and takes a big bite of a breakfast burrito. "PPS has never invited YIKESSS to anything before. Why now?" he asks with a full mouth.

"Does there have to be a reason?" Charlie shrugs. "Maybe the human principal just thought it would be a nice thing to do."

Bella, who is attempting to study for an afternoon exam in Humans 101, snorts like that's a preposterous idea. In the front row Crypta Cauldronson looks up from her eyephone and turns around. "I heard PPS has a new principal this year. He just moved to town. He's a *widower*, poor guy."

Bella looks up from her flash cards and narrows her eyes at Crypta. "How do you know all that?"

Crypta smiles and flicks her shiny brown hair over her shoulder. "My mom. As president of the Creepy Council, it's kind of her job to know stuff like that."

"Oh, really?" Bella replies, trying to seem

nonchalant, though Dee notices that Bella is gripping her flash cards rather tightly. "If she knows so much, then why was *I* the one to tell you about the dance?"

Crypta scowls at Bella and turns back around.

"Nice one, Maleficent." Eugene holds up a hand to high-five Bella, still balancing in his chair. Suddenly a line of red sparks appears like a lasso and wraps itself around the chair's front legs. It yanks the chair back down onto all fours, making Eugene drop his burrito onto the floor.

"Are we going to make this a daily occurrence, Eugene?" Professor Belinda calls out from the front of the room. Her hand is in the air, and red sparks sizzle on her fingertips. "Perhaps I should send you to test out the chairs in Principal Koffin's tower, instead?"

Dressed in one of her signature floral maxi dresses and adorned with an armful of silver bangles, Professor Belinda looks like a harmless hippie. But to underestimate her would be a grave error, as she's the most powerful witch in all of Peculiar.

"No, ma'am, that won't be necessary." Eugene picks up his burrito and dusts it off. "Five-second rule," he says, and then takes another big bite. Bella, watching him, makes a disgusted face.

The raven in the corner squawks three times to signal the start of the morning announcements. It opens its mouth wide, but instead of another squawk, Principal Koffin's voice comes out.

"Good morning, students," she begins, and every ear in the room perks up. Is she going to talk about the dance?

"Before we begin with the day's usual announcements, I'd like to first address something that was brought to my attention this morning."

Bella and Dee exchange an excited glance.

"Professor Berry's fairymouse has gotten out

of its cage again," Principal Koffin says, and the entire classroom groans. "If anyone finds Twinkle, please return her to the fae wing immediately."

"That's the third time in a week," Charlie whispers, shaking their head. "They have got to get a better cage."

With a deep sigh that's audible through the raven, the principal continues. "By now I'm sure you've all seen the flyer that's been circulating through the school grounds advertising the Peculiar Public School fall dance, and the fact that YIKESSS students are, quote, 'welcome' to attend."

The classroom goes silent with anticipation.

"First, I feel I should share something with you all. I received this flyer in the mail last week, along with a note from the rather . . . *enthusiastic* new principal at the public school, encouraging us to attend. The truth is, I had no intention of addressing it. In my opinion, mingling with our human neighbors off school grounds is a situation ripe for disaster. With no magical veil to protect you, you'll be vulnerable. You'll be putting yourselves, the humans around you, and the supernatural community as a whole at risk. It's my job to keep you all safe. Why would I *ever* condone such an event?"

As Principal Koffin speaks, the students' anticipation deflates, and Bella's and Dee's looks of excitement turn into grimaces.

"But *then*, without my knowledge or approval, someone had the flyer distributed around town, at locations where they knew YIKESSS students would be able to see it. Now it seems my approval is no longer deemed necessary. The cat's out of the bag, as they say, and it can't be shoved back in no matter how hard you push, or how many spells you try—"

The principal pauses, presumably to compose herself.

"What I mean to say is that, if you want to go to this dance, I no longer feel I have the right to stop you. Therefore, you have my permission to attend, on the obvious condition that you remain on your best behavior. YIKESSS is not liable for any werewolf tantrums or magical misfires that may occur."

The classroom erupts into cheers.

"Listen carefully now." Principal Koffin sounds considerably less excited. "There shall be no magic or any other acts of the supernatural performed in the presence of the humans. *No* exceptions. Any student caught breaking this rule will be punished to the fullest extent. If you're thinking about ignoring this rule, remember: I will be there, and I will be watching you."

"You hear that, Bella?" Dee whispers. "No magic!"

"Yeah, yeah." Bella rolls her eyes. "I'll be perfectly boring."

"Tomorrow afternoon I will be hosting a school-wide assembly in the cafeteria that will be mandatory for all students who want to attend the dance. We'll be going over some rules for the evening, and it will be a chance

for you to ask any questions you might have."
She pauses, and then clears her throat. "In
other news, auditions for the winter play, *A
Midsummer's Nightmare*, will take place in the
amphitheater after school today. Students
wishing to . . ."

"Whoa," Eugene whispers over the
announcements. "Seems like the human principal went over Principal K's head with this
whole thing. Brave guy."

"She doesn't seem happy," Bella agrees, and
then shrugs. "Oh well. I mean, she's still going
to be supervising. How much damage could we
actually do?"

Dee raises an eyebrow. Eugene and Charlie
both struggle to keep straight faces.

"So we're going to meet at the witches' house
before the dance, right?" Charlie says, switch-
ing gears.

"Of course." Bella puts away her flash cards,
now having much more pressing matters to

discuss. "And we all have to go thrift shopping to look for outfits!"

Dee thinks about Sebastian. He said he would see her at the dance, which means he's going to see her outfit, too. She *has* to look breathtaking. "Totally," Dee agrees, and then blushes into her lap.

Bella catches her. "Why are you making that face?"

Dee doesn't meet her sister's eye. "I don't know what you mean." She flips to the next page of the comic. Bella watches her for a long moment, taking in the red face, the *Howler* comic, and the lie.

"Oh, for the love of everything unholy," Bella says, exasperated. "You *do* have a crush on that human!"

Dee gasps. "Do not!"

"Do too!"

"What human?" Charlie asks, leaning in to better hear the gossip.

"The son of the human mayor, who almost caught us with Cornelius," Bella says, her voice sour. "He was snooping around the pharmacy yesterday."

"His name is Sebastian!" Dee says. "And he wasn't *snooping*. He was buying a comic."

"He's pretty cute, if I remember right," Charlie says. "Is he going to be at the dance?"

"Charlie!" Bella hisses. "Don't encourage her!"

"I agree with Maleficent on this one," Eugene says, gesturing to Bella as he munches the rest of his breakfast wrap. "Crushing on humans is dangerous business. Sooner or later some truths are going to slip out and hit the fan."

"That's not how that expression goes," Bella mutters.

"Can everybody please relax?" Dee closes the comic book. "I don't have a crush on him. I just think he's . . ." She smiles to herself, remembering. "Creepy."

"Maleficents," Professor Belinda says from her desk. She points to the raven, which is still broadcasting the morning announcements, and then the professor holds a finger up to her mouth. "Shh!"

Bella turns around with a sigh and picks up her flash cards again. Dee listens to the rest of the announcements with a smile on her face.

There's a palpable energy in the air when Principal Koffin arrives in the cafeteria for the assembly the next afternoon. Having little experience with human events in general, most of the sixth grade has shown up, bright-eyed and eager to learn the ins and outs of a real human dance.

Bella and Dee, despite having spent the last five years at school with humans, are just as clueless as the other monsters in the room. Peculiar Elementary School never put on any dances, but even if they had, it's unlikely the twin witches would have been welcome. Bella and Dee's classmates, and more specifically their classmates' parents, often did everything they could to keep the twins—whom trouble *did* always seem to follow—away from social events.

The YIKESS students quiet down as Principal Koffin walks to the center of the cafeteria and steps onto the podium that was magically erected by Professor Belinda. A moment later Argus the four-eyed crow lands on her shoulder and calls the room to attention with a squawk. Bella, Dee, Charlie, and Eugene are seated at a table nearby.

"Good afternoon, students," the principal says, smoothing back her sleek blond bun. Her voice is amplified not by a microphone but by the podium's magic.

"What do you think she'll teach us first?" Bella whispers excitedly. "How to beat the humans in a dance-off? What to do if there's a ghoul in the hallway?" She smiles at the thought, knowing how ghouls like to haunt highly populated areas to mess with humans. "I've always wanted to meet one."

"We're supposed to blend in with the humans, not compete with them," Dee whispers back. "Now shh! I don't want to miss anything."

"Yeah, listen up, Dee." Crypta, seated across the table from the twins, leans forward. "You'd better learn how to blend in with the humans, because you're never going to fit in with us."

Dee's jaw drops in shock. What is *that* supposed to mean? Bella whips her head around and stares daggers at Crypta.

"At least we're not going to give ourselves away, little miss Creepy Council Junior. You couldn't pretend to be human if your life depended on it."

Crypta rolls her eyes and turns her attention back to the assembly. While most witches start to show signs of manifesting their powers around age nine or ten, Crypta manifested much earlier, at age four. As a result she never went to human elementary school and has spent less time around humans than any of the other witches at YIKESSS.

"Don't listen to her, Dee," Charlie whispers. "You're the creepiest witch I know."

"Yeah, she's just jealous." Bella nudges her sister. "And besides, wherever I fit, you fit."

Dee smiles weakly at her friends, touched even though they're trying too hard to make her feel better.

Sure, Dee thinks, she may not be as smart as Bella, or as good at flying, or as quick to learn spells . . . but she's still a Maleficent. A *witch*. Whether or not she gets along with humans doesn't change that.

So why do Crypta's words still scratch like a wolf at the door of Dee's brain?

"I'd like to start today's assembly by asking

for a volunteer," Principal Koffin says from the podium. She looks around the room, waiting for someone to raise their hand. "Ah, Gregory Tremble. Thank you."

Everyone looks across the cafeteria at Gregory, a ghost. "Um." He struggles to speak, becoming a little more transparent than usual. "I—I didn't volunteer."

"Not to worry, I'm sure you'll do just fine." The principal extends a long, slender hand and waves him forward. "Come along, quickly."

Gregory floats reluctantly into the center of the room.

"Excellent. Now, Gregory. Pretend I am a human child. I have just approached you and asked you to dance. How do you respond?"

A few giggles emerge from various places around the room. Gregory's bright white eyes dart around anxiously. If blood ran through his veins, he'd surely be blushing. After several long moments of silence, his nerves get the better of him and he disappears completely.

The room erupts into laughter, including Bella and Eugene. Charlie and Dee cringe with secondhand embarrassment.

Principal Koffin is unfazed, her face like stone. "Can anyone tell me what Gregory did wrong?"

Bella's hand shoots up into the air. She answers without waiting to be called on. "He floated instead of walking, and then he disappeared when he got nervous."

"Indeed." The principal nods. "Gregory followed his supernatural instincts. For him that means disappearing when the situation gets uncomfortable. For a vampire it might mean shape-shifting. A witch might cast a spell of protection or diversion. You all understand, I think, where I'm going with this." She looks at the spot where Gregory disappeared. "You may be seated now, Mr. Tremble."

Bella and Dee feel a whoosh of wind brush past them.

"Here at YIKESSS you are encouraged to

follow your supernatural instincts. But out there, in the presence of humans, you must actively fight against them. I understand if this seems confusing. One day you will all be able to control your instincts enough to use them to your advantage, but for most of you"—here Principal Koffin looks directly at Bella and Dee—"that day is still far off. Therefore, at the dance, discretion will be of the utmost importance."

Bella sticks her hand straight up in the air again. "What happens if we see a ghoul in the hallway? I'm *dying* for some haunting tips."

The principal gives Bella a disapproving look. "You will do nothing, because there will be no ghouls, gremlins, poltergeists, or the like haunting the halls that night."

Bella looks skeptical. "How do you know? The handbook says ghouls like to hang out in schools and hospitals."

Principal Koffin nods. "That's right. But fortunately for you students, Professor Belinda is already hard at work on a magical veil of protection that will keep such creatures at bay. It will be placed over PPS on Friday."

"Similar to our own protective veil, think of this one as a safety blanket." Professor Belinda speaks up. She's standing with Vice Principal Archaic and a few other members of the faculty by the door. "It will snuff out sparks of magic, put a glamour over supernatural traits like wings or extra eyes, and repel malevolent creatures."

"Uh-oh, Crypta," Bella says over her shoulder. "No malevolent creatures. That means you won't be able to get in."

Next to Bella, Eugene laughs.

Crypta sends red sparks shooting out of her finger and right into Bella's book bag, knocking it off the table and spilling its contents all over the floor. "Oops." Crypta shrugs. "My finger slipped."

"My Divination flash cards!" Bella frets, kneeling down while Dee glares at Crypta. "They were in alphabetical order."

From his perch on Principal Koffin's

shoulder, Argus flaps his wings toward Bella and Crypta and lets out a squawk to quiet them down. The principal turns her attention back to Professor Belinda.

"Let's continue. Professor, the music, please."

Professor Belinda sends blue sparks into the air, and a popular song by a human band starts playing from nowhere and everywhere.

"In order to act with discretion," Principal Koffin says over the music, "you must learn to partake in appropriate human dance. For many of you that will require a certain reining in of strength and skill. For instance, Wendy Fang—"

Everyone turns to look at Wendy, a werewolf who's on the scream team with Bella and Crypta and is known for her ability to land backflips from the top of the pyramid. She stands up timidly.

"Please show me how you might normally dance."

Wendy laughs and looks around uncomfortably. "By myself?"

"Certainly not," Principal Koffin says, and then lifts her wings off her back. "I'll dance with you."

The principal flies into the air and then starts swaying her hips to the beat, ignoring the waves of laughter coming from the students. Wendy, looking uncertain, forcefully starts bobbing her head.

"Come on, give it your all," Principal Koffin says, spinning around in the air.

Wendy starts dancing for real, throwing her whole body into the beat and jumping around. Eventually she jumps so high that she does two consecutive backflips. When she lands on her feet, the cafeteria bursts into cheers and applause, and Wendy lets out a long howl of satisfaction.

The music stops and Principal Koffin returns to the podium, composing herself. "Thank you, Wendy. That was a perfect example of what *not* to do at the dance."

Wendy's smile fades, and she quickly sits back down.

"You see," the principal continues, "human children can't jump that high, and they definitely can't do aerial tricks. You'll all have to restrain yourselves to the floor, I'm afraid."

Collective groans move across the cafeteria. In the back a pink hand is raised in the air. "What do human dance moves look like, exactly?" the hand's owner says.

"I'm glad you asked." Principal Koffin nods at Professor Belinda, and the music starts up again. "I will now demonstrate some acceptable human dance moves. First we have the sprinkler." She puts one hand behind her head and stretches the other one out in front, then moves her arm to the beat. "Next, the shopping cart." She puts both hands in front of her like she's holding a cart handle, then rhythmically extends her arms as if she's grabbing items off a shelf. "Another is the chicken dance."

Bella wrinkles her nose. "Her moves are a little outdated, don't you think?"

"I kind of like this one," Charlie says, shimmying their shoulders. Principal Koffin has moved on to the jazz square.

After a few more questionable dance moves, Professor Belinda changes the music to a slower song, and Principal Koffin splits the room into groups. "Find a partner," the principal instructs the students. "One of you place your hands on your partner's shoulders, and the other put your hands on your partner's waist, far away, like so." She holds her arms all the way out in front of her. "Some humans call it leaving room for the holy spirit, which is absurd, of course, as spirits do not enjoy dancing to loud music."

Everyone stands up. Eugene looks at Bella. "What do you say, Maleficent? Want to be partners?"

"Sorry." Bella links arms with Dee. "Dee and I are always partners."

179

Dee smiles apologetically at Charlie, who was clearly about to suggest partnering up. "Next time?"

Charlie shrugs like it's no big deal and then turns to Eugene. "Partners?"

Eugene plops his hands onto Charlie's shoulders. "Sorry if I step on your feet," he says. "I've never danced like this before. I *can* do a pretty wicked worm, though."

"The worm? That's cute," Charlie says. "Did I mention I could moonwalk—"

"*Yes,*" Eugene interrupts.

"—upside down? Only in bat form, but I'm still working on it."

Eugene's pointy ears droop just a little. "Show-off."

Bella's hands go onto Dee's shoulders, and Dee's hands to Bella's waist. They start swaying back and forth.

"What do you mean, 'next time'?" Bella asks, referring to what Dee said to Charlie. Dee can hear the hurt in her voice. "You and I pinky-swore we'd always be partners."

"I know," Dee says. "But don't you think it might be good for us to partner with other monsters sometimes? You know, to meet new friends?"

Bella makes a face. "What do I need new friends for? I have you."

"Ow!" Charlie yelps next to the twins. "My foot!"

"Sorry." Eugene shrugs. "At least I warned you."

Dee bites her lip, unable to meet her sister's eye. "I just think, if we want to fit in, we should get to know other people too."

Bella's eyes spark with recognition. "You're still thinking about what Crypta said." She shakes her sister's shoulders, urging her to snap out of it. "Dee, seriously, don't listen to her. You're a witch. Of course you fit in."

"But maybe she has a point," Dee falters. "I mean, it doesn't really *feel* like I fit in. Besides Charlie and Eugene, I don't know anybody else here. At least you've got friends on the scream team."

Dee thinks about Sebastian again, about the easy way they fell into conversation at the pharmacy. She has always had an easier time relating to humans than other monsters.

"The girls on the scream team aren't my friends," Bella insists. "They're, like, my colleagues. I just need them to like me so they'll vote me captain."

Suddenly the music stops playing. "Great work, everyone," Principal Koffin calls out from the podium. "Now return to your seats, and we'll discuss the human oddities otherwise known as corsages and boutonnieres."

Bella squeezes Dee's shoulders. "Don't worry, Dee. You've got plenty of time to find a place for yourself." Then the sisters break apart. "It's all going to work out. You'll see."

CHAPTER 5

After school on Friday, Bella and Dee rush back to their home in Eerie Estates to get ready for the dance. Thanks to their pop Ron's keen decorative eye, the girls' bedroom resembles a beautiful nightmare, perfectly suited for a couple of blossoming witches. Their beds are adorned with iron headboards and dark canopies that sparkle like the night sky. The deep purple walls and black shag rug are magic-absorbent, so any spells that might accidentally ricochet and make a mess will instead sink in and disappear. Plus, each sister has her own personalized casting vanity and cauldron, hot pink for Bella and green for Dee. The witchy possibilities are endless.

Their dads have already agreed to let Charlie and Eugene come over early on the condition that the twins clean their room first, so Bella conjures a dusting charm and gathers old cups of water while Dee picks up dirty clothes from the floor and puts them into the hamper. Cornelius, meanwhile, chases and swats at his red ribbon, which Dee has enchanted to move around on its own. Then the twins play a round of rock, spider, scissors to see who has to vacuum the floor.

"Spider covers rock," Bella says. "I win."

Dee groans. "Best two out of three?"

Bella grins and shakes her head.

When their room is clean, Bella blasts some music while Dee pulls their outfits out of the closet and drapes them across her bed. Cornelius promptly stops playing with his ribbon to jump onto Dee's dress and curl into a little ball.

Bella picks up her outfit, a sharp pair of overalls with black and green pinstripes, and a turtleneck underneath—"Beetlejuice chic," Dee declared the look when Bella stepped out of the dressing room at the thrift store. With her favorite black leather booties and her crescent moon necklace, Bella thought she looked *very* chic, indeed. She taps herself on the shoulder, conjuring purple sparks and zapping the outfit onto her body. The uniform she was wearing replaces the overalls on the bed.

"Eek!" Bella squeals, spinning around to look at herself in the mirror. "We are going to be the creepiest witches at the dance."

"You mean the coolest," Dee reminds her, fiddling with her own star necklace. "That's what the humans would say."

"So what?" Bella fixes the part in her straight black hair so it's centered. "You can spend your whole life worrying about what every human thinks of you, or you can choose not to care, like me."

Dee purses her lips. Part of her knows Bella is right, that she shouldn't care what every human thinks of her, but another part of her recognizes that for the first time in their lives, Bella doesn't quite understand what Dee is going through. Bella is the perfect witch: strong, smart, and brave. She doesn't have to worry about fitting in with the humans because she already fits in so well with the monsters. Unlike Dee, Bella is sure of her place in the world.

Not to mention the fact that Dee actually *likes* humans. She's pretty sure she wants to work in the human world as a meteorologist one day, now that her talent for controlling the weather and conjuring natural disasters has been revealed, but she hasn't told Bella yet.

Choosing a life away from witchcraft is something her sister *definitely* wouldn't understand.

Dee scoops up Cornelius and puts him on her pillow, then brushes the cat hair off her dress and zaps it onto her body the same way Bella put on her outfit. It's got green and black stripes, just like Bella's overalls, plus sheer green sleeves that sparkle and a bright green tutu skirt. When she spins, the skirt billows out around her knees and the sparkles gleam in the light. Best of all, it even has pockets.

She approaches the mirror, looks at her reflection next to Bella, and takes a deep breath. She wonders if Sebastian will think her dress is as "cool" as she does.

"Wait," Bella says, studying Dee's reflection. She moves behind Dee and starts fussing with her sister's curls, taking two handfuls of hair from the sides of her head and braiding them together to create a fancy half-up, half-down style. Then she puts her hands over Dee's head and rubs her fingertips together, conjuring silver sparks that fall into Dee's hair like tiny pieces of glitter.

"There," Bella says, stepping back to survey her work. "Now you're ready to dance under a disco ball."

An over-the-moon Dee grins at her reflection in the mirror, then throws her arms around her sister and hugs her tight. "Thanks, Bells."

Downstairs the doorbell rings, and the sisters swap excited glances.

"Girls!" Ron calls out. "Charlie and Eugene are here!"

Bella and Dee run into the hallway and lean over the banister. Ron opens the front door, and their friends step inside. The first thing Bella and Dee notice is Eugene's hair. It's even bigger than usual, possibly the result of a teasing comb and his mother's hair spray, and it perfectly matches the orange sweater-vest he bought for tonight. He stands out against the black and blue tiles that line the foyer.

Beside him, Charlie's black hair is slicked

back with gel, and they've traded the dark dress cape they usually wear for a bright red one Dee found in the racks at the thrift store. "It brings out your eyes," she said, urging them to try it on. After a moment of hesitation— bright colors draw attention, and Charlie doesn't usually like wearing anything other than black—they agreed.

"Wow," Bella calls out. "You two look great!"

"You witches look pretty spooktacular too," Eugene replies, smoothing up his hair. As the member of the group with the most experience around humans, Eugene is the least nervous, and therefore not very worried about blending in.

"Hi there," says a voice. A moment later Bella and Dee spot a woman in high-waisted jeans and a T-shirt moving slowly through the doorway. The twins take a closer look and realize that half her jaw and a cheekbone are poking out of her skin.

"I'm Vicky, and this is my husband, Ted." Ted sticks his head through the doorway and waves a pale, skeletal hand. "We're Eugene's parents."

"They *insisted* on coming along to take pictures," Eugene says, rolling his eyes.

"As they should," Ron says. He shakes both their hands. "Nice to meet you. I'm Ron. My husband, Antony, should be here any minute."

"Hey, creepy Halloween decorations, Mr. M," Charlie says, looking around the foyer and into the living room. The holiday is still weeks away, but the Maleficents take Halloween very seriously and like to decorate early. Their home, which is usually adorned with dark and mystical artifacts, gets transformed into a monster's worst night terror around the holidays. Picture lots of pastels, rustic wooden signs, and plenty of cute figurines of creatures and humans hugging.

"Thanks, Charlie." Ron smiles, though it's kind of hard to tell behind his bushy werewolf facial hair. He points to a big wooden sign above the fireplace that says LIVE, LAUGH, LOVE in cursive. "The girls picked that one out."

"Super scary," Eugene agrees. He picks up a smaller sign on the table by the door that says HOME IS WHERE THE HEART IS. "This one too."

Bella and Dee join everyone downstairs, with Cornelius not far behind. "Dee!" Charlie gasps when they see her. "You're so sparkly!"

"It was Bella's idea." Dee spins in a circle, letting her dress and hair shimmer in the light.

Bella grins. "I used a sparkle charm."

"You two look so beautiful." Ron puts a hairy hand to his chest and shakes his head in disbelief. "I can't believe you're going to your first dance. Where did the time go?"

"Don't cry, Pop!" Dee hugs him around his waist. "If you cry, I'll cry!"

"I'm *not* crying," Ron says, and then turns his head to discreetly wipe a tear from his cheek.

"Oh, jeepers." Bella rolls her eyes. Dee is only five minutes younger, but sometimes Bella thinks it feels more like five years. "We're only going to be gone for two hours."

Eugene takes a step forward. "Hey, witches,

check this out." He pulls something out of his pocket, a little black box with a red button on top.

"What is it?" Bella asks. "Jewelry?"

"Better." Eugene smiles wide. "It's a 3-D printer. I programmed it to print a corsage that matches your outfit. I call it . . ." He thinks for a moment. "Well, I haven't actually come up with a name yet." He holds the box out to Bella. "Go ahead, push the button."

Bella raises an eyebrow, considering, then shakes her head. "No, thanks. Flowers don't really go with this outfit."

"I want to try!" Dee takes the box from Bella. She presses the button, then feels the box start to warm up. She hears some bleep-bloops and feels the turning gears. Finally the box dings.

"That means it's ready," Eugene explains. "Open it."

Dee lifts the lid and pulls out . . . well, she's not sure exactly. "What's this?" she asks, holding up some sort of purple-and-white vegetable attached to a ribbon.

"It looks like a turnip," Vicky says, leaning a little closer. "Oh dear."

"Hobgoblins." Eugene's ears droop. He snatches the box from Dee and starts turning it over in his hand. "It's supposed to print flowers, not vegetables!"

Ron shrugs. "Close enough. They both grow in the ground." He smiles at Eugene. "That's some really impressive magic, kid."

Eugene puts the box away, obviously disappointed. "It's not magic." He mopes. "It's code."

"It's still awesome," Dee says. She hands the turnip corsage to Ron and holds out her wrist. "Will you help me tie it on, Pop?"

Suddenly Antony appears next to Charlie, making the skittish vampire scream in surprise. Ant closed the pharmacy early so he could get home to see the twins off, and in his haste decided once again to float through the wall instead of using the door.

"I'm here!" Ant says, looking around at the kids. "I came as fast as I could!"

"You're just in time for pictures, hon," Ron says. "Meet Eugene's parents, Vicky and Ted. I'm going to go get the camera."

"I'm so pleased to meet you," Ant says. He looks at Charlie. "Where's your mom tonight?"

"She's still on a haunting in Mexico," Charlie says, noticeably glum. "Her assignment keeps getting extended."

Charlie is used to their mother traveling all around the world for work—as a banshee, it's her job to haunt the homes of people who are going to die soon—but this is the longest she has ever been away.

"We spoke to Esmeralda on the phone earlier and promised we would send her some photos," Vicky explains. "She's devastated that she can't be here."

"Will you take some pictures on my phone too?" Bella gives her eyephone to Ant, then backs up and fixes her hair.

When Ron returns with his camera, the group lines up in the foyer underneath the crystal-ball light fixture. Eugene throws one arm around Bella's shoulder and the other around Dee's, while Charlie, the shortest of the bunch, stands next to Dee with their shoulders back and their head held high to appear taller. Ron points the camera at the group and says, "Say 'skeleton key'!"

"Skeleton key!" they all echo with smiles on their faces as Ron, Ant, and Vicky start snapping photos.

Dee feels Cornelius pawing at her leg. He looks up at her with big, sad eyes and lets out a forlorn meow.

"What's up, buddy?" She bends down to scratch his head. "You want to come to the dance too?"

"Bad idea," Bella says, widening her eyes at Dee. "Or did you forget who's going to be there tonight?"

Dee feels herself blush. She *definitely* didn't forget. "Nobody will recognize Cornelius," she replies instead of answering. "I'll keep him with mc the whole time."

"Take him," Ron says, putting down the camera. "Dad and I are going out for dinner, and I can't have him scratching up any more art while we're gone."

Cornelius meows in agreement.

Dee smiles and picks him up. "Okay, Corny boy, you're coming with me."

"You're just going to carry him?" Bella asks, eyebrow raised.

"If I had to guess," Charlie says, "I'd say the human school probably has a rule against bringing pets to dances."

"So we're sneaking him in?" Eugene's pointy ears perk up. "Wicked."

Dee shifts Cornelius in her arms and considers her options. She could bring a bag, but that would be obvious, and anyway, he'd get bored in there pretty quickly. If only he were a little bit smaller, she thinks, and she could just stick him into her dress pocket . . .

"I know!" Dee puts him on the ground, sticks her pointer finger into the air, and spins it in a counterclockwise circle, conjuring yellow sparks that sprinkle down over Cornelius and turn him into a tiny black kitten. Cornelius looks down at his fuzzy paws, then up at Dee. He lets out a squeaky little meow of approval.

Charlie gasps. "Cornelius! You're the cutest kitten I've ever seen!"

Dee picks up Cornelius and gently tucks him into her pocket. "There you go," she coos. She looks up at Bella and their friends. "Is everybody ready?"

"Yeah!" Bella claps.

"I guess so," Charlie says, uneasy. "I really hope I don't get nervous and accidentally turn into a bat."

"Don't worry, Charlie," Eugene says. "Blending in with the humans is gonna be a piece of cobweb cake."

One by one the monsters walk out the door, ready for whatever the night has in store.

~~~~~ **CHAPTER 6** ~~~~~

When Bella, Dee, Charlie, and Eugene get
dropped off at the dance, they're surprised to find themselves standing outside the
Peculiar Public School cafeteria.

"The cafeteria?" Bella says, glancing back at
her dads in the car. "This is where the dance is?"

"Where did you think it would be, Bella

Boo?" Ron asks through the window, and Bella's expression turns into a grimace. He knows how she feels about being called that in public. "The gymnasium?"

Bella shrugs. She hadn't thought about it, but she supposes the cafeteria makes sense, much to her dismay. It's not like humans can just conjure a ballroom the way YIKESSS does whenever they have events.

"I'm sure it will still be awesome." Dee loops her arm through Bella's. "We're going to be the creepiest witches at the dance, remember?"

Bella gives her a sly smile. "The *coolest*."

"The cafeteria, all right!" Eugene glances eagerly toward the entrance. "I bet there's going to be a *ton* of food here."

"I hope there's no garlic," Charlie says. "Otherwise, I'm going to be sneezing all night."

Ant and Ron blow kisses and drive away, and the friends begin to move up the sidewalk. They pass a small cluster of humans hanging around by the doors. Their outfits, Bella notices, are dreadfully boring, made of all the same light colors and flat, uninteresting shapes—the exact opposite of Bella's and Dee's outfits. Bella smiles to herself, satisfied. She and her friends are definitely going to be the best-dressed at the dance.

"Nice hair, soft serve," one of the boys calls out to Eugene, with a smirk on his face. His friends all laugh.

"Thanks!" Eugene says earnestly. He nudges Dee. "Did you hear that? That kid thinks my hair looks soft."

"No." Bella glares at the kid. "He's saying your hair looks like soft-serve ice cream. He's being *mean*."

"Bella . . . ," Dee warns, knowing where this is headed. "Don't make a scene."

Bella waits until the boy makes eye contact with her, then lets her hair fall in front of her face and does her best Bloody Mary glare. The boy, so smug a moment ago, jerks back, frightened.

"Jeez, Bella." Charlie looks a little unnerved too. "You've been practicing."

"Of course I have." Bella fixes her hair and returns to normal. "If I'm going to be the youngest Bloody Mary in history, I have to be the scariest, too."

They show their YIKESSS IDs to the human woman seated at the doors, and she lets them pass. In her pocket Dee scratches kitten Cornelius behind the ears to keep him calm and out of sight. It's not until they're all safely inside that she lets him stick his head out and look around. When he does, he squeaks out an unenthusiastic meow.

"Cornelius is right," Bella says, taking in the room and scrunching up her nose. "This is totally *blah.*"

It's common knowledge in the supernatural community that YIKESSS events, no matter how big or small their purpose, are always something of a spectacle. Decorations are enchanted to move and change, long tables are filled with grand feasts on self-heating (or cooling) platters, and everyone comes dressed in their most sinister attire. This human dance is a bit less vibrant. The balloons and streamers sort of sag, and the snack table—which appears to hold little more than punch and pretzel bites—can't be more than a few feet long.

"Where's the disco ball?" Dee looks up at the ceiling. "I thought human dances had disco balls."

"Why did you think that?" Charlie asks, looking nervously toward the kitchen for any signs of garlic.

Dee shrugs. "I saw it in a movie once."

"Aw," Eugene groans. "The kitchen is closed! There's no pizza or ice cream here at all."

Bella smirks and holds up a finger. "We could always conjure some."

"No magic!" Dee whispers, pushing down Bella's hand. "Don't even try. Look who's here." She points toward the snack table, where Principal Koffin, by far the tallest one in the room, stands behind a large glass bowl, scooping some orange punch into a cup and talking to a man. She's wearing a black pantsuit, and her wings are tucked behind her back so that they look like a cape. Perched at the window behind her, Argus the crow blinks his two sets of eyes and surveys the room, seemingly acting as lookout.

"Who's that she's talking to?" Charlie squints into the distance. Like all vampires, Charlie has excellent night vision, but the man is hard to distinguish through the crowd, and only his back is visible to the group.

"Maybe the principal," Bella guesses. He's wearing a crisp, expensive-looking suit, and when he turns his head, she can make out a straight nose and a sharply cut jaw. Then Bella notices Professor Belinda at the opposite end of the table, looking fabulous in a chic velvet robe that matches her wavy black hair. When Professor Belinda catches Bella looking, she smiles.

"Note to self," Bella says, waving back innocently. "Avoid that corner of the room." The teachers would all certainly be watching the group's every move.

Eugene, more concerned with what's on the table than who is behind it, lets out a groan. "That doesn't look like witch's brew punch," he says, and pouts. He's right—witch's brew punch is dark and smoky, and it bubbles. This drink is just Sprite and pineapple juice with sad, melty globs of sherbet.

"Come on, you guys," Dee says, trying to keep the mood up. "We knew it was going to be a little different from what we're used to. That's part of the fun!"

"Fun for who?" Eugene mutters. "Not my stomach."

"I agree with Dee," Charlie says, adjusting their cape. "Let's try to have some fun. At least the music is funky, right?"

"Right!" Dee grabs Bella's hand. "Come on, let's dance."

Dee drags Bella to the center of the room, and Charlie and Eugene follow close behind.

As the friends move, they notice many of their classmates lingering at the edge of the crowd, seemingly too nervous to mingle with the humans. When the twins reach the dance floor, they realize that none of the humans are even dancing. The kids are just huddled together in small circles, talking loudly over the music. Many of them stop their conversations to glance at Bella and Dee as they pass. Bella doesn't seem to notice, but Dee does.

Bella spots Crypta in the crowd, wearing a simple black dress and flats. "Wow," Bella says, surprised. "Look who decided to dress like a human. I have to admit, I didn't think she had it in her." Bella meets Crypta's eyes and waves. Crypta ignores her, opting instead to whisper something into their classmate Jeanie's ear.

The song changes, and all four friends recognize it instantly. "I love this one!" Bella shouts. She starts dancing, trying out the sprinkler first, and then forgoing Principal Koffin's suggestions altogether and jumping around instead.

"Me too!" Charlie agrees, dancing in a jazz square. Dee falls into step with them for a few beats, laughing as she sashays in her dress. Then Charlie stops and shouts, "Everybody, look out!" They grab their cape, spin around, and bust out an awesome moonwalk.

"Oh yeah?" Eugene crosses his arms. "That's pretty good, but you haven't seen my moves yet. Hey, witches." He looks at Bella and Dee. "Check this out." Then he drops to the floor and starts doing the worm.

Bella laughs. Dancing with her friends *is* pretty fun. It makes her forget all about the boring decorations. She grabs Dee's hands, spins her around in a circle, and then dips her down so far that she almost touches the ground. Dee shrieks with a mixture of fear and delight.

When she stands up, they do it again, but this time Dee spins and dips Bella. A few songs pass this way, with all four friends laughing together and dancing without a care in the world. Dee is having such a blast, she almost forgets to look for Sebastian—though she can't help but sneak a peek every now and then, hoping to spot his curly hair or contagious grin.

It's during one of these "sneak peeks" that Dee notices a group of human girls glancing over and laughing at them. She looks back at her friends but can't figure out what they're doing wrong. Have they revealed themselves as supernatural somehow?

Dee stops moving and takes a look around. Everybody else is still standing in small circles, talking or drinking melty sherbet punch and acting like they're too cool for dancing. It's obvious now that Dee and her friends are the only ones dancing like nobody's watching, when in fact *a lot* of people are watching.

She feels a swell of humiliation rise up inside her chest. In all her research on cool human dance moves, never once did it say that the coolest move of all was *not* dancing. Then she takes in everybody's plain pants and simple dresses. She looks down at her own dress, which suddenly appears much too poufy and too green. It seems she got that wrong too.

Dee looks back at the gossiping human girls. One of them makes eye contact with her and giggles again, and Dee's heart sinks. She hears Crypta's words in her head again: *You're never going to fit in with us.*

Dee's face starts to burn bright red. She already doesn't fit in with the other monsters. Now it seems she's failing at blending in with the humans, too.

That's when Dee notices Sebastian. He's standing not too far from the human girls, holding a cup of punch and chatting with a friend. Dee feels her pulse quicken. When he sees her, is he going to laugh at her too?

Without a word to Bella or her friends, Dee runs off the dance floor and out of the cafeteria.

~~~~~••• CHAPTER 7 •••~~~~~

In the bathroom Dee puts Cornelius in the sink and studies her reflection in the mirror. Her outfit, which looked so fun and funky at home, just looks childish to her now. Beetlejuice chic—what was she thinking? Humans only dress like Beetlejuice to go trick-or-treating, and even then they don't add sparkles and tutus. Of *course* those girls were going to laugh at her.

Afraid to get caught breaking the rules by using magic, Dee tries to shake some of the sparkles out of her hair. Then she yanks at the green taffeta lining of her tutu. None of it does any good. She still feels as silly as she looks.

She lets out a frustrated huff. How is she supposed to work in the human world as a meteorologist if she can't even blend in for a couple of hours at a school dance? Not for the first time, she's jealous of Bella's aspirations to be the next Bloody Mary. More specifically, she's jealous of her sister's certainty. Bella is meant for scaring, the same way a fish is meant for swimming or a ghoul for haunting. Dee's purpose in life is still much less certain.

She hears Crypta's voice again, seeming to echo throughout the room. *You're never going to fit in with us.*

With Cornelius occupying the sink in front of her, she moves over to the next one and splashes cold water onto her face. Then she looks at herself in the mirror again.

"Bella is going to be Bloody Mary," she says, her hands gripping either side of the sink. "What will I be?"

In the mirror a figure appears behind Dee. She's wearing a dirty, tattered nightgown, and her long, dark hair hangs menacingly over her face. Dee jumps and then glances behind her. There's nobody there.

"Donna Maleficent," the figure in the mirror croaks. "How may I assist you this evening?"

"Bloody Mary?" Dee asks, surprised. She leans closer to the mirror, so close that her nose almost touches it. "What are you doing here?"

Mary tilts her head to the left. "Whatever do you mean, child? You summoned me."

"Oh," Dee says, confused. She didn't mean to summon anyone. She only said Mary's name once, under her breath, when the lore clearly states you're supposed to say it ten times, with the lights off and a candle burning. She knows because she has seen Bella try it over and over. Could the lore be mistaken?

"Well?" Mary says, impatient. "Do you want my assistance or not?"

Dee looks at Cornelius. His eyes are wide as he stares into the mirror. He sees Mary too, but he doesn't seem afraid. Just alert.

Dee looks at Mary again. "Sure, I guess. But don't you have scaring to do?"

"Eh." Mary shrugs. "Slow night."

"Huh." Dee thinks about Bella. "My sister is *not* going to believe this. She's kind of your biggest fan." She glances toward the door. "Could I maybe go get her?"

Mary shakes her head. "Only one at a time. That's the way it works."

Dee frowns. *Now* Mary wants to follow the rules. "Okay, well, I don't need to scare anyone, but maybe you could give me some advice?"

Bloody Mary takes one step closer to Dee, so that her face hovers just inches from Dee's cheek. Dee sees her chapped, bloody lips form a small smile.

"Very well." Mary's voice is somewhere between a whisper and a growl. "Speak."

"Okay," Dee begins, inching away from Mary. "It's just that I'm at this dance with Bella and my friends, trying to have fun, but the humans are laughing at me."

Mary is unimpressed. "And?"

"And . . . well, I don't want them to laugh at me." Dee bites her lip, feeling something like shame.

"Would you like me to unleash my vengeance upon them?" Mary raises her hands and hooks her fingers so they look like claws. "I could take their tongues, and they will laugh no more."

"*No,*" Dee says urgently. "No vengeance. I want them to like me."

"Dear girl," Mary coos, and Dee can feel her breath, hot and foul, hit her cheek. "Whatever for? You're a witch. Be proud of your power!

They should fear you, and you should revel in their fear, as I do."

Dee makes a face. "Yeah, but scaring is more my sister Bella's thing. I want to use my powers to help humans."

"*Help* humans?" Mary repeats, and then puckers her lips in displeasure. "How very strange."

Suddenly the door opens, making Dee jump again. Mary disappears.

Crypta Cauldronson walks in, carrying a little black clutch. When she sees Dee, she stops.

"What are you doing?" she asks, raising one perfectly arched eyebrow. "Hiding from the humans?"

Dee shrugs. "Something like that."

Crypta moves to stand at the sink next to Dee. She looks in the mirror and starts reapplying her cherry lip gloss. "Well, you're not exactly trying to blend in, are you?" She smacks her lips together and then applies another layer. "That dress practically glows in the dark."

Dee stays silent as she looks at Crypta in the mirror. Crypta, with her shiny straight hair and perfectly plain dress, looks exactly like a human. *Typical,* Dee thinks. Just as Crypta fits in with the monsters better than Dee does, she can blend in better with the humans, too.

Dee feels overwhelmingly like a failure. There were plenty of dresses that looked just like Crypta's at the thrift store. She even tried a few of them on. *Why* hadn't she bought the pale pink one with the bow on the back? That one was nice enough. If she had, maybe Sebastian would have spoken to her by now. Maybe she looked so ridiculous that he was avoiding her on purpose.

From his place in the sink, Cornelius meows disapprovingly. He seems to know what Dee is thinking.

"Aw, is this your familiar?" Crypta asks.

Dee nods. "Cornelius."

"My mom says most witches don't connect with a familiar until they're older." Crypta smiles down at Cornelius, making Dee consider that maybe she isn't as heartless as she seems. *Maybe.* "You're lucky."

Lucky. Dee doesn't feel lucky. She feels foolish and embarrassed.

Crypta puts her lip gloss back into her clutch and fluffs up her hair. Then she pulls out her eyephone and takes a few mirror selfies. The blue eye blinks with each picture she takes.

"What you said at the assembly," Dee says quietly. "You really hurt my feelings, you know."

Crypta furrows her brow. "What did I say?"

Dee stares for a moment in disbelief. Of course Crypta doesn't remember. She's never thought about the consequences of her own actions before, Dee thinks. Why start now?

Still, Dee presses on. "You said that I would never fit in."

Crypta snorts. "That's it? Lighten up, Dee. It's just a joke." She puts her eyephone away and checks herself out in the mirror one last time. "You're so sensitive. Are you sure you're a witch?"

Crypta leaves the bathroom. Dee stares after her for a moment, stricken. Then she looks at herself in the mirror, silently mulling over Crypta's question. *Well, are you?*

"*Meow,*" Cornelius insists, judgment in his eyes.

"Don't look at me like that," Dee whispers. "If I'm not a real witch, then maybe I should just be a human."

Dee holds her own gaze in the mirror. She doesn't care anymore if she gets in trouble and has to leave YIKESSS. At least then she won't have to worry about fitting in where she clearly doesn't belong.

She taps herself on the shoulder and spells the pale pink dress from the thrift store—or one just like it, with pockets—onto her body, along with a pair of white ballet flats like the black ones Crypta wears.

Dee does a little spin, surprised the spell worked. The protective charm Professor Belinda put over the school is supposed to make doing magic impossible. Perhaps there's a loophole that allows her to cast in the bathroom, or in case of an emergency? Which, according to Dee, this most definitely is.

Dee looks at herself and sighs. She got what she wanted. She'll finally be able to blend in with the humans. So why doesn't she feel better?

Cornelius meows again. Instead of responding, Dee picks him up and gently places him back in her pocket.

❧ CHAPTER 8 ☙

Dee returns to the cafeteria, but this time she doesn't join Bella, Charlie, and Eugene in the middle of the dance floor. She scans the room for the human girls who laughed at her before, and spots them by the punch table, refilling their cups. Without a second thought she walks over.

"Hi," she says, smoothing down her dress.

The girls turn to look at her, and then exchange surprised glances among themselves. For a moment Dee worries they might recognize her.

A girl with red hair and bangs is the first to speak up. "Um, hi. Do you go to YIKESSS?"

Dee hesitates. She looks over at Bella and her friends, who are all watching her with wary expressions on their faces. Then she looks back at the girl and shakes her head.

"I just started at PPS," Dee lies. "I'm Donna."

In her pocket Cornelius lets out a small, disgruntled meow.

"I'm Katie," the girl replies. She gestures to the other two. "This is Emily and Jessica."

Jessica picks up a cup of punch from the snack table and offers it to Dee. "I *love* your dress."

"Thanks!" Dee, pleased with herself, takes a sip of the punch and winces. *Blech.* It's all sugar, no fizz, but she smiles and pretends to like it anyway.

In the middle of the dance floor, Bella, Charlie, and Eugene have all stopped dancing. It's the most human they've looked all night.

"What is she *doing*?" Bella, confused and a little irritated, watches Dee talk to the humans. Here they are, having a great time dancing with the humans, *just like* Dee wanted, and then all of a sudden she runs off with no explanation. It doesn't make sense. "And where did she get that dress?" Bella's face falls. "We don't match anymore."

"It looks like the one she tried on at the store," Charlie decides, shuffling their feet. "The one you said made her look like a human."

"Because it *did*," Bella says. She sees her sister glance back at her and then quickly look away, as if Bella doesn't even exist. "It *does*." Bella crosses her arms, trying to disguise the hurt she feels.

"It's a downgrade, for sure," Eugene agrees. He's still slightly out of breath from doing the worm for twenty minutes straight, and his poufy hair has deflated and gone lopsided. Sort of like a melted ice cream cone, Bella thinks regretfully. "Hey," Eugene adds, "maybe she's playing some kind of game?"

"Like what?" Bella scoffs, keeping all ice cream thoughts to herself. "The Ignore Your Friends game? What's fun about that?"

"She's probably just trying to see if she can fit in with the humans," Charlie observes, shimmying to the beat now. "Dee wants to be friends with everyone. You know how she is."

I thought I did, Bella thinks. Deep down she knows Charlie is right, but at the same time, Dee being friends with everyone usually doesn't come at Bella's expense. Her sister never excludes her.

Bella lets out a huff of frustration. "I don't understand what's so great about being human. You have way less power."

"*And* way less responsibility," Charlie points out. "Not everybody wants to be the next Bloody Mary, you know."

Bella shrugs. "Not everyone can be. Charlie, you should know. Your mom is one of the best scarers in the world."

"Yeah, which is why she's still in Mexico and I never get to see her. Sometimes less responsibility is a good thing."

Charlie, fully dancing again, moonwalks right into a human. The person turns around, and the friends recognize him as the man Principal Koffin was talking to earlier.

"Whoa there," he laughs, and Bella's eyes are drawn to his teeth, which are bright white and perfectly straight, almost artificial-looking.

"I'm so sorry," Charlie says, taking a step back. "I guess I just got carried away by the rhythm."

"That's all right. Happens to the best of us." He looks around at the group. "You kids are from YIKESSS, right? Having a good time?"

The group nods. Bella takes in his PPS STAFF badge, hanging from a lanyard around his neck. She reads his name, typed in bold print:

PRINCIPAL OSWALD PLEASANT. *Aha*. They were right before: This is the PPS principal.

"Wonderful," says Principal Pleasant, seeming to genuinely mean it. "I think it's so important for our two schools to join together as one community, don't you? We have so much to learn from each other."

The group nods again. "Totally," Bella adds, cracking a small, private smile. If only he really knew.

"Well, I'm off to the punch table," the principal says. He gives the group a wave. "Until we meet again!"

The group stares after him. "He seems nice enough," Charlie says.

"Definitely enthusiastic," Eugene adds. "Like Koffin said." He looks at Bella. "Anyway, I think it's okay that Dee is doing her own thing. You know, it's sort of like how—"

"But she's *not* doing her own thing," Bella interrupts him, remembering where their conversation left off. She feels a new wave of anger swell up inside her. "She's doing what the humans want her to do. Otherwise . . ." She looks down at her striped overalls, which she picked out specifically because they matched Dee's dress, and she clenches her fists. Bella knows how much Dee loves that stripy green dress, and how excited she was to wear it out tonight. "Otherwise she wouldn't have changed outfits."

Bella feels her magic flicker on her palms, the way it tends to do when her temper flares up. She takes a few deep breaths and lets them out slowly, the way Professor Belinda taught her.

"What I was *going* to say," Eugene continues when Bella is calmer, "is that as a goblin, everyone expects me to become a trickster. But *I* want to be a pilot."

Bella and Charlie share a look of surprise. They assumed Eugene would become a trickster not because he's a goblin but because of how much he likes mischief in general.

"You do?" Charlie asks.

Eugene smiles proudly and nods. "I'm going to be the first goblin pilot ever. Pretty cool, huh?"

"Aren't goblins afraid of heights?" Bella asks. She's pretty sure she read as much in her Supernatural Cultures textbook.

Eugene sighs. "All I'm saying is that wanting to fit in with humans doesn't mean I don't care about my monster friends. It just means I have other interests too."

Bella looks at Dee again. She's laughing with the humans, sipping sherbet punch and pretending to be too cool for dancing. She appears to be having a great time without her monster friends.

"Fine," Bella says as the song changes. "If she's having fun without us, then we can have fun without her, too." She starts dancing just as wildly as before. After only a moment of hesitation, Charlie and Eugene follow her lead.

Over with the humans, Dee is laughing at a joke she doesn't understand. Emily just showed the group a short video on some app that seems to be a lot like WitchStitch, but without any of the magic. Dee wishes she could show them a video she saw yesterday of a ghost dog fetching an enchanted tennis ball in the sky. Instead, when they ask Dee for her username, she can only say she doesn't have one.

"Really?" Katie says. "Wow, you must live under a rock."

Dee shakes her head. "I live in Eerie Estates."

That makes the girls laugh, which makes Dee smile, even though, once again, she doesn't understand what was so funny.

Two boys join them, and Dee recognizes one of them as the human who made fun of Eugene's hair outside.

"Mike, Wyatt, this is our new friend Donna," Katie says to the boys. She turns to Dee. "She's *hilarious*. Donna, tell him the joke you told us earlier. The one about the witch garage."

"Oh." Dee raises her eyebrows. "Um, it was just that witches don't have garages. They only have broom closets."

227

The whole group bursts into laughter, and Dee takes a satisfied sip of her drink. She hadn't been telling a joke, simply stating a fact, but the humans don't need to know that.

"Oh, man." Mike nudges Katie and gestures to the dance floor. "The YIKESSS weirdos are at it again."

Dee turns around to see Bella, Charlie, and Eugene dancing up a storm in the center of the room. Everybody around them has taken a few steps back to watch—also, probably to avoid accidentally getting hit by Eugene's unpredictable worm movements. Dee even sees a few human cell phones out, recording the whole thing.

Emily puts a hand over her mouth, stifling laughter. "I'm not sure what's more embarrassing, his dancing or his orange Hershey's Kiss hair."

"Probably his dancing," Jessica says.

Katie shakes her head. "His hair, all the way."

The girls look at Dee, expecting her to weigh

in. Dee bites the inside of her cheek. She knows she should say something to defend Eugene, but if she does, it will just give away the fact that she's lying about going to PPS, and she can't have that.

"His hair, totally," Dee agrees. She looks down at her cup of punch, not wanting to meet their eyes. "It's, like, as bright and melty as this sherbet."

Everybody laughs, and Katie turns to Mike. "What did I tell you?" She puts a hand on Dee's shoulder. *"Hilarious."*

Dee forces out a laugh even though her heart is pounding. It didn't feel good to say those things about Eugene. It definitely didn't feel "hilarious." She puts her hand into her pocket, and Cornelius nuzzles his tiny kitten head into her palm, making her feel a little better.

"You're right," Mike says to Katie, but he's looking at Dee. "Donna, you should hang with us at school on Monday. We have an extra seat at our lunch table."

"What's your schedule?" Katie pipes in. "Maybe we'll have a class together."

"My schedule?" Dee hurries to think of something to say, but her heart is still racing, and her lies are catching up to her. "Um . . ."

She takes a step backward and feels her ankle collide with another student's shoe. She reaches out for something, or someone, to steady herself with, but nobody comes. With a shriek she falls backward into the snack table, knocking it to the ground and spilling the entire bowl of punch all over her pink dress. Cornelius, sensing alarm, manages to hop out of her pocket just in time to avoid the splash.

The music stops, and Dee looks up from her place on the floor to see that everyone, human and monster alike, is staring at her, their expressions varying between laughter, annoyance, and secondhand embarrassment. She doesn't look long enough to see if Sebastian is among them.

"Oh my gosh." Jessica rushes over and crouches down next to Dee. "Are you all right?"

Dee lets Jessica help her up. She looks down at her dress, which is sopping wet and ruined, and then looks back up and locks eyes with Bella, who hasn't moved from her place in the center of the dance floor.

The sisters hold each other's gaze for one, two, three seconds.

Then Bella looks away.

Dee runs out of the cafeteria and into the hallway, with kitten Cornelius right on her heels. Bella, Eugene, and Charlie watch them go.

"Do you think we should go after her?" Charlie asks, their red eyes wide with concern.

Bella shakes her head. "Let her new human friends be the ones to help."

The music resumes, and Bella, Charlie, and Eugene continue to dance.

~~~•❀ **CHAPTER 9** ❀•~~~

The hallway is empty, dark, and quiet, save for the dance music coming through the open doors. Dee rounds the corner to a vacant row of lockers and sits down on the floor. Cornelius catches up a few moments later.

Dee looks back down the hallway, waiting for Bella, Charlie, Eugene, or even one of the humans to appear and ask if she's all right. But they never do. She and Cornelius are all alone.

Dee puts her head in her hands. What is she supposed to do now? She abandoned Bella and her friends for those humans, made fun of Eugene, and then lied to the humans about going to school with them. Not to mention that she and her clumsy legs spilled the sherbet punch *and* ruined her pink dress. That's four strikes. If this were a flyball game, she would be out.

Cornelius meows and brushes up against the side of her leg. Dee scoops his tiny kitten body up in her hands and kisses the top of his head. "At least we have each other," she whispers. Cornelius meows in agreement.

Dee looks down at her dress and sighs. It really *is* ruined. And yet she's surprised to find that she doesn't care one bit. She much preferred the green-and-black dress in all its poufy, stripy glory. She should never have changed outfits to begin with.

In fact, Dee thinks, she should never have come to the dance at all. Of course she was going to embarrass herself—she almost always does something embarrassing! She was never actually going to fit in with the humans. *Why* didn't she listen to Ant when he tried to tell her that going to a human dance wasn't a good idea?

She squeezes her eyes shut and wishes she were at home right now. Or anywhere but here, for that matter. Preferably someplace that doesn't have fragile objects, as her clumsiness would probably cause her to break something there, too. Jeepers, she wishes she weren't so clumsy. She wishes she were something more graceful, like a princess, or a gazelle, or . . .

She opens her eyes and sees the turnip corsage on her wrist. A turnip! Turnips *can't* trip. They don't have legs.

That's it, Dee thinks, letting out an unenthusiastic sigh. She wishes she were a turnip.

And then—*POOF!* In a burst of green magic, Dee is no longer sitting by the lockers. It seems she is lying down, and perhaps maybe even rolling? She catches a glimpse of Cornelius, who has grown ten times his kitten size. He lets out a panicked meow, and it sounds low and loud.

Oh no.

Cornelius hasn't grown larger at all. It's Dee who has shrunk, and with a sinking feeling she realizes . . .

She has accidentally turned herself into a turnip.

⤑⤑⤑⤑ CHAPTER 10 ⤛⤛⤛⤛

Cornelius approaches Dee. He blinks his big
yellow eyes curiously and touches her turnip greens with his nose.

"Cornelius!" Dee shouts up at him in her
squeaky turnip voice. "Go get Bella!"

Cornelius cocks his head like he's listening,
but he doesn't move.

"Cornelius, go find help!"

But instead of finding help, Cornelius starts playing with Dee, batting her back and forth between his paws. Dee lets out a groan of frustration. Kitten Cornelius is an even worse listener than the fully grown version.

Dee tries to reverse the spell by silently wishing herself back to normal, but it doesn't work. Perhaps because she doesn't have hands to conjure sparks? Or maybe Professor Belinda's protective charm *does* work, but only on intentional magic? Dee sighs. Whatever the reason, it seems she's stuck.

She listens closely for any sounds of life approaching, but the halls stay still and silent. What to do now besides get pushed around and hope that someone finds her? Someone supernatural, that is. If a human stumbles upon her, she'll have to stay quiet and act like a turnip. Dee can't go exposing the supernatural community over something so silly—she's already caused more than enough trouble for one night.

Cornelius swats her a little too hard, and she rolls away from him, behind a trash can, where she gets wedged between the can and the wall.

"Cornelius!" she yells out, struggling to wiggle herself free. "I'm stuck back here!"

Grunting and writhing, Dee tries to move with all her might, but it's no use. She isn't going to be able to get free on her own. She pauses to catch her breath and looks around.

That's when she notices the spiderwebs. They're scattered all around her, looking shiny, taut, and sinister.

Dee's tiny turnip heart begins to pound. She thinks about the decorative spiderweb article in the newest issue of *Haunted Housekeeping*, which encourages readers to hang their webs in a disorganized fashion to create the illusion of decay. These webs are much too pristine to be decorative.

On the other side of the trash can, Dee thinks she sees four pairs of eyes blinking at her in the darkness. She squeezes her own eyes shut, trying to convince herself she imagined it.

It could be worse, she reassures herself. She could be down in Eugene's basement again, holding that spider doll. Or worse still: taking a Potions exam.

When she opens her eyes, something brown and fuzzy is standing over her. A dog? No—she's three inches tall. A dog would be much bigger. This only seems like a dog to Dee because she's so small. The fuzzy creature backs up, revealing eight long, hooked legs. It blinks all eight of its eyes again.

Never mind, Dee thinks. *This is the worst scenario of them all.*

She screams at the top of her lungs, and the huge spider rears back. Then a fluffy black paw comes from out of nowhere and bats her away from the spider, back into the center of the hall.

"Cornelius!" Dee cries, relieved. "You saved me! You're such a good boy!"

He meows happily, and then immediately resumes playing with her.

"Ouch," she shouts. "Watch the face!"

Eventually Cornelius rolls Dee to the cafeteria doorway, where she has the chance to observe the dance going on without her. Most of the humans still aren't dancing or enjoying the music, opting instead to stand around drinking icky punch or scrolling on their phones. It all seems so terribly boring to Dee now. She can't remember why she ever wanted to be part of it in the first place.

She quickly spots Bella, Charlie, and Eugene, as her friends are the only ones in the whole room who are really dancing, and Dee is struck immediately by how awesome they look. She sees other students around them, both humans *and* monsters, whispering and laughing at the group's over-the-top and outdated moves. More important, she sees how Bella and her friends don't pay them any attention. All they care about is having fun, and clearly they are. From where Dee stands (or rolls), they seem to be having a blast.

In that moment she no longer cares whether she fits in with the humans or the monsters. She fits in with her friends, and that's all she needs. Bella, Charlie, and Eugene are the creepiest—no, the *coolest*—ones at this party. They're the ones other people should want to be liked by. Dee could be out there having fun with them right now if she hadn't been so concerned with what the humans thought of her.

And who knows? If she had stayed true to herself, maybe there's a human here who would have liked her anyway.

Just then Dee spots Sebastian. He's bobbing his head to the music while his eyes scan the crowd as if he's looking for someone. Dee's pale turnip cheeks turn bright red.

It's official: she really messed up.

~~~~~•••~~~ **CHAPTER 11** •••~~~~~

When a slow song comes on and the humans begin to pair off, Bella finally takes a break from dancing.

"Why are you stopping?" Charlie asks, their cape billowing as they sway to the soft rhythm. "I like this one."

"Me too," Eugene says. He looks down at his

shoes and then glances up at Bella. Is she imagining things, or is he nervous? "Hey, Maleficent, want to dance with me?"

Bella's eyebrows shoot up in surprise. Hasn't she been dancing with him the whole night? She looks around at the humans, how they've coupled up to rock back and forth while holding on to each other, the way she practiced with Dee at the assembly. Then she glowers. Thinking of her sister makes her feel a fresh wave of hurt.

"No, thanks." She shakes her head, and Eugene deflates just a little. "I'm going to find the bathroom."

"Right," Eugene says, laughing uncomfortably. "Totally get it. When you gotta go, you gotta go."

"Keep an eye out for Dee," Charlie reminds her. "I haven't seen her in a while."

Bella resists the urge to roll her eyes. "I'm sure she's fine."

"A bowl of punch spilled on her," Charlie points out. "In front of the whole school."

243

"*Two* whole schools," Eugene adds, swaying in time with Charlie.

"She's a klutz," Bella says. "It's nothing new."

Charlie and Eugene look at each other, both clearly holding their tongues.

Bella sighs, exasperated. "Fine, I'll look for her. But I'll bet one of her boring human friends let her borrow another one of their *boring* human dresses, and they're off somewhere talking about . . ." Bella pauses, thinking. "I don't know, whatever boring stuff humans talk about."

"Taxes?" Eugene guesses.

"Maybe." Charlie doesn't sound convinced. "Or maybe she's hiding somewhere, embarrassed?"

Eugene nods in agreement.

Bella replies with a dismissive wave of her hand. Then a human girl with braces and a red bow in her hair taps Charlie on the shoulder.

"Hi," she says, her voice shy. "I like your cape. Would you want to dance?"

Charlie looks back at Bella and Eugene, who

give encouraging nods. When Charlie returns their attention to the girl, they smile so wide that both of their fangs poke out. The girl doesn't seem to notice.

Bella leaves her friends and moves through the crowd, not caring that some people's eyes linger on her as she passes. Following the signs for the bathroom, she wanders into the hallway. She's about to turn left, toward the bathroom, when she spots Cornelius off to the right, by himself.

"Cornelius?"

The kitten doesn't notice her. He's too busy playing with something small. Confused, Bella gets closer. The object between his paws appears to be a vegetable, maybe an onion, or a radish? Then she hears a small, squeaky sound. It takes her a few seconds to realize that the sound is coming from the radish.

"Bella! It's me!"

Bella's eyes widen. She leans over and nudges Cornelius away from the radish—from

Dee?—and then picks her up and dusts her off.

"Thank *badness* you're here!" Dee squeaks. "Cornelius was making me really dizzy."

"Dee?" Bella says, squinting down at her sister. "Why are you a radish?"

"I'm not a radish," Dee says, more than a little irritated. "I'm a turnip."

Bella covers her mouth with her hand as she resists the urge to laugh. "Sorry. Why are you a turnip?"

Turnip Dee puffs out her cheeks. "I was embarrassed, so I wished I was a turnip, and then I became one, and I can't figure out how to change back!"

Now Bella does laugh. She can't believe she was worried Dee had abandoned her for the humans, when the truth was, she had become a turnip.

"*Ha, ha, ha,*" Dee mocks. "It's so funny. Would you *please* help change me back?"

"That depends," Bella says, smirking. "Have you learned your lesson?"

"Bella!"

"Okay, okay," Bella says. "But honestly I have no idea how to fix this. I'll take you to Professor Belinda." She puts Cornelius into the front pocket of her overalls and cups Dee between her palms.

"Thanks," Dee says. "And, Bella, I *am* sorry. I shouldn't have ditched you or changed outfits."

"Don't worry about it," Bella says, walking back to the cafeteria. "Although, you're right about the dress. Pink lace? That *bow*?"

"I know," Dee admits. "I think the punch was actually an improvement."

With that, both sisters laugh, and everything is back to the way it's supposed to be.

Well, aside from the fact that Dee is still a turnip.

Bella finds Professor Belinda monitoring the snack table, which has been restored to its former punch-and-pretzel glory.

"Professor," Bella says, and her voice wavers. Will Dee get into trouble for this? The rules

247

were clear: they weren't supposed to use *any* magic on PPS grounds. And Bella and Dee were already on thin ice with the principal.

Professor Belinda, who has been dancing to the music with her eyes closed, spins around quickly, as if Bella has awoken her from a dream. "What is it, Bella? Another spill?"

"It's, um . . ." Bella glances down at Dee. "Well, I'll just say it. My sister accidentally turned herself into a turnip."

Professor Belinda looks surprised. "I'm sorry?"

Bella opens her palms to reveal Turnip Dee. "Hi, Professor!" Dee squeaks.

"Oh, my!" Professor Belinda's eyes widen. She takes Dee from Bella and examines the girl turnip between her fingers. "Hmm. Good over-all size and coloring. I must say, Dee, it seems you're a perfect turnip! Well done."

"Um," Dee says. "Thanks?"

"So, we won't get into trouble?" Bella clarifies.

Professor Belinda shakes her head. "This is a

simple fix. Now, if you had turned yourself into a rotting turnip, *that* would have been cause for concern."

"Phew." Dee smiles, relieved. Professor Belinda winces.

"Gah!" She holds Dee a little farther away from her body. "A turnip with teeth! What an unsettling sight."

"Hey!" Dee squeaks.

Professor Belinda looks at Bella. "Come along. Let's move into the hallway, and I'll lift the veil of protection. She'll be a witch again in no time."

In the hallway a few minutes later, Professor Belinda recites an incantation that temporarily lifts the veil of protection, then changes Dee from a turnip back to a witch. Dee, once again wearing her green-and-black stripy dress, does a little spin, glad to be normal again. That is, with the exception of a new streak of green in the front of her hair, which resembles the exact color of the leafy green part of a turnip.

"Creepy!" Bella says, reaching out to touch the streak. She takes a step back and examines her sister fully. "You know, it actually suits you."

"A small side effect from your time as a vegetable," Professor Belinda says. "A simple turmeric-and-star-salt potion should turn it to black again."

Dee thinks about it for a moment and then shakes her head. "I think I'd like to keep it."

Professor Belinda smiles. "Of course. Very witchy, indeed." She turns to go, but then looks back at the twins. After a beat of hesitation, she says, "One last thing. As I'm sure you're aware, it is most unusual that Dee managed to break through the veil of protection, even accidentally. The charm I created was a powerful one. It should not have been possible to penetrate it."

Dee raises her eyebrows, while Bella looks down at the floor.

"I'm going to investigate how this could have happened," Professor Belinda continues.

"But in the meantime, I think it's best not to mention this little kerfuffle to Principal Koffin, hmm? She's got enough in her cauldron as it is."

The twins nod in unison.

Professor Belinda returns to the cafeteria, and Dee gives Bella a big hug. "I'm so glad you found me. I thought I was going to be stuck as a turnip forever."

"What was it like, being that small?" Bella replies.

Dee thinks about the spider behind the trash can and shudders. "You don't want to know."

Bella glances through the doorway into the cafeteria. "Before we go back in, I have a confession to make."

Dee frowns. "What?"

From her pocket Bella pulls out a small drawstring velvet pouch. She unties the drawstring, and the contents spill onto her palm, revealing a tablespoon or so of black salt.

Dee's jaw drops open in shock. "You didn't."

Bella's face is apologetic. "What if something bad happened, and we needed to use our powers to protect ourselves?"

Dee shakes her head in disbelief. Bella came to the dance with enchanted salt in her pocket, which shielded her from the effects of Professor Belinda's magical veil. "Wait," Dee says. "*Our* powers?" She checks the other pocket of her dress, the one Cornelius wasn't hiding in all night, and feels the grainy texture of salt brush against her fingertips.

Bella shrugs. "I didn't have time to make you a bag, so I just poured some in there when you weren't looking."

Dee knows she should be mad about Bella's recklessness, but mostly she's just relieved there's an explanation for what happened. The idea that her magic could be strong enough to penetrate the veil on its own would be frightening if it weren't so preposterous. She still has so much to learn.

"Should we go back inside?" Dee asks, changing the subject. The dance is almost over, but she's only just getting started.

"Yes!" Bella agrees, and then turns to go in.

"Wait." Dee glances around to make sure nobody is coming. Then she grabs a section of Bella's hair and tugs on it once, turning it hot pink. Bella gasps in delight.

"There." Dee grins. "Now we're matching again."

~~~•••• CHAPTER 12 ••••~~~

By the time the DJ announces his last song of the night—"Thriller" by Michael Jackson—Bella, Dee, Charlie, and Eugene are having so much fun dancing that they've all but forgotten about Dee's brief experience as a turnip. Even better, a few other humans and monsters have joined them on the dance floor, so the event is actually starting to resemble a real school dance.

When Eugene gets on the ground to do the worm, a circle forms around him, and everybody starts clapping to the beat. Soon Charlie moonwalks their way into the center, and after that a human kid jumps in and starts flossing. Before they know it, a full-on dance-off is taking place. Cornelius sits on top of a speaker nearby, watching it all from a safe distance.

Meanwhile, Bella and Dee spin and dip and flip each other, laughing the whole time. At one point Bella spots Crypta on the sidelines, watching them. Bella waves her over, but Crypta quickly looks away, pretending not to see her.

"Your loss!" Bella calls out.

When the song ends, everybody on the dance floor groans in unison. A few YIKESSS kids try to start a "One more song" chant, but a stern look from Principal Koffin quiets them down immediately. Then the lights turn on, and it's official: the party is over.

"Whew!" Eugene says, panting. His hair has gone back to its natural wild state, and sweat glistens across his green forehead. "I don't know about you ghouls, but I'm exhausted."

"Me too," Dee agrees. She looks around for Cornelius, who jumps from his perch on top of the speaker over to her shoulder. She tucks him safely back into her pocket.

"That was *amazing!*" Charlie bounces on the balls of their feet, still full of energy. "I feel like I could dance all night."

"That's because you're technically nocturnal," Bella points out, a little out of breath herself.

"So are you," Charlie reminds her. They look at Eugene. "By the way, can I still sleep over at your house tonight?"

"Yeah!" Eugene nods eagerly. "I've gotta get your opinion on my newest experiment. Picture this—" He holds up his hands. "A machine that reads books for you."

Bella puts a hand on her hip. "An audiobook?"

Eugene points at her. "No. This reads the book *for* you, and then you press a button and the words get transferred into your brain!" He looks around at his friends eagerly.

"That actually works?" Dee asks, intrigued by any invention that would make her homework easier.

"Well, not *yet*." Eugene grimaces. "But once I work out the kinks, it will."

Suddenly and silently, Principal Koffin appears behind him, making Dee and Charlie jump in surprise.

"It is time to clear the premises," she tells them. "Did you all have an enjoyable evening?"

"The best!" Dee says. She links arms with Charlie and Bella, who then links arms with Eugene. "I'm so glad we all got to be here together."

"Without using any magic *at all*," Bella adds with her most innocent smile.

Principal Koffin replies with a simple "Mhm." And yet something about the way she says it makes Bella and Dee suspect she knows about everything that went on tonight.

"Well," Principal Koffin finishes. "I hope you all have a pleasant weekend." She nods her farewell and leaves just as quickly as she came. For a moment they all stare after her.

"What do you think she does on the weekends?" Bella asks.

"Who knows?" Eugene says. "Frankly, I'm surprised she even exists outside of YIKESSS. The harpy is practically part of the architecture."

"I'll bet she's got lots of stories to tell," Charlie says, and the rest of the group nods in agreement.

With linked arms all four friends head for the exit. They're almost to the doors when Dee notices Sebastian standing nearby with some friends. Before she has time to think about what to do next, his eyes meet hers.

"Dee!" He waves, and then walks over. "Hey. I was hoping to see you tonight."

Dee feels the bats in her stomach, pumping their wings as fast as they can.

"You look awesome," he says. "I like your hair. Very *creepy*," he adds with a wink.

Dee blushes. "Thanks." Cornelius pokes his head out from her pocket and meows, and Sebastian's face lights up.

"Wow, what a cute kitten! What's its name?"

"Cor—" Dee starts, and Bella widens her eyes in warning. "Cory. His name is Cory."

"Hi, Cory." Sebastian smiles and scratches him on the head. Cornelius purrs contentedly, like Sebastian is an old friend.

Which is exactly what he is, Dee quickly realizes. In fact, maybe *that's* why Cornelius has been so grumpy lately. He misses his pal Sebastian.

"So." Sebastian glances back at his friends, who are clearly waiting for him. "See you around?"

"Yeah." Dee smiles wide. "You most definitely will."

Dee, Cornelius, and her friends leave the cafeteria. It isn't until they're outside under the stars, a safe distance away from the humans, that Charlie asks in a hushed voice, "Was that the mayor's son?"

"Sebastian," Bella tells them. "And in case it wasn't obvious, Dee thinks he's the banshee's knees."

"It's obvious." Eugene nudges Dee playfully. He looks toward the parking lot and points at a black car that resembles a hearse. "Hey, there's my mom. Let's go, Charlie."

Charlie hugs Bella and Dee at the same time. "See you Monday!"

Bella and Dee watch their friends go, and then sit down on a bench while they wait for their dads.

"What a night," Dee says. She pulls Cornelius out of her pocket and holds him in front of her face. "Did you have fun, buddy?"

Cornelius meows happily. It seems his interaction with Sebastian has brightened his spirits.

"That makes two of us," she whispers.

"I danced more tonight than I ever have in my entire life!" Bella swoons, and then makes a displeased face. "Although, I was really hoping to meet a ghost. I wanted some haunting tips."

"Oh, by the way," Dee says, "I saw Bloody Mary."

Bella's jaw drops. "WHAT?" She puts her hands on Dee's shoulders. "Where? *How?*"

"In the bathroom," Dee says. "I said her name and she just appeared."

"Jeepers creepers! I've tried to summon her hundreds of times, and nothing happened, and you get to meet her on your first try?" Bella's jealousy morphs into admiration. "You know, she doesn't come for just anybody when they call. You must have caught her attention somehow."

Dee shrugs. She didn't think much of it before, but now that Bella mentions it, Dee can't help but wonder: Why *did* Bloody Mary choose her?

Dee grabs two fistfuls of her tutu. "Maybe it was my dress," she says jokingly.

Bella laughs. "Probably."

A familiar three-beat honk catches their attention, and the sisters look up to see their dads' white car idling in the parking lot.

"You have to tell me everything," Bella says, standing up. "What was she like?"

"I'll tell you all about it in the car." Dee stands up too. "But first let's ask if we can stop at Scary Good Shakes on the way home. I need to get the taste of turnip out of my mouth."

Bella giggles. "Deal."

~~~~~ EPILOGUE ~~~~~

A man walks into a windowless room. He shuts the door and locks it before turning on the light.

A fluorescent bulb illuminates the bare white walls. The room appears to be an office, albeit a very plain one. The only furniture inside is a desk, three chairs, and an empty bookshelf. There is also a narrow wooden door on the back wall, which presumably leads to a coat closet. Since the room has no windows, it's impossible to know for sure what time of day it is. But judging by the dark circles under the man's eyes, and perhaps also by the way he has haphazardly loosened his tie, it is likely very late, or even very early. Either way, it has been a while since he last slept.

The man walks to the desk in the center of the room. There is a computer on the desk, plus a stapler, two framed photographs of a woman and two small children, and a brass nameplate. He removes the ID badge from around his neck and drops it just behind the nameplate. Both say the same thing: PRINCIPAL OSWALD PLEASANT.

He pulls a set of keys out of his pocket and unlocks the second drawer on the desk's left side. He rifles through the contents of the drawer until he pulls out another, smaller set of keys. Then he stands up and moves to the closet. When he unlocks the door, he smiles.

The closet contains only one thing: a large wooden filing cabinet—an antique, by the look of it. Each drawer seems to have its own unique set of locks. The man examines the second key chain until he finds the two keys he needs. He inserts the keys into the locks, turns them simultaneously to the left until he hears a click, and then slides the drawer open slowly. When he lays eyes on what's inside, he lets out a small sigh of satisfaction.

The device he removes from the cabinet is small, black, and rectangular. He pushes a button and a screen lights up. He pushes another button, and the device starts to ring. It rings and rings until finally a woman's voice, distant and muffled, comes through the line.

"Beta." The man's voice is hardly above a whisper. "It's me."

The woman speaks softly too. It's impossible to make out her reply.

"I know," the man says. "It took longer than I anticipated, but the wait is over. I found her."

The man is quiet then. There's a noise in the distance, a sort of rumbling that could be coming from a machine. He doesn't seem to hear it, or else he's not bothered by it. He is focusing very hard on what the woman has to say. Finally he smiles, emphasizing his sharp jaw and large, straight teeth.

"That's right," he says. "The banshee is in Mexico."

He starts fiddling with a ring on his finger, a large silver thing with some sort of crest engraved on top. He raises his hand to his lips and kisses the ring once.

"You know what to do," he says to the woman. "I'll see you soon."

MONSTROUS MATCHMAKERS

⤳⤳⤳• CHAPTER 1 •⤳⤳⤳

A black cat in a green collar moves through the shadows down Franken Lane, his fur illuminated by the dim light of the crescent moon. There are no lamps on this street, nor anywhere else inside the gates of Eerie Estates. The supernatural creatures who call this neighborhood home much prefer the darkness.

At the end of the road, the cat makes a right onto Stein Street, then ducks behind a row of shrubs and disappears. It's his piercing yellow eyes that give him away again a few minutes later, when he emerges two blocks westward, on the front lawn of the black house at 333 Quivering Court. He walks up the path to the porch and then hops onto the sill of an open window, where he can hear muffled voices and see the flickering blue glow of the living room TV. After pausing a moment to lick his paw, he slinks inside, and the window closes behind him.

On the other side of the wall, the young witch Bella Maleficent sits cross-legged on the couch in her bright green pajamas, with a bowl of popcorn in her lap. She leans forward, her eyes glued to the TV. To her left her sister, Dee Maleficent, slouches between two cushions, scrolling on her green eyephone while her feet rest on the black coffee table in front of her. The cat jumps down from the windowsill onto the back of the couch, and then crawls over Dee's shoulder to rest in her lap.

"There you are, Corny boy." Dee scratches behind Cornelius's ears and kisses him on top of the head. "I thought Eugene might've kidnapped you."

In the months since Cornelius came to live with them, he's gotten quite comfortable venturing around their gated community on his own. Eugene even texted the twins an hour ago that the cat had shown up on his doorstep to say hello.

Bella reaches down absently and grabs a handful of popcorn, then shoves the whole thing into her mouth. *"Ugh,"* she groans between chews. On the screen a woman with hair as red as the crushed velvet couch she sits on is pleading her case. "Serafina'll say anything to get a broom."

Dee puts down her eyephone and focuses on the TV. The twins are watching *Which Witch Is the One?*, their favorite supernatural matchmaking show. On this episode Alistair must take two contestants on a single date and then eliminate the one he likes the least.

"I could really see myself falling in love with him," says Serafina, one of the witches chosen for the date. She's speaking to the camera in a confessional-style setting. *"From day one I've trusted in this process, and I've been one hundred percent genuine. I think Alistair can feel that I'm here for the right reasons."*

From his place drying dishes in the kitchen, they hear their dad Ron snort. "Yeah, right. She's there to become WitchStitch famous."

"Totally, Pop," Bella agrees. She reaches for more popcorn, but her hand hits the bottom of the bowl. She uses her pointer finger to zap it full of a fresh batch, and is pleased when every kernel is perfectly popped, no burnt pieces to be seen. Since their disastrous first day at YIKESSS, with practice the twins have been able to master simple spells with a much lower rate of chaos or destruction.

"So what?" Dee says. "That doesn't mean she isn't there to find love, too."

"That's right, honey," says their dad Antony, appearing in the doorway between the kitchen and living room. "We shouldn't judge other creatures before we get to know them."

"Come on, Dad. She *wants* us to judge her," Bella argues. "Why else would she have gone on supernatural television to find love?"

The camera switches to the other contestant, Helena. *"When I started this journey, my cauldron was empty. Then Alistair filled it up. I know it's taken me a little longer than most of the other witches here to let down my walls, but now that I have . . ."* She pauses to wipe a tear from her cheek and compose herself. *"I don't want to go home tonight. Alistair has my heart."*

"Why does everyone have to be so cheesy?" Dee says, checking her phone and then immediately putting it down again. "Nobody talks like this in real life."

"Love makes people do strange things," Ron

says, joining Ant in the doorway. "Look at your dad and me. I moved to the *suburbs* for him."

Ant smiles and shakes his head. "The Enchanted Forest was no place to raise a family."

"You were right," Ron says, putting an arm around his husband. Over time, ghosts naturally become more solid around people they love. In the comfort of his own home, Ant is so solid that he can almost pass for human. "What else is new?" They exchange a quick kiss, and Bella and Dee both groan.

"Right in front of us?" Bella says. "Unbelievable."

"So embarrassing!" Dee adds.

Their dads look at each other and laugh, and the twins exchange a small smile. Bella and Dee would never admit it to Ant and Ron, but they know how lucky they are to have two parents so in love.

"Bed in ten minutes," Ant says. He moves across the living room, toward the stairwell in the foyer.

Ron shuts off the lights in the kitchen. "Good night, girls," he says, following Ant. "We love you."

"Love you," the girls both say at the same time.

Bella waits until their dads get all the way up the stairs before she smirks at Dee. She knows what her sister is looking for every time she checks her phone. Or rather, *who*.

"I'll bet you'll be just as *in lurv* as Dad and Pop after your movie date tomorrow."

Dee feels her cheeks heat up. Over the weekend, Sebastian visited the pharmacy while Dee was stocking shelves and told her about the new *Space Wars* movie that just came out. He said he was seeing it with a couple of friends on Tuesday afternoon at the Manor Theater and asked if she would like to come along. In a bout of nerves Dee stammered that *actually* she and her friends were planning to see that movie on Tuesday too. What were the odds! They agreed to meet there and then exchanged phone numbers, *just in case*. So far she hasn't received so much as a text, but that could change at any moment.

"It's not a *date*," Dee says, stroking Cornelius's back and smiling to herself. "It's a friendly gathering. That's why you're coming."

"Right," Bella says. "And I'll be there for you, of course. But, Dee, you know you don't need me. You never have trouble thinking of what to say when Sebastian comes to visit you at the pharmacy."

"I know," Dee says. "But that's when it's just the two of us. This time his human friends will be there. What if I say the wrong thing?"

"You won't," Bella assures her. "Charlie and Eugene, on the other hand—"

Hearing Eugene's name, Cornelius lifts his head and meows. He gives Dee a meaningful look.

"What is it, buddy?" Dee looks at Bella. "I think he needs to tell us something about Eugene."

"Wait, Alistair is about to give out his

broom!" Bella squeals, returning her full attention to the TV, where the three witches are seated on a picnic blanket in the woods. "Cornelius can tell us during the commercial."

"This was not an easy decision to make," says Alistair in an accent veering toward Hungarian. *"You've both sacrificed so much to come on this journey with me, and you've trusted the process even through times of uncertainty. Serafina, I love how easily we click. You make me laugh, and we have so much fun together, but there's still a part of me that worries you're not ready for commitment. And, Helena, it has been such an incredible experience getting to know you. I've seen how much you've tried to open up these last couple of weeks, and I've appreciated—"*

"Jeepers creepers," Bella groans. "Get on with it already!"

"But I do feel like there's still a part of you that you're holding back. You've lowered your walls, but you haven't knocked them down completely. I need a witch who isn't afraid to show me who they really

are. *That being said . . .*" Alistair turns to Serafina. *"Serafina, will you accept this broom?"*

Bella and Dee gasp. A kernel of popcorn falls out of Bella's mouth.

Serafina smiles wide. *"I will."* She takes the red broom. Then Alistair picks up his own broom, and the two fly away together holding hands, leaving Helena behind as she bursts into tears. The show cuts to commercial.

"No, he didn't!" Bella says, at the same time Dee says, "Big mistake, Alistair!"

"Meow!" Cornelius insists, looking from Dee to Bella.

"Okay, okay." Dee holds up a finger and zaps a notebook and pen onto the coffee table. Cornelius jumps from the couch onto the table, picks up the pen with his tail, and starts writing.

"Wow," Bella says, peering around the cat. "Your lessons with him are really starting to pay off."

"That's because he's the smartest boy in the whole world, *yes he is*," Dee coos. It's normal for witches to find creative ways to communicate with their familiars, but not many can successfully teach them to write. Such a task requires great patience and trust from both parties.

Bella, still watching Cornelius, cocks her head. "Is that supposed to say 'Eugene'?"

Dee sits up and takes the note, which looks like it was written by a small child. "He's still getting the hang of it," she reminds Bella, and then she reads the note out loud. "It says, 'Youjeen grounded. No movy.'"

Dee squints at the paper. "I think that means Eugene is grounded and can't go to the movies tomorrow."

Cornelius meows happily at his job well done.

Bella scratches him on the head and then pulls her pink eyephone out of her pajama pocket. When the eye at the top of the screen opens, she says, "Call Eugene. Speakerphone."

Eugene picks up on the third ring. "Yes, I'm grounded," he says instead of hello. "For a week. The TrashEater6000 sort of backfired.

Two weeks' worth of trash exploded all over the kitchen." He lets out a heavy sigh. "Who'd have thought a machine could get indigestion?"

"So you can't come with us to the movies?" Dee whines. "But I need moral support!"

"Sorry, Dee. Nobody's more bummed than me. I love *Space Wars*." Eugene is obsessed with anything involving flying and laser beams.

"What about the flyball game on Friday?" Bella says. "It's my first game as scream team captain, and we're debuting some routines that will *really* get the crowd roaring."

"I'll try my best to be there. Maybe Mom will lighten my sentence for good behavior," Eugene says. "Speaking of which, I've gotta get back to cleaning up. Part of my punishment is that I have to get rid of the trash myself, instead of asking one of you to spell it away for me. Mom's got one of her eyes on the table, watching me."

Bella wrinkles her nose, grateful that neither of their dads is a zombie.

"Okay," she says. "See you tomorrow at school." She hangs up.

"What a bummer." Dee slouches into the couch again as *Which Witch Is the One?* returns from commercial break. "At least you and Charlie will still be there." She scoops a handful of popcorn from the bowl on Bella's lap. "Maybe you'll even hit it off with one of Sebastian's friends."

"His human friends?" Bella scoffs. "Not likely."

"Come on, Bella," Dee urges. "Remember what Dad said? Don't judge a creature before you get to know them. Maybe they'll surprise you."

"I'm never surprised," Bella says. "Especially not by humans."

On the TV, Helena is crying in the back seat of a carriage. *"I've never let down my walls like this before, and it was all for nothing. Will I ever love again?"*

"Maybe you just need to let down your walls," Dee teases. Both sisters laugh, but deep down

Dee thinks there might be some truth to the idea. She wouldn't admit that to Bella, though. When it comes to matters of the heart, Bella can be more tightly wound than a mummy.

"Girls," they hear Ron calling out from his room upstairs. "You know what time it is."

"Boo," Bella calls out, and then points a finger at the TV and zaps it off. They don't need to bother trying to be sneaky by lowering the volume. As a werewolf, Ron has excellent hearing.

From his place on the coffee table, Cornelius meows and pushes the notebook forward with his paw. Dee picks it up and sees that he's written something else.

Giv catnip plees.

CHAPTER 2

The next day the twins take their seats in Potions class to find their professor, a troll named Professor Daphne, writing the words *Cup of Cheer* on the board at the front of the room.

Dee sighs in relief. "We finally get to make something happy."

Bella and Dee's Potions class is in the middle

of their unit on mood-altering potions. Yesterday they learned how to brew the recipe for Sips of Sadness, which is so potent that one small whiff can cause twenty-four hours of gloom. Just ask their classmate Jeanie, who forgot to put on her mask and accidentally inhaled the vapors from her cauldron. Jeanie's mother had to pick her up at lunch after nearly two hours of uncontrollable crying.

"Yawn," Bella says, pushing her cauldron out of the way to rest her elbows on the table. She closes her eyes. "I could brew this in my sleep. Wake me up when we get to shape-shifting."

The raven perched in the corner by the door lets out a loud squawk, making the girls jump in their seats. The bird waits until it has the full attention of the class, and then opens its beak to project Principal Yvette Koffin's voice.

"Excuse the interruption, Professor Daphne," the principal says. "But I wanted to ensure that all of your students are properly masked before brewing today."

Professor Daphne frowns and crosses her arms. True to the nature of trolls, she's perpetually grumpy and has a problem with authority. She likes it even less when her own authority is questioned. "As always, they will be masked when the lesson begins."

When Principal Koffin speaks again, her tone is sharper. "Considering what happened yesterday"—several pairs of eyes in the room flick toward Jeanie, who slouches behind her cauldron in embarrassment—"that's not exactly a guarantee, is it?"

A dark cloud passes over Professor Daphne's face, and the twins exchange a nervous look. Their professor's nickname during medieval times used to be Daphne the Defiler, and she had quite the reputation before settling down to teach at YIKESSS. When she gets angry, she'll pick up whatever is closest to her and throw it a great distance. It doesn't matter what—or in the case of one student from the YIKESSS class of 1968, *who.*

"I appreciate your *concern*, Yvette," Professor Daphne spits, not sounding appreciative at all. "But I know how to lead my class."

"It doesn't seem that way to me," Principal Koffin snaps back. "In fact, it *seems* like you couldn't lead a ghoul to a graveyard, even if it gave you a map."

For a moment the room is shocked into silence. Everyone is used to Principal Koffin's strictness, but they've never heard her be so unnecessarily mean before—not to anyone, but especially not to Daphne the Defiler.

Professor Daphne lets out a roar and stomps toward the exit, leaving the floor indented in her wake. She kicks down the door, knocking it off its hinges, and continues roaring into the hallway.

Through the raven the class can hear Principal Koffin's heavy sigh. "Turn to page forty-two in your textbooks and begin brewing," she instructs. "But first, masks *on*. Is that understood, Jeanie Jenkins?"

At the table behind Bella and Dee, Jeanie looks down and nods.

"I can't hear you!"

"Yes, ma'am," Jeanie says quickly. The raven closes its mouth, ending the broadcast. It takes a few moments for the students to relax and start chattering among themselves again.

"Okay," Dee says. She pulls her textbook out of her bag. "Is it just me, or did Principal Koffin wake up on the wrong side of the tower today?"

"She definitely seems crankier than usual," Bella agrees, zapping her textbook open to the correct page. "I said hi to her this morning when I saw her in the hallway, and she totally ignored me." Then Bella perks up with an idea. "Hey, maybe if I give her my Cup of Cheer, she'll give me extra credit?"

"Listen to that, Jeanie," says Crypta Cauldronson from behind the twins. "Bella is trying to cheat to get ahead. What else is new?"

"Poor Crypta," Bella says to Dee without bothering to turn around. "Still bitter that I was voted captain of the scream team and she wasn't." She flicks her ponytail over her shoulder in satisfaction. The election was held on Friday afternoon at the flyball field, and to the surprise of Bella and Crypta, Bella won by a landslide.

Crypta snorts. "I know you cheated. What did you offer them in exchange for their votes? Magic mice? Contraband pixie dust?"

Dee, who has been sneakily checking her phone, pockets it and turns around. "Crypta, you know Bella wouldn't bribe the squad for votes. That's unethical."

"No," Crypta says. "That's politics." She narrows her eyes at Bella. "I'll figure out how you did it somehow. Just wait."

Suddenly Argus, Principal Koffin's telepathic four-eyed crow, sweeps into the room and perches on the back of Professor Daphne's desk chair. It seems the principal sent him to keep watch over the class while Professor Daphne lets out her anger. As if the bird senses the tension coming from their corner of the room, his eyes land on Bella and Crypta.

"Jealousy is an ugly emotion, Crypta," Bella whispers. "Keep it up, and you'll be greener than the Wicked Witch of the West." She turns to Dee. "Okay. Let's brew."

Bella puts on her safety mask and then conjures orange sparks to ignite a small, controlled fire underneath the cauldron. She squints down at the instructions in the textbook. "Let's see, we need to start with two teaspoons of crushed lavender, a vial of dill, and some bottled baby giggles. Dee, can you get that stuff from the supply closet while I heat the cauldron?"

Dee doesn't reply. Bella glances up to find her smiling down at her eyephone, mask still off.

"Dee, hello?" Bella waves her hand in front of her sister's eyes. "Are you even listening? Put your mask on!"

"Sorry," Dee says, though she doesn't sound it. She hurries to put her mask over her nose and mouth. "What do you need?"

Bella cocks her head. "What are you looking at?" Without waiting for a response, she snatches Dee's phone out of her hands.

"Hey!" Dee tries to take it back, but Bella, the slightly taller twin, holds it just out of reach. After a few seconds of struggling, Dee gives up and Bella smiles, satisfied. Then she looks at the screen, and her smile quickly disappears.

"You're texting Sebastian?" Bella practically shouts. She isn't sure what's more upsetting: the fact that her sister is being so careless with the rules—which clearly state no texting during class—or that Dee has been keeping this a secret from her. "Do you know what will happen if Professor Daphne sees? Your phone will get punted to the other side of Peculiar."

Bella's eyes skim the exchange. Sebastian texted first, just this morning. Can't wait for the movie later ☺. Dee replied, Same!!! ☺. They established a meeting time at the Manor Theater, and then Sebastian asked what her favorite movie snacks are. And in case ur wondering, he added, I'm a Milk Duds kinda guy.

Bella shoves the phone back into Dee's hands. "That settles that. You hate Milk Duds."

"Well," Dee says, "I don't think I've ever tried them."

Bella groans. "Dee, focus!" She snaps her fingers in front of Dee's face. "We have a potion to brew! Sebastian will still be there when we're done."

"Sebastian Smith?" Crypta chimes in, putting a hand over her chest as if in shock. "Mayor Boris Smith's son?"

Dee and Bella look at each other, their faces expressionless. If Crypta knows that Dee was texting a human, that means soon the whole school would know too.

"You shouldn't be texting the human mayor's son," Crypta chides. "You're putting us all at risk of exposure."

"It's none of your business, Crypt Keeper," Bella says.

"Actually"—Crypta raises her brow—"if it involves supernatural-human relationships, it *is* my business. Or should I say"—she leans across the table with a smug little smile—"my *mother's* business."

Bella whips her head around. "You wouldn't."

Crypta shrugs. "I might." She looks down at her textbook, feigning nonchalance. "Unless, of course, I'm too busy with all my duties as captain of the scream team."

Bella practically jumps out of her seat. "Over my undead body!"

Dee glances around the cauldron at Argus the crow. He's watching them, which means Principal Koffin probably is too.

"Fine." Crypta crosses her arms. "Co-captain?"

"Come on, Crypta," Dee sighs, keeping her voice down. "That's low, even for you."

"Maybe so," Crypta says. "But I'll go as low as I need to in order to get what I want. That's the difference between you and me."

Over at Professor Daphne's desk Argus the crow squawks in their direction. It's a warning, Dee is pretty sure. *"Okay,"* she says, picking up her textbook. "What ingredients did we need again, Bella?"

But Bella doesn't answer. She's too busy scowling at Crypta with her fists clenched. Dee can see angry red sparks shooting out from between Bella's knuckles.

Dee puts a calming hand on Bella's shoulder, though her own heart is pounding hard in her chest. "Bells, breathe," she says. "Let's get back to the potion. The cauldron fire has almost gone out."

Bella hesitates for a moment. Then, snapping out of it, she blinks and relaxes her fists. "Right," she says, returning to stoking the cauldron. "We need lavender, dill, and baby giggles, stat!"

Dee nods once, satisfied. She knows that the only thing strong enough to distract Bella from her rage is the threat of a bad grade. Dee hurries over to the supply closet and rushes to acquire the necessary ingredients. She hopes that if she throws herself into the task, perhaps she won't have time to think about what her new-found friendship with Sebastian may cost her sister—not to mention the entire supernatural community in Peculiar. And even scarier: the fact that despite everything she knows, she still doesn't want to give Sebastian up.

She returns to the table to find Bella eye level with the flames at the base of the cauldron, coaxing them into submission. Her green irises are reflecting a watercolor of oranges and reds as she concentrates. "Start with the dill," Bella instructs. "Then the baby giggles to dull the sadness, then two teaspoons of lavender for inner peace."

Dee does as she's told. When brought to a boil, the dill produces a purple steam, which the baby giggles soften to a pale pink. Even behind her mask, Dee can't help but smile when she sprinkles them in. Bella smiles too, though not because of the giggles. The potion is coming along perfectly. They're well on their way to an A+.

As Dee prepares to add the lavender, she feels her eyephone buzz in her pocket. *Not now, Sebastian,* she thinks, though she can't help but feel the bats in her stomach anxiously taking flight. In a few hours she will be with Sebastian at the movies—maybe even sitting next to him. What if he tries to hold her hand? She blushes at the thought, hoping that if Bella notices, she chalks it up to heat from the flames.

Dee dumps two tablespoons of lavender into the cauldron. Then the potion darkens, and the bubbles start to build up at an angry rate.

"Hmm." Bella frowns, confused. She lets her sparks sizzle on her fingers, lowering the flame, but it does no good. The bubbles continue to rise until they spill over the edge of the cauldron and onto the table, staining their textbooks and filling the room with a mood-numbing steam.

Bella looks at Dee. "What happened?"

"It wasn't my fault!" Dee looks at the measuring spoon in her hand. "The recipe called for—"

"Two *teaspoons*," Bella says, her eyes narrowing in on the spoon. "That's a tablespoon."

Dee deflates. "Oops." Behind them Crypta snickers.

"Jeepers creepers." Bella rubs her temples. There's no way they'll have time to clean this up *and* brew a satisfactory potion from scratch. Like her textbook, her perfect record will be stained.

Without missing a beat Argus flaps his wings and soars out of the room. A few moments later Principal Koffin comes barreling through the doorway.

"That's quite enough," she says, widening her wings behind her. She looks a bit unlike herself, Bella notices. Her red pantsuit is wrinkled, and her bun, usually so pristine that there isn't a hair out of place, appears unkempt and frizzy.

"Donna Maleficent," Principal Koffin's voice booms. "Not only have you brought failure upon yourself and your sister today"—hearing the word "failure" makes Bella drop her hands and widen her eyes in horror—"but your carelessness has created a noxious gas that could have harmed your classmates. What do you have to say for yourself?"

"I didn't do it on purpose," Dee says, taken aback by Principal Koffin's extreme reaction to such a small mistake. "I'm sorry."

"Look me in the eye when you are talking to me, girl!" Principal Koffin says.

"I'm *sorry*!" Dee says again, looking up warily. "I mean, all I did was spill a little bit of cheer. Is that really so bad? I'll clean our cauldron, and everything will go back to normal."

"You dare talk back to me?" The principal's wings extend even farther, which only happens when she is at her most vengeful. A few students at the front of the classroom cower back.

"Dee," Bella whispers. "Ix-nay on the acktalk-bay."

Dee furrows her brow. "What?"

"Very well," Principal Koffin continues. Her eyes are dark and unrelenting. "You'll clean your cauldron, and all the others on the grounds, in detention after school today."

Dee sits back in shock. YIKESSS probably has at least a hundred cauldrons. "But—but that will take hours!" And she has plans with Sebastian!

"Perhaps you should have thought of that before," the principal says.

Bella slowly raises her hand. "Um, Principal Koffin? Since I wasn't the one who messed up the proportions, do you think maybe I could have another chance to brew the potion?" She smiles guiltily at Dee and adds, "No offense. You know I'm on your side."

Principal Koffin raises her chin and looks down her nose at Bella. "There will be no second chances today." Bella slumps into her seat, and the principal looks at Dee again. "I'll see you back here at three o'clock, sharp." With one final scowl and a *whoosh* of her wings, she sweeps out the door.

CHAPTER 3

*C*leaning cauldrons? Majorly nasty! I think I'd rather be grounded.

In Humans 101, while they're supposed to be reading about sewing machines, Dee reads a note from Eugene under her desk. She sighs and zaps her reply onto the paper in purple ink.

The worst part is that I have to bail on Sebastian.

Bella, Charlie, will you two still go to the movies so he doesn't think I hate him?

Dee uses her magic to fold the note into a tiny butterfly and sends it fluttering over to Bella. When Bella reads it, she lets out a small but pointed snort.

No way, Bella replies in black ink. She's still miffed at Dee for being so clumsy with the proportion of lavender, and for giving Crypta something to blackmail them with. *I'm not hanging out with humans without you!* Bella spells her note into a tiny comet and sends it shooting to the back of the room, where Charlie sits.

If Bella isn't going, I'm not going alone! Charlie adds. *What if there's a scary part, or something jumps out at me, and I accidentally shape-shift?* They use their new compulsion powers to add legs to the note and make it scurry over to Eugene.

Still bogus of Koffin to give you detention for a little cauldron spill, Eugene writes. *I mean, considering she didn't even give you detention when you nearly burned down the school in Spell Casting . . .*

He flicks the note to Dee.

I know, she replies. *Something's up with her. But what?*

The paper butterfly begins its journey to Bella, but halfway there it stops midair and disintegrates.

"Dee, Bella," Professor Belinda says, barely looking up from the scrolls on her desk. Every head in the room turns toward them. "Charlie and Eugene. You know the rules about notes. Principal Koffin's office, now."

"Wait!" Bella sits up straight. "Can't we work something out?" Professor Belinda raises one skeptical eyebrow, and Bella elaborates. "Principal Koffin is scary today. And *not* in a good way."

Professor Belinda tucks a strand of long dark hair behind her ear and ignores Bella's plea, though something in her eyes suggests she doesn't disagree with Bella.

"I'll give the principal notice that you're on your way," the professor says simply, and then returns her attention to the stack of scrolls on her desk.

The four friends make their way to Principal Koffin's tower office, Bella grumbling with her arms crossed every step of the way.

"Great, just *great*," she says. "I was supposed to be at the top of the Horror Roll this quarter, and now that's going to be ruined."

"At least you can try again next quarter," Eugene says, his ears drooping. "When Mom hears about this, her head is gonna roll. I'll probably be grounded forever."

"You don't know that," Charlie says. "Maybe Principal K will let us off with a warning?"

Even Dee looks skeptical. "I don't know. You should have seen her this morning. She was . . ." She trails off, thinking of the best way to describe the frenetic aura that surrounded their principal. "Stressed out! And *mean*."

"She definitely wasn't herself," Bella says as the group turns into the main corridor. Suddenly Dee lets out an ear-piercing scream.

Waiting around the corner is Vice Principal Augustus Archaic, and he's stretched his ghostly face into a big, sinister grin. He giggles. "I got you!" he says, putting his hands on his cheeks and pushing his face back to its normal proportions. "You were so frightened!"

"Good one, VP," Eugene says, grinning, as Charlie hides behind him, flapping their wings in bat form.

"Sorry, Vice Principal, but this really isn't a great time," Dee says. "We're on our way to Principal Koffin's office."

The vice principal's face turns grave. "Oh, dear me," he says, and then floats to the side. "Well, best be onward. And good luck to you all."

None of the friends like the sound of that.

Several minutes later the group reaches the top of the long, winding staircase that leads to Principal Koffin's tower office. Bella, ahead of the pack, walks up to the wooden door and taps the iron knocker three times. The door creaks open on its own, and one by one the friends step inside.

"Man, I'm out of shape," Eugene huffs, bringing up the rear. "I've never actually been here. I didn't know there'd be so many stairs." When he steps into the office, the door closes behind him.

"She's not here," Bella says, looking around. "Neither is Argus."

"Leaving her office unattended doesn't seem like Principal K," Charlie says, their red eyes gazing up at the tall windows, the towering bookcases. They let out a sigh of admiration. "I bet there's lots of secrets in these books. You know, I read over the summer that those stairs were built to slow down enemies if they ever try to break in."

"What kind of enemies?" Eugene says, kneeling to study a rusted contraption that looks like some sort of medieval machine.

"Humans, obviously," Charlie says. "Monsters have magic. They don't need to take the stairs."

"Great point." Eugene stands up. "Any one of you could have flown me to the top."

"If I had known you were going to complain so much, I would have," Bella says. She sits down on the bench in the center of the room. "This is the worst day *ever*."

Dee is quiet, hovering by a small portrait hanging near Principal Koffin's desk. She feels responsible that they all ended up here. Even though it was *technically* Bella who sent the first note, they had been discussing Dee's misstep in Potions. If she had only paid more attention to which measuring spoon she picked up—if *only* she weren't such a klutz—she could still be going to the movies after school.

"What am I going to say to Sebastian?" Dee looks around at her friends. "I obviously can't tell him the truth."

"Sebastian is the least of our worries," Bella says. "Or did you forget where we are right now?"

"Just tell him you got detention." Eugene shrugs. "Happens to the best of us."

Dee bites her lip. "But what if he asks why? I'm not so great at lying to him."

"Dee," Charlie says. "No offense, but if you're going to start spending time with a human, you'll have to get used to lying."

The group hears a squawk in the distance, coming from the corridor. "Shh!" Bella says. "They're coming."

The other three rush to sit down on the bench. A moment later the door opens and Argus swoops inside, then lands gracefully on his perch behind the desk. Principal Koffin moves swiftly into the room behind him.

"Dee Maleficent," she says as she takes a seat. She looks and sounds burned out. "Haven't you had enough punishment for one day?"

"Yes," Dee says. "As a matter of fact, I have. Which raises the question, do I really *need* to be punished again?"

On a normal day such a tongue-in-cheek remark might have garnered a small smile from the principal, but today her face remains as cold and hard as stone.

"Well, let's see." The principal rests her hands on the desk, interlocking her long, slender fingers to emphasize her sharp talons. "Passing magical notes, was it? Is such an activity not against the rules during class?"

Dee fidgets in her seat. "Well, yes, it is. But—"

"And were you not warned by Professor Belinda on the first day of school that getting caught passing notes during class would result in immediate disciplinary action?"

"Yes," Dee says again. "I was."

"*And* were your friends here not *also* aware of the repercussions of magical note passing during class?"

Dee glances at her friends. "Yes, they were."

"So, Dee. You tell me." The principal leans forward in her seat, her gaze piercing. "Do *you* think you deserve to be punished?"

Dee glances over at Bella and drops her voice to a whisper. "A little help here?"

Bella doesn't reply. She sits on her hands and grinds her teeth. She's afraid that if she says one word, her magic will explode. Next to her, Eugene casts his eyes downward, apparently fascinated by a loose thread on his blazer.

Dee sighs and looks back at the principal. "This feels like a trick question."

Charlie puts a cold hand on Dee's shoulder. "We're really sorry, Principal Koffin," they say. "We knew it was against the rules to pass magical notes, but we did it anyway. We deserve whatever punishment you think is fair."

Bella looks at Charlie in disbelief. "You Benedict Arnold!"

Dee frowns. "Who?"

"Perhaps if you spent less time passing notes and more time paying attention in Humans 101," Principal Koffin says irritably, "you would know."

"I pass notes *and* pay attention," Bella pipes in. "Doesn't that count for something?"

Principal Koffin stares blankly at Bella. "No."

Bella slumps in her seat as the principal returns her attention to the group. "Now let's discuss your punishment. . . ."

CHAPTER 4

I was right," Eugene says, frowning down at a filthy cauldron and holding a slimy sponge that's even greener than his hand. "I *would* rather be grounded than doing this."

In addition to extending Dee's detention another day, Principal Koffin looped in the rest of the gang on cauldron-cleaning duty. Even worse, since they were caught passing notes while they were supposed to be learning about humans, Principal Koffin is making them learn how to *clean* like humans instead. Now Bella, Dee, Charlie, and Eugene are each seated at their own table with a basket of sponges and a couple of buckets of soapy water. Professor Daphne snores at her desk, wiped out from her day of rampaging around the grounds.

"But you already *are* grounded," Charlie points out, their voice echoing off the inside of the cauldron as they scrub at a tough stain on the bottom.

"Yeah." Eugene's pointy ears droop a little. "Lucky me."

"Look on the dark side," Dee says, her tone optimistic. "With all four of us cleaning these cauldrons, it won't take nearly as long as it would have if I were here by myself."

Bella laughs, but there is no humor in it. "I'm so glad we could get detention to make your life easier." Some sludge splashes onto her blazer as she scrubs. "Oh, *gross*." With a huff of frustration, she throws the sponge into the cauldron. "We have to do something about Principal Koffin's bad mood."

Dee raises her eyebrows. "What could we do?"

Bella cocks her head, thinking about it. "We could try brewing another Cup of Cheer. We're already in the right place." She gestures to the cauldron in front of her.

"And get in even more trouble?" Dee shakes her head. "I can't handle *another* day of detention."

"Dee's right," Eugene says, putting down his sponge. "And anyway that would only work for a day or so, until the potion wears off. To really cheer her up, we'd have to know what's making her so cranky in the first place."

"Good point," Bella says. She looks around at her friends. "Any ideas?"

They're all quiet for a moment. Then Charlie says, "Maybe it's the weather? I get grumpy when I'm cold too."

"Or maybe she got jury duty," Eugene tries. "That happened to my mom last year, and she was peeved for days."

They all look at Dee to hear her idea. She's hiding behind her cauldron, typing on her eyephone with a smile on her face.

"Dee!" Bella snaps.

"Sorry, sorry." Dee hurries to put her phone away. "But guess what? Sebastian's not mad that I can't make it to the movies! He said we should go together another time instead. Isn't that great?"

"Spook*tacular*," Eugene says in a dry voice. Charlie mumbles their agreement.

Bella's attention stays fixed on her sister, who is blushing and practically bouncing in her seat. Despite all the awful things they've been through today, one text from Sebastian has made Dee positively giddy.

Bella gasps, emitting a burst of yellow sparks from her fingers that makes the light fixture over her desk flicker. "That's it! Maybe

Principal Koffin just needs a little bit of love in her life!"

Dee, Charlie, and Eugene exchange uncertain glances. Nobody says a word.

"Think about it," Bella says, standing up. She starts pacing back and forth. "She's always alone. She's a workaholic. There's no *way* she'd be this grumpy if there was somebody out there sending her cute messages."

Charlie looks at Dee, seeming to understand Bella's train of thought. "You might be onto something," they say. "But what can we do about it? It's not like we can just set her up with someone. . . ."

Their voice trails off when they see the scheming smile forming on Bella's face.

"Oh, no," Dee says. "No! You can't be serious. How would we go about finding a match for the most particular monster in all of Peculiar?"

Bella shrugs. "I don't think it would be that hard."

"Once again I'm going to have to side with

Dee," Eugene says. "We don't really know anything about Principal Koffin."

"We know that she's a harpy," Bella says. "We know that she has a passion for education—"

"Eh," Charlie says. "That's debatable."

"We don't know what her type is," Eugene says. "Like, does she like funny people? Tall people? Dead or undead people?"

Bella brushes Eugene's concerns away with a wave of her hand. "We could find all that stuff out."

Eugene seems skeptical. "How?"

"That depends." Bella gives him a mischievous look. "How fast can you pick a magic-proof lock on an iron bolt?"

❧❧❧ CHAPTER 5 ❧❧❧

Ten minutes and one half-formed plan later,
Bella, Dee, and Eugene sneak out of detention and head west through the empty halls,
toward Principal Koffin's tower. Charlie, who
firmly believes there is no such thing as *too careful*, elected to stay behind to keep watch over
Professor Daphne, lest something happen to

rouse her from sleep and they need to explain their friends' absences. Trolls are notoriously deep sleepers, and under the right conditions they can remain in a slumbering state for quite some time. So Charlie found a music playlist on their eyephone called "Peaceful Bedtime Piano," pressed play, and wished their friends good luck.

Bella, Dee, and Eugene arrive at the entrance to the tower stairwell. There is a sign posted on the door, the same sign that pops up every day around this time. It's written in Principal Koffin's careful, slanted script: *Office Closed*.

"What if she's still in there?" Dee says with a worried crease in her brow.

"She's not," Bella assures them. "Every day at three thirty she takes a walk around the grounds, and Argus goes with her. I always see them during scream practice. We're good for at least another half hour."

Bella pushes open the door confidently, and

then abruptly stops. "Well," she sighs. "I didn't see this one coming."

The three friends look up at the long, winding stairwell to find that it's not a stairwell at all but a slide. The steps have been magically flattened down.

"What the . . ." Eugene trails off. He walks up to the flattened stairs and tries to climb them, but immediately loses his footing and slides back to the bottom. "Slippery." He glances back at the twins. "I'll bet she does this whenever her office is closed."

Bella remembers what Charlie said earlier, about the stairway being built to prevent enemies from breaking into the tower. Despite the risk of what they're doing, Bella gets a little excited, curiosity tingling in her belly. What could Principal Koffin be hiding in there?

"We'll have to fly to the top," Bella says. She looks at Dee. "Did you bring your broom? I left mine in my bag."

Dee reaches into her blazer pocket and pulls out a tiny, palm-sized broom. She taps it once, and in a burst of pink sparks, it grows to its full size. She looks up. "I can probably only fit one of you at a time."

"Take Eugene first," Bella says. "He can get started on the lock."

"You got it, Maleficents," he says with a salute. Then he climbs onto the back of Dee's broom. "Uh, just out of curiosity, have you ever flown anyone on this thing before?"

"Nope," Dee says with a grin. "Hang on tight. It might be a bumpy ride."

With jerky, bumblebee-like movements, Dee flies Eugene up to the top of the tower. He hops off the broom onto the landing, rubbing his head in the spot that bonked the wall about twenty feet below.

"Sorry!" Dee says, flying back down to pick up Bella. By the time the twins arrive at the top, Eugene has finished picking the lock and is sitting on the floor, scrolling on his eyephone.

"Just once I'd like a challenge," he says, then pockets his phone and stands up.

The heavy satin curtains are drawn inside Principal Koffin's office, shrouding the room in a still, silent darkness. Dee lets out a small sigh of relief. Until this moment she was convinced the principal would be at her desk, waiting to catch them.

Eugene moves to take a step toward the light switch, but Bella reaches out a hand to stop him. "Wait," she says. "There might be some sort of alarm. I have a feeling she didn't stop at the stairs."

Bella extends an arm like she's holding a torch. "Magic," she says, her voice steady and strong, "reveal yourself."

Blue sparks shoot out from her fingertips and form a smooth, controlled flame, illuminating the friends' faces and the area around them. A few moments pass before two thin blue lines appear at floor level across the center of the room, cutting it into four equal parts.

321

One of them is hardly an inch from Eugene's sneaker. When he realizes, he jumps back.

"I'm guessing we probably shouldn't touch those," he says, ears pointed on high alert.

"Or anything glowing blue," Bella adds, taking in several enchanted objects around the room. One of which, she notices with a satisfied smirk, is the light switch. What would her friends do without her?

"Dee, some light?" Bella says. "I have to keep hold of this flame, or else the magic markers will disappear."

Dee holds her hands slightly apart in front of her, palms facing each other, and focuses very hard on the space between them. Conjuring pure light, which is different from flames, is one of the most difficult and dangerous spells for a witch to master. When a witch masters the light, she has as much power as the moon itself. She can illuminate the world or plunge it into darkness.

A bead of sweat forms on Dee's brow as she

conjures a ball of light no bigger than a marble. Before it can fizzle out, she sends it shooting toward the antique lamp on Principal Koffin's desk. It lands in the bulb, and the lamp lights up.

"Nice!" Bella says, impressed by her sister's control.

Dee wipes the sweat from her forehead and grins, feeling drained but proud of herself.

Eugene takes a careful step to his right, over the blue line. "Okay, so what exactly are we looking for here? I doubt Koffin keeps a diary where she gushes over crushes."

"Anything personal." Bella's eyes sweep the room. "Anything that tells us about who she is, or what she likes."

"Easier said than done." Eugene looks warily at a tall glass cabinet full of crystals, talismans, and other magical objects. "This place is like a museum."

"Literally," Dee agrees. "Everything in here seems at least a hundred years old." She approaches the wall of dusty-looking leather-bound books and leans forward to read the spines. *"Sixteenth-Century Astronomy. Seventeenth-Century Herbal Medicine. Bird Feeders: A Comprehensive Guide."* Dee scrunches up her nose. "Boring."

"Okay, so she likes history," Bella says. "That means she would probably want to be with someone who's been around for a while, so they can swap stories."

"And she likes reading," Eugene says, gesturing to the wall of books. "I mean, obviously."

"Look." Dee spots a small book resting horizontally on top of several others on the shelf. "A book from this century." She holds it up: *Eddie Gory's Bloody Good Book of Jokes.*

"Ha!" Eugene says. "So she's into humor. Kind of ironic, considering I don't think she's ever laughed a day in her life."

Bella, examining an old tea set, simply shrugs. "Everybody wants to be with someone who can make them laugh."

"Really?" Eugene says, raising an eyebrow.

"Hey, have you ever wondered why the broom was late for work?"

Bella pretends to consider. "Hmm . . . no, definitely not."

"It overswept!" Eugene bursts into laughter. "Get it?"

Bella just shakes her head, but Dee giggles as she makes her way from the bookcase toward Principal Koffin's desk. She glances over the belongings scattered on top. There are some folders, a set of quills, an old-timey pair of glasses. Dee pushes the glasses aside and reads the handwritten letter resting underneath.

"What's that?" Bella asks.

"It's from Principal Oswald Pleasant." Dee skims the note. "He wants YIKESSS and PPS to have another joint event later in the year, after he returns from a . . . what's a 'sabbatical'?"

"Not that," Bella says. "I mean that glowing thing."

She points at a leather-bound book on the far side of the desk, haloed in a forbidding

325

blue glow. Dee leans in to get a closer look but doesn't dare touch it. "It's got her initials on it," she says. "Maybe a day planner?"

"You know, none of this stuff is very personal," Eugene says. He's inspecting what appears to be a sliver of shattered witch glass. "Like, there are no pictures anywhere in here. It's as if she doesn't have any friends or family."

"Maybe she doesn't," Bella says. "When was the last time you saw her hanging out with a friend? When have you even seen her off school grounds?"

"Actually, there is one picture." Dee points at a small portrait hanging on the wall behind the principal's desk, one she noticed earlier but didn't pay much attention to. Strangely, it also glows blue.

"Who would want to steal this?" Bella asks, coming closer. It's a medieval-style painting of three women, a man, and a dog. The women are all tall and severe and dressed in black, with shimmering wings tucked tightly behind their backs. They are all harpies, Bella realizes. She has never seen another harpy besides Principal Koffin before.

Her eyes travel to the center of the photo, where the man sits on a golden throne. His hair is so bright and wild that it looks like fire. He has one hand resting on the dog's head.

"Is that . . . ," Dee says, pointing at the woman on the far left.

"Principal Koffin," Bella replies, eyes wide. In the portrait she looks a little younger, and her hair hangs down loosely to her waist, but otherwise she's the same. "Who are the other two?"

Dee takes a step closer to get a better look and accidentally trips over a leg of the desk chair. She almost falls directly into the painting but catches herself just in time.

"Phew," she says. "That was a close one."

Bella gasps. "Dee!" She points downward. "Your foot!"

Dee looks down to find that in the process of

catching her balance, she stumbled right across a blue line.

"Eugene," Bella snaps. "Put that ancient relic down. We've got to get out of here."

Eugene puts the Walkman he's holding back where he found it and hurries toward the door. He throws it open, preparing to dive headfirst into the slide-stairs, but stops himself just in time.

"Uh-oh," he says, because the slide has sprouted big spikes, transforming once again. "Guess we're flying down."

Dee pulls her broom from her pocket and zaps it to its full size. There's no time now to worry about whether it can support everyone at once. "Everybody, on!" she says as she mounts. Bella and Eugene both climb onto the back and hold on tight, and Dee propels them off the railing. They fall, swift and hard, but just before they reach the bottom, Dee manages to gain control of the broom and stick the landing.

"Wicked," Eugene says, his balance a little

wobbly as he dismounts. "You know, for a second there I thought we were all going to die."

"We can worry about death later," Bella says. "We need to get back to detention."

They hurry out of the stairwell and across the main corridor, where they turn down a hallway and run, for the second time that day, right into their vice principal—quite literally *into* him this time, as he is a ghost.

"Good heavens!" Vice Principal Archaic says, picking up the book he dropped and adjusting his top hat. "You got *me* this time. Well done."

"We weren't trying to scare you," Dee says, and then immediately regrets it.

"Oh?" the vice principal says. "Where are you students off to in such a rush?"

"Uh . . ." Bella racks her brain for an excuse. "Bathroom. It's *urgent*."

The vice principal raises one skeptical bushy brow. "All three of you?"

Bella, Dee, and Eugene all nod in unison. "We

had the stew for lunch," Bella explains further. "They don't call it *radioactive* for nothing."

Augustus makes a sympathetic face. "Quite right." He nods and steps out of their way. "Well, carry on. And do try to be mindful of other ghosts on your journey, hmm? We aren't as corporeal as everyone else, but we're still here!"

As he turns to go, Bella gets a good look at the book he's holding: *Birds of the Americas*. Dee and Eugene continue down the hall, but she stays put.

Dee and Eugene stop running when they realize Bella isn't with them.

"Bella!" Dee whisper-shouts from down the hall. "What are you doing? We're going to get caught!"

Bella zaps herself to where they're standing. "Vice Principal Archaic! He's the one!"

"Wow," Dee says, amazed at how easily her sister just carried out a Level 5 traveling spell. "Since when can you beam?"

"I've been practicing." Bella runs a casual

hand through her hair. The group starts moving again. "Anyway, Archaic."

Eugene makes a face. "That Monopoly man? No way Koffin will go for it."

"Eugene," Dee chides. "That's not a very nice thing to say."

"He's not a Monopoly man," Bella interjects as they turn a corner. "He just wears old clothes. But that's perfect for Principal Koffin, because she likes history, and Archaic is older than time itself. They'll have *lots* to talk about."

"He's got that Monopoly man hat," Eugene mutters, putting a flat hand above his head and raising it up to indicate great height. "We'll have to get rid of that."

"It's not a bad idea," Dee says, ignoring him. "I mean, if Principal Koffin wants someone who likes to joke around, there's nobody better."

"Plus, they both love birds!" Bella adds, getting excited now. "It's perfect!"

"Okay, okay. I see your point," Eugene admits. "So how do we make it happen?"

They return to the Potions classroom to find the door closed. As quietly as she can, Bella opens it a crack to see Professor Daphne still asleep at her desk, snoring loudly to soothing piano sounds. She opens the door all the way, and then she and the others tiptoe inside.

"Looks like Charlie's plan worked well," Eugene says, pausing at the front of the classroom.

"A little too well," Bella agrees. The three friends look at Charlie, who has their head on the table and is fast asleep.

CHAPTER 6

Bella and Dee are standing at their lockers in the witch wing the next morning when Principal Koffin passes by, looking frazzled. Dee, rummaging through her books to find the Supernatural Cultures homework she misplaced, doesn't notice, but Bella seizes the opportunity. She zaps her locker shut and hurries to fall into step with the principal.

"Wicked morning, Principal Koffin," Bella says, hurrying to keep up. "How are things?"

"Horrible, if you must know," the principal says, facing straight ahead. From this angle it's easy for Bella to see the dark circles around her eyes. "Someone broke into my office yesterday after school."

"Oh." Bella puts a hand over her mouth, feigning surprise. "That *is* horrible. Do you know who it was?"

"That remains to be seen." She shoots Bella a suspicious glance. "I don't suppose *you* have any idea who it might have been?"

"What? Me?" Bella forces out a laugh to conceal her pounding heart. "I don't know a thing."

"Perhaps you saw someone hanging around the corridor after school hours?" the principal presses.

Bella shakes her head firmly. "I didn't see

anyone. I was scrubbing cauldrons, remember?"

Principal Koffin doesn't reply. As she turns a corner into the fae wing, she quickens her pace even more.

"So listen," Bella says, practically running now. "I was talking to Vice Principal Archaic earlier, and he told me that he thinks you're the *creepiest*."

The principal's face doesn't change. "Is that so."

"It *is* so!" Bella says. She swerves to narrowly avoid a fairy flying toward her. "The creepiest monster he's ever met—that's what he said."

"Hmm" is the principal's only reply.

"He really respects you," Bella continues. "And Argus, too. He *loves* birds. In fact—"

"Miss Maleficent." Principal Koffin stops walking. "I'm terribly busy. I suggest you make your way to Professor Belinda's classroom now. The homeroom ravens are about to caw."

Instead of waiting for a response, Principal Koffin ruffles her wings and continues on, leaving Bella standing alone in the middle of the hallway.

A smile forms on her face as she watches the principal walk away. *It's a start!*

When she returns to the lockers, she finds that Dee has emptied her entire bag onto the floor and is frantically searching through its contents. "I can't find my homework anywhere. I think Cornelius might've been sleeping on it this morning."

Bella shakes her head. "That cat will sleep anywhere besides his bed." She points a finger in the air and casts a retrieving spell. A few seconds later a worksheet appears in Dee's hands.

Dee smiles, then blows some stray cat hairs off the paper. "I *knew* it." She looks at her sister. "Since when can you do that?"

Bella waves a hand like it was nothing. "I checked out some advanced-spell books from the library. No big deal."

In homeroom Bella, Dee, Charlie, and Eugene huddle together at their desks.

"How did it go with Koffin?" Eugene asks. "Is she in love with Archaic yet?"

"Not exactly," Bella admits. "She basically ignored me when I tried talking to her."

"Same with Gus," Charlie says. "We did what you said—we told him Principal K thinks he's creepy and suggested he should ask her on a date, and he got all nervous and disappeared."

Dee rests her elbows on her desk and puts her chin in her hands. "I never would've thought someone who loves scaring so much could be frightened off by a little romance," she says. Unwittingly her eyes flick to Bella.

Bella exhales quickly and decisively. "Well, we're just going to have to try harder." She looks around at her friends. "Are we ready for phase two?"

Eugene raises his eyebrows. "Phase two?"

Bella nods once. "Operation Get Archaic and Koffin Together, No Matter the Cost."

"Operation *GAKTNMC*?" Charlie recites, frowning. "Doesn't exactly have a ring to it."

The group considers for a moment. Then Dee says, "How about 'Operation Love Spell'?"

Bella, Charlie, and Eugene exchange a look, and then everyone nods their agreement.

"Okay," Bella says, putting her hand in the center of the huddle. "To Operation Love Spell."

The others add their hands to the pile. "Operation Love Spell," they all echo.

The first mission is assigned to Dee, who takes a detour to Principal Koffin's office on her way to class. She cuts across the main corridor and slips through the entrance at the bottom of the tower. Pausing at the foot of the winding staircase—which has returned to its usual, steplike form—she removes her tiny broom from one pocket and an even tinier bouquet of black roses from the other. Bella plucked them from their dads' garden this morning and then shrank them with magic. "To Yvette. Love, Gus," she said with a pleased grin.

Dee zaps the broom and the flowers to their full size and flies to the landing at the top of the stairs. She places the bouquet in front of Principal Koffin's door, adjusting the stems until the roses are arranged nicely, and then gives the door two swift knocks. As fast as she can, she jumps over the edge of the landing with her broom and hides beneath the stairs, hovering in the air.

She hears Principal Koffin open the door. A few moments pass. Then Dee hears the principal say, "Gretchen?"

The heavy clacking sound of high heels approaches the landing, followed by a voice. "Well, well, what do we have here?"

Dee claps a hand over her mouth. She'd recognize Gretchen Cauldronson's snooty, high-pitched voice anywhere.

"I'm not sure," the principal says, her voice taut, maybe even a little distressed.

Gretchen speaks again. "Do you think these flowers have anything to do with—"

"*Shh,*" Yvette hisses, cutting her off. "Anyone could be lurking. Do me a favor and incinerate them."

Dee hears a *whoosh*, followed by the smell of smoke and the sound of a slammed door. She hears the locks in the door click, then waits a few moments in silence before peeking over the edge of the landing.

The roses are on the floor, reduced to a crispy pile of ashes.

Dee winces. Maybe she should've added a note.

Meanwhile Charlie stands outside the vice principal's office, taking a few deep breaths for courage. When they work up the nerve, they pull an envelope out of their blazer pocket with the words *From your secret admirer* printed on the outside, enchanted by Bella to mimic Yvette's careful writing. They place it right outside the door and hurry away.

A few moments later the door opens, and out steps Eugene with the vice principal. Only, he doesn't quite look like the vice principal. Gone is his top hat, revealing a shockingly full head of wavy brown hair, and he wears a fashionable sport coat and tapered trousers that appear to be from this century. From this *decade*, even.

"Are you sure I don't look foolish?" Augustus says, self-consciously touching the top of his head, then his freshly shaved face. "I haven't gone without my mustache since Lincoln was in office. And I feel so . . . underdressed."

"What did I tell you?" Eugene says. "It's going to be so much easier to scare people if you blend in with them. You've got the element of surprise on your side now."

The vice principal nods. "I suppose I can't argue with you there." He looks down at his outfit. "I certainly won't miss that blasted cummerbund." Then he notices the note on the floor. "Hmm, what's this?"

He bends over to pick it up. When he recognizes the handwriting, his face immediately goes two shades paler.

"What is it, Mr. A?" Eugene peeks over the vice principal's shoulder, feigning interest.

Augustus tucks the note into his coat pocket. "Nothing to concern yourself with, Eugene. I think it's time you head back to class."

"Sure thing, big A," Eugene says with a dramatic wink. "By the way, can I get an—"

The vice principal retreats into his office and slams the door.

Eugene's ears droop. "Excuse slip?"

When the clock strikes twelve, all four friends, located in various wings around the school, put in their blueteeth to regroup.

What's everyone's progress? Bella thinks from a bathroom stall in the witch wing.

Charlie, returning to their Compulsion class in the vampire wing, is the first to reply. *Archaic got the note, but he still hasn't left his office. I just did another walk-by.*

He's probably waiting for the right time to ask Koffin out, Eugene thinks, slouching into his desk in Supernatural Cultures. *Don't worry, Maleficent. The makeover I gave him is so good, there's no way she'll be able to resist him.*

Excellent. Bella smiles. *Dee, did Koffin like the flowers?*

NO. Dee's thoughts come through like a shout. *SHE BURNED THEM.*

What do you mean, she burned them? Charlie thinks.

And why are you yelling? Eugene adds.

I'M A LITTLE BUSY AT THE MOMENT, Dee replies. *I'M TRYING NOT TO GET HIT WITH A CREAM PIE.*

We're doing UFO drills in Met Ed today, Bella explains to Charlie and Eugene. Once a week their Metaphysical Education teacher makes them mount their brooms and dodge whatever object she feels like throwing at them, so they can practice agility. Today that object is cream pies. It's why Bella is hiding in the bathroom. *Dee, remember to relax your grip! The broom can sense your fear.*

Once again Charlie asks, *Why did Principal Koffin burn the flowers?*

SHE DIDN'T KNOW THEY WERE FROM

ARCHAIC, Dee thinks. *SHE WAS—AH, MY SHOE—SUSPICIOUS.*

Bella groans. It feels like they're getting nowhere. *Okay,* she thinks as she emerges from the stall. *We need a new plan, stat. Dee, I'll meet you in the locker room.*

With missions one through three of Operation Love Spell complete but yielding little in the way of results, a frustrated Bella decides she can't wait around for fate to bring the principal and vice principal together—she'll have to do it herself.

At the beginning of lunch, Bella eagerly takes off in the direction of Principal Koffin's office, while Dee, slightly *less* eager because the mission is cutting into her favorite time of day, sets out to locate the vice principal.

Bella finds Yvette first, crossing the main corridor. "Principal Koffin!" she calls out from some distance away, urgently waving her arms. "Come quick!"

The principal lets out an irritated sigh that echoes off the walls. "What *now*?"

"Someone accidentally created a portal to another dimension in the botanical wing!"

The principal's eyes momentarily widen with alarm, and then narrow skeptically. "By 'someone' do you mean yourself?"

Bella shakes her head vigorously. "I was on my way to the cafeteria when I saw it. Room 314. I think someone is trapped in there!"

Principal Koffin hesitates for a moment, like she's unsure whether to believe Bella. Then she decisively flaps her wings and takes off in the direction of the botanical wing. Bella runs after her, pumping her legs as fast as she can to keep up.

On the other side of the school, Dee finds the vice principal in his office, reading and rereading one single page of creased paper. When he sees Dee coming, he hurries to fold the paper up and shove it into his desk drawer.

"Dee Maleficent," he says by way of greeting. When he gets a closer look at her face, his forehead creases with concern. "What's the matter?"

"There's a black hole in the botanical wing!" she says, and then backtracks, forgetting this part of the plan. "Er—wait. It might also be a portal to another dimension? I forget."

Without any hesitation the vice principal gets up from his desk and hurries out of the office, blurring his corporeal form to float as fast as he can toward the scene.

"Oh, room 314!" Dee calls out after him.

Principal Koffin is the first to arrive at the classroom, rushing through the doorway and frantically looking around for any signs of an interdimensional portal. Vice Principal Archaic arrives a few moments later.

"Yvette!" he says. When he sees her, his skin gets a little more transparent—the ghostly equivalent of blushing. "Did—did you already remove the black hole?"

"Black hole?" She looks suspicious. "I was

told it was a portal." Then, seeming to notice him for the first time, she looks him up and down. "Augustus," she says, taken aback. "Your clothes."

Before he can respond, the classroom door shuts and locks behind him. He glances at the door, and then back at Principal Koffin. "Did you do that?"

Bella snickers into her hands on the other side of the wall, just out of view.

"Now they'll *have* to fall in love!" she whispers to Dee, who just arrived and is still panting from running all over the school. "Did you see the way she looked at him? It's *just* like Helena and Alistair."

"I guess," Dee says. "Besides the fact that Alistair kicked Helena off the show."

Suddenly the door bursts off its hinges and into the hallway with a heavy gust of wind. Bella rushes to take cover, while a frightened Dee can't help but scream.

Principal Koffin relaxes her wings as she

steps through the doorway. When she sees the twins, she raises her wings back to their full, intimidating height.

"You two!" she roars, angrier than the twins have ever seen her. "I should have known. *What* is the meaning of this?"

"Um . . ." Dee laughs nervously. "I guess the portal fixed itself?"

The principal puts her hands on her hips and glowers down at the girls. Bella and Dee inch closer together, bracing themselves for the worst.

"Your antics this week have been entirely unacceptable," she says. "You've given me no choice but to—"

Vice Principal Archaic appears behind her and taps her on the shoulder. "Excuse me, Yvette?"

She shoots him an irritated glance. "Not now, Augustus."

"I apologize for my most untimely interruption, but I've got to get down to the cafeteria for lunch monitor duty," he says. "I was just wondering if . . . if perhaps you'd like to accompany me to lunch sometime?"

The twins let out gasps of delight, while Principal Koffin blinks in surprise.

"There's this quaint little sandwich shop just outside of town," the vice principal continues, talking through his nerves. "Perhaps we could—"

The principal's face hardens. "No," she says, turning up her nose. "I'm afraid I can't."

"What?" Bella whines. "But, Principal Koffin—"

"*Enough,*" the principal snaps. She turns to Vice Principal Archaic, who has all but sunk into the wall of lockers with embarrassment. She softens her tone just a little. "I'm sorry, Augustus, but it would be impossible."

"Not to worry," he says, and lets out a discomfited little laugh. "Not to worry. I'll just . . .

erm, I had best be off." He floats away as quickly as he can, without another word.

Principal Koffin watches him go for a moment, still a little stunned, and then composes herself. She turns the full weight of her fury back on to Bella and Dee. "Now, where was I?"

This is so unfair," Bella grumbles into the cauldron she's scrubbing. "We try to do something nice for Principal Koffin, and this is how she repays us? With *more* detention?"

Bella and Dee are in their Potions classroom, cleaning cauldrons after school for the second day in a row. Professor Daphne, acting once again as their detention monitor, sleeps soundly at her desk, not to be disturbed, no matter how many times Dee accidentally sends a sudsy cauldron crashing to the floor.

"She wasn't nice to Vice Principal Archaic, either," Dee says as she squeezes her sponge over a bucket. "Poor guy. Did you see how sad he looked?"

Bella recalls the crushed expression on Archaic's face when Principal Koffin refused him—just like Helena when Alistair gave his broom to Serafina on Monday's episode of *Which Witch Is the One*? "Yeah. She could've at least come up with an excuse, instead of just saying no." Bella channels her frustration into her sponge by squeezing and scrubbing harder. "And what did she mean by 'it would be impossible,' anyway? What's impossible about lunch?"

"Take a breath, Bella," Dee warns. "Or else you'll zap that cauldron to smithereens."

"I'm just *saying*." Bella continues scrubbing. "Operation Love Spell worked perfectly on Vice

Principal Archaic. What's Principal Koffin's problem? Why is she *so* against falling in love?"

Red sparks sizzle on Bella's fingertips, and the cauldron cracks beneath her hands. She groans. Fortunately, Professor Daphne is unfazed, still snoring softly at her desk.

Dee shrugs. "Maybe she's not against it. Maybe it's just a little harder for her." She feels her eyephone buzz in her pocket and blushes, guessing who it might be without having to look.

"What do you mean?" Bella zaps the broken cauldron pieces into a nearby trash can and then crosses her arms. "And why is your face all red?"

Dee puts a hand to her cheek self-consciously. "I mean . . . we don't know what she's been through. Maybe something happened in her past that made her put walls up." She picks up her sponge and gets to work on a new cauldron. "Maybe she's had her heart broken. Like Helena."

The anger falls from Bella's face as she considers this. "Jeepers creepers, it *is* just like Helena and Alistair. She still had walls up from her last relationship, so Alistair couldn't get close to her, and that's why he sent her home!"

Dee raises an eyebrow. "What's your point?"

"My point," Bella says, dropping her sponge, "is that Principal Koffin will never be able to fall in love if she keeps her walls up. We have to help her!"

"Right," Dee says, her voice flat. She's resisting the urge to check her eyephone notifications. "I thought that was what we've been doing all day today with Operation Love Spell."

"But there's one thing we still haven't tried." Bella's eyes brighten. "A love spell!"

Now Dee drops her sponge too. "*No.* Or are you trying to turn our detention into an expulsion?"

"But why not?" Bella presses. "We've got everything we could possibly need to cast the spell right here." She gestures to the supply closet of ingredients at the back of the room. "We could do it fast."

Dee glances at Professor Daphne. "We can't perform a love spell while she's sleeping right there. What if she wakes up?"

"She's not going to wake up," Bella assures her sister. "See?" She picks up the cauldron she just started cleaning and throws it down onto the floor so that it shatters. Professor Daphne doesn't stir.

Dee bites her lip and says nothing.

"Dee, come *on*," Bella begs. "If we don't do this, Professor Koffin could stay in this bad mood forever, and who knows how many more detentions we'll get?" She looks at the broken cauldron pieces by her feet and zaps those into the trash with the others. "I *can't* clean any more cauldrons. I'll lose my mind."

Dee looks down at her hands. She wants Principal Koffin to cheer up just as much as Bella does. She certainly doesn't want any more detention. But how can they guarantee that this spell will do the trick?

"Okay," Dee says. She feels her phone buzz in her pocket again. "But we have to be as specific as possible. We can't leave any room for loopholes."

"I'm with you." Bella gets her Level 1 Spell Casting handbook out of her book bag and uses magic to flip through its pages. "I'm pretty sure there's nothing in here that will help us." She pauses on page 102, which includes a charm for attracting woodland creatures, and then slams the book closed. "*Ugh.* We need a higher-level casting book."

"How are we going to get one of those?" Dee asks.

Bella shakes her head. "We can't. At least not right now." Then her gaze lands on a set of shelves across the room, where about two dozen Potions textbooks, Levels 1 through 5, sit unattended. A wicked smile spreads across her face. "But I'll bet we can find something in there."

Dee bites her thumbnail, feeling uncertain. "Are you sure this is a good idea? I can barely brew a Level One potion."

"Oh, it will be fine," Bella says, already moving toward the books. "I've been doing a lot of extra reading lately, remember?"

Approximately forty-three snores from Professor Daphne later, Bella finds a recipe for a Potion of Vulnerability in the *Love Spells* section of a Level 3 Potions book. "'A potion for letting down one's defenses to reveal the truth of the heart within,'" Bella reads. She looks up at Dee. "That seems like it could do the trick. What do you think?"

"Yeah," Dee says, her eyes on her phone and her fingers flying across the keypad. She and Sebastian are planning another trip to the movies. "Totally."

Bella narrows her eyes. "Did you even hear what I said?"

"*Yes,*" Dee says, though really she only heard about half of it. She puts her phone away and looks at Bella. "Potion of Vulnerability. Let's do it."

Bella conjures a flame beneath a cauldron at the back of the room while Dee gathers the necessary supplies. She lists the ingredients as she places them on the table. "St. John's wort, crushed rose petals, moondust, and eggshell. The only thing missing is fresh tears." She looks at Bella. "How are we going to get those?"

Without taking her eyes off the flame, Bella holds one hand up in the air and zaps an onion from their pantry at home into her palm. Dee looks at it, confused. Then the onion starts peeling itself, and almost as quickly, Dee's eyes begin to water.

"Hey!" Dee scolds, putting her hands over her eyes.

"Sorry," Bella says, a guilty look on her face. "Quick, grab a vial and catch some tears while you're still crying."

With the last ingredient secured, Bella and Dee get to work brewing the potion, following the directions as carefully as they can. By the time they get to the last step, when everything is boiling in the cauldron, they're both sweating, and the steam has frizzed up their hair.

Dee looks down at the textbook. "It says we have to say an incantation into the cauldron," she reads. "So the potion can absorb its 'true purpose.'" She puts the last bit in air quotes.

"What kind of incantation?" Bella asks, stoking the flame with her sparks.

Dee makes a face as she skims the page. "Doesn't say. I think you're just supposed to tell it what you want it to do."

"Okay, then." Bella stares down into the honey-colored liquid boiling inside the cauldron. "Potion, please make Principal Koffin let down her walls—"

"No, not like that," Dee says. "Like an incantation. Give it *rhythm*."

Bella takes a deep breath. She looks into the potion and tries again.

"Yvette Koffin," Bella whispers. "Let down

your walls so your vulnerability shines through, and you'll find a love that's strong and true."

She looks up at Dee, who shrugs and says, "Seems good enough to me."

Bella nods, satisfied. "Okay. All we have to do now is let it brew for ten minutes. Then we sprinkle a little bit on her doorknob, and voilà!" She claps her hands together in excitement. "As soon as she touches it, the potion will seep into her skin, and Operation Love Spell will officially be a success."

The girls both look down into the potion, which swirls and sparkles like liquid gold. Then they look at each other and smile.

⤳⤳⤳ CHAPTER 8 ⤳⤳⤳

Bella and Dee enter homeroom the next day in high spirits. When they sit down at their desks, looking confident and relaxed, Eugene and Charlie swap a puzzled glance.

"You witches are surprisingly calm this morning," Eugene says. He looks at Bella.

"Especially you. I would've thought you'd be on the warpath after two days of detention."

Bella shrugs and starts fiddling with her hair. "Principal Koffin's bad mood is yesterday's news. I have a feeling that today things will be different."

"Really?" Eugene leans forward in his seat. "What did you do?"

"Nothing against the rules, I hope," Charlie says, not looking up from the homework they're rushing to finish.

Bella's smile is small and smug. "Let's just say we got her to let down her walls." Behind Bella, Dee giggles into her *Howler* comic.

"Sounds like it was against the rules," Eugene mutters to Charlie, who nods in agreement.

"Speaking of letting down walls," Charlie says. "Did you hear about the pixie-dust spill?"

Dee's jaw drops. "The *what*?"

The raven in the corner caws to signal the start of the morning announcements. "Quiet, everyone!" Professor Belinda calls out from her desk. She's slumped forward, clearly exhausted. Before the twins have time to wonder why, Principal Koffin's voice echoes through the raven, and the intensity behind it sends a shiver down every spine in the room.

"Students and faculty, listen up, *now*," the principal snarls, and Bella winces. That's certainly not the way someone who's madly in love is *supposed* to sound.

"I have some distressing news. In the early hours of this morning, the fae wing had a security breach. The vault containing our school's entire supply of pixie dust was broken open, causing a major leak."

Bella widens her eyes. Without a fairy to control it, pixie dust is pure chaos magic. A leak in the school would mean halls turning into mazes, lockers that move and change, erupting candle fire—anything to sow fear and confusion. As far as she knows, a leak like this has never happened at YIKESSS before.

"Luckily," the principal continues, "we were able to contain the dust and repair the vault before any major damage was done. *Unluckily*, that doesn't change the fact that someone deliberately tried to wreak havoc on school grounds, effectively putting all of you in danger."

Murmurs spread across the classroom. Was it a prank gone wrong? An accident? It couldn't *possibly* be a real intruder, could it?

As the principal continues, her voice gets even more grim. "Were this an isolated incident, I would be less concerned; I'd perhaps even chalk it up to some misguided young monster looking to cause a stir. However, this leak comes on the heels of another concerning event. Two days ago my office was broken into after school hours, and the culprit still has not been found."

Bella looks around at her friends, who are all wearing the same panicked expressions. When Dee meets her eye, Bella knows they're thinking the same thing. *We are so getting into trouble.*

"Your safety is my top concern," Principal

Koffin says. "Therefore, I have no choice but to cancel next week's Harvest Moon Feast, and any other YIKESSS events moving forward that could put you in harm's way, until whoever is responsible comes forward."

The class lets out a collective groan, Eugene loudest of all. The Harvest Moon Feast is the supernatural equivalent of a Thanksgiving feast for humans, and Eugene was looking forward to setting the record for most cauldron cakes eaten in a single night.

"In the meantime it's important that you all stay vigilant," the principal continues. "If you see something suspicious, it is your *responsibility* to tell someone."

She hesitates, as if debating whether to say more. Finally she says, "That's all for today." The raven closes its mouth, and she's gone.

"We didn't do it!" Dee says, quickly closing her comic book. "Right?"

"We *did* break into her office," Charlie points out, clearly worried.

"*Shh!*" Bella hisses at them to be quiet. "That doesn't have anything to do with the pixie-dust leak. They're two separate incidents that just *happened* to take place two days apart." She shrugs. "It could happen to anyone."

"Hey." Eugene grins. "Whoever broke into the vault of pixie dust will probably get blamed for breaking into her office, too, right? Then we'll be off the hook."

"Or *maybe* whoever broke into her office will also get blamed for the pixie dust," Dee says with a concerned crease in her brow. "I can't get another day of detention! My hands are starting to prune from all the cauldron scrubbing."

"Don't worry, Dee." Bella keeps her voice low. "Eugene's right. We just have to make sure whoever leaked the pixie dust gets caught first."

Charlie sighs. "And *how* are we supposed to do that?"

"By keeping our eyes open," Bella says. "And our heads down."

Charlie puts their head on the desk and mumbles into their worksheet. "Why can't we ever just have a normal day at school?"

When Bella, Dee, Charlie, and Eugene leave for their first classes, they're on the lookout for even the smallest signs of trouble. As it turns out, the group doesn't need to look for very long. They're all only a few steps out the door when they hear screaming in the distance, coming from the direction of the botanical wing.

"Those don't sound like shrieking sunflowers to me," Eugene says, his ears perking up. He looks at Bella. "What do you say, Maleficent?"

Bella doesn't hesitate. "Let's go." She turns on her heel and leads the way. As they hurry toward the commotion, they pass crowds of students rushing in the opposite direction.

"Remind me why we're running *toward* what everybody else seems to be running away from?" Charlie says, their voice fraught with worry.

"Aw, c'mon, Charlie," Eugene urges, excitement in his eyes. "We're monsters. Sometimes we've gotta live life on the edge."

"Tell that to my stomach," Charlie says. "It really doesn't care for surprises."

When they get to the botanical wing, they realize the noises are coming from the greenhouse, home to the school's extensive supply of plants, herbs, and flowers. The screaming has stopped, replaced by other strange noises like hissing and growling. The friends pause just outside, unsure of what they might be walking into. Have the magical creatures escaped from the stables somehow? Is Professor Daphne in another one of her moods?

"I have a strange feeling," Dee says. She's not sure how, but she knows that the plants inside the greenhouse are angry. "I don't know if we should go in there."

Bella ignores her and rushes through the door. When she sees what's inside, her jaw drops.

"Jeepers—" she starts but doesn't finish, because a vine extends from out of nowhere and snatches her up.

"Bella!" Dee rushes in after her sister to discover that the entire room has come alive. All around her, plants thrash, writhe, and roar like vicious toddlers throwing a tantrum. She watches Bella scream as she gets tossed around in the air by several tenacious vines as tall and thick as tree trunks. Everything has grown to five or six times its normal size. Some plants have even grown teeth.

"Put me down!" Bella pounds her fists into the vine around her waist and conjures flames, scalding the plant and forcing it to relax its grip as it shrivels back in pain. But it's no use: when one vine drops her, another simply catches her midair. It doesn't take long for her to realize that there are too many vines to fight off this way.

"Don't worry, Bella!" Dee calls out, trying to ignore how very worried *she* is. "We'll find a way to get you down!"

Devil's ivy snakes across the floor nearby, and when Eugene and Charlie follow Dee into the room, they accidentally step on a few leaves. The angry ivy hisses, rears up, wraps itself around Eugene's and Charlie's ankles, and squeezes tight.

"Oh no!" Charlie wails as the ivy creeps up their legs. "They've got me! This is how it ends!"

Eugene shakes his head at Charlie's fear. "Wouldn't you rather die doing something exciting than live a boring life forever?"

"No!" Charlie yanks at the ivy, but it won't budge. "I want to read books in a cozy coffin. That's it."

They're both distracted by Bella's scream as a vine spins her in the air. Eugene winces. "At least we're not up there."

As soon as he says it, the ivy gathers below Eugene's and Charlie's feet and raises them both up to the ceiling. "Oh great," Charlie says, the vines taking over their arms now. "The plants have a sense of humor."

As her friends get lifted above her head, Dee notices a few tiny, shimmering specks of gold raining down from the devil's ivy. She gasps. "It's pixie dust!" Then she says more loudly, so the others can hear, "Somebody used pixie dust to enchant the plants!"

"Does that mean a fairy will be able to— *ouch!*—stop them?" Bella asks, as the vine around her waist squeezes tighter.

"Maybe," Dee replies. "I'd better go get Principal K—" Her sentence gets cut off as a tree branch wraps itself around one of her ankles and then lifts her into the air so that she's dangling upside down. Dee screams.

"Charlie," Bella shouts. "Turn yourself into a bat, and you'll slip out of the ivy!"

Charlie looks anxiously down at the vines creeping across their chest. "I don't know if I can! I'm too nervous."

"Yes, you can!" Eugene says, the ivy tangling across his limbs. "Pretend we're at a flyball game. You have to turn, or else you can't play."

Charlie squeezes their red eyes shut, concentrating. After a few seconds they disappear, then reemerge from the ivy as a small, red-eyed bat.

"I did it!" They smile, and the sun glints off their tiny fangs. They rapidly pump their wings to stay in the air. "Okay, I'll go get help. Hang on!"

Bella snorts, clutching the vine that holds her hostage. "Like I have a choice?"

Across the room Dee struggles to free herself from the twisted branch, only to realize that freeing herself would mean crashing headfirst into the ground. "Tree, put me down! Please!" She looks around for a vine to grab on to, or anything that might be able to help her. That's when she sees it.

In the corner, a smoky shadow of a man, giggling into his hands.

"Poltergeist!" she yells, pointing at the monster.

"Poltergeist?" Bella looks where her sister

points, but the monster is already on the move. Poltergeists are nefarious tricksters whose sole purpose in the afterlife is to cause trouble. When Bella finally spots it, her eyes widen with understanding. "Oh. Well, that explains it."

"But what is it doing *here*?" Eugene asks from the ceiling, the ivy now wrapping up his chest.

Dee purses her lips, thinking. Poltergeists, as well as all other malevolent monsters, are usually kept away from YIKESSS by the protective veil that surrounds the school. Maybe this one found a crack in the foundation somehow?

Suddenly Dee realizes she's once again just a few feet off the ground. She was so busy thinking about the poltergeist that she didn't notice that the tree had listened to her when she'd told it to put her down. The branch relaxes its grip on her ankle, and Dee slides out of it easily.

"Thanks, tree," she says, standing upright. "Um, could you maybe ask your plant friends to let the others go too? They're my friends."

The branch shrinks back toward the trunk of the tree. A few moments pass, and then, slowly, the other plants start to calm down. They lower Bella and Eugene to the ground and unravel their vines.

"Whoa," Dee says. "Who'd have thought that all we needed to do was ask them to let us go?"

Eugene stretches out his limbs while Bella leans forward with her hands on her knees, looking a little green. "I *did*," she says.

"But you didn't ask nicely," Dee recalls. "Plants are living beings too, you know. They probably have feelings."

"Whatever." Eugene pushes a section of ivy aside like a curtain and heads for the door. "Let's just get out of here."

Bella groans. "We're going to be *so* late for class." She stands up and starts to follow him, then changes her mind and leans against a tree trunk. "On second thought maybe I should go to the nurse."

Dee drapes Bella's arm over her shoulders. "I'll take you," she says. "Eugene, you should go catch up with Charlie and tell them the poltergeist is the one who broke into the pixie-dust vault."

"On it," he says, quickening his pace.

"I can't believe you're not more freaked out right now," Bella says to Dee as they move slowly after him.

"Principal Koffin can handle one poltergeist," Dee says, brushing a vine out of her way. "She'll get rid of it, and everything will go back to normal."

"Not about that," Bella says. "I'm talking about the fact that you just told a roomful of enchanted plants what to do, and they *listened*."

"Oh," Dee replies. "Yeah. When you put it like that, I guess it does seem a little unusual."

"A little?"

The girls are interrupted by Principal Koffin and Professor Belinda bursting into the greenhouse.

"Girls," Professor Belinda says, startled to see them. "What are you still doing here? Go, quickly!"

Holding on to each other, Bella and Dee hurry out of the room without another word, the plants bending and shifting to clear a path as they go.

CHAPTER 9

The poltergeist is no match for Principal Koffin and Professor Belinda. As it turns out, they were already on their way to the botanical wing when they bumped—or rather, *flew*—into Charlie, who rushed to fill them in on what had just transpired in the greenhouse. After Bella and Dee make their escape, the principal and professor corral the poltergeist into a corner so that Professor Belinda can zap it back to the ether where it came from.

The twins hope that after the poltergeist is banished, everything will return to normal and Principal Koffin can finally focus on opening her heart to Vice Principal Archaic. Unfortunately, things in Peculiar are rarely so simple. Over the next few days a slew of strange occurrences continues to plague YIKESSS, sending the principal into full-on crisis mode.

More dark creatures show up and start causing trouble: sprite gremlins pick a food fight in the cafeteria, ghouls hide in lockers to steal screams, *another* poltergeist breaks into the Potions supply closet to mix up ingredients. A third-year kelpie even dives into the swimming pool only to be surprised by a horned hydra napping in the deep end.

But the worst comes on Monday morning, when Bella discovers that a video of Friday night's flyball game has been circulating on the internet—not the monsternet but the *human* internet. Apparently, a human out for a walk noticed the shimmering flyball in the distance and decided to climb the hill up to YIKESSS for a closer look. *I had to film this so other people would believe me,* reads the caption on the video post. *And so I would believe my own eyes.* Since it was posted Saturday morning, the video has racked up hundreds of thousands of views.

"How is this possible?" Bella asks, pulling her phone closer to her face to get a better look. The video shows Charlie, in bat form, passing the flyball to their classmate Mildred on her broom, and then the two teams racing to the goalposts, which float in midair. Mildred passes the ball to Drake, who passes back to Charlie, who then uses their wing to smack the ball past the goalie and into the net for five points.

"Nice shot," Dee says to Charlie, watching over Bella's shoulder. Behind her a nervous Charlie smiles into their lap.

"Lucky shot," Crypta mumbles with an eye

roll. Since Professor Belinda is away dealing with the crisis of the hour—a swarm of pesky nettleflies in the metaphysical education wing this time—the entire class has their eyephones out to watch the video.

"She's just jealous," Eugene assures Charlie with a pat on the shoulder. "She knows you're the best, and she *wishes* she could do that."

"Oh yeah," Crypta says. "I *wish* I were exposing our secret to the entire world. You got me."

"Back off, Crypta," Bella snaps, as Charlie sinks lower into their seat. "I'm sure the Creepy Council is already working on fixing it. By tomorrow, I'll bet none of the humans will even remember."

"And it's not Charlie's fault," Dee adds. "Humans aren't supposed to be able to see past the veil."

Charlie considers this and then sits up a little straighter. "Yeah. It's *not* my fault. It's like the veil is malfunctioning or something."

Next to them Eugene nods. "Actually, you've

got a point. All the weird stuff that's been happening lately should be impossible because of the veil."

"And if the veil *did* get knocked down," Charlie continues, "we'd have no way of knowing. We'd just be sitting ducks, vulnerable to whatever comes our way."

Bella turns Charlie's words over in her mind and then widens her eyes. She turns to Dee, who's looking back at her with the same panicked expression.

"You don't think—" Bella begins.

"Is this because of the spell?" Dee finishes her thought.

"A *spell*?" Charlie repeats. Bella and Dee both shush them.

"Oh no," Eugene says. "*What* did you witches do now?"

Bella puts a finger to her lips, motioning for her friends to be quiet. She glances back at Crypta, who is definitely trying to eavesdrop. She lowers her voice and begins twirling her finger through her hair. "Nothing much. We just brewed a little love potion to get Principal Koffin to let down her walls."

"Only, now it kind of seems like the *wall* we let down," Dee says, putting air quotes around "wall," "is the veil of protection." She starts to feel a little sick.

"You know, two months ago my biggest problem was my garlic allergy." Charlie says, shaking their head. "Those were the days."

"Ugh!" Bella groans and throws her hands up. "We should have been more specific!"

"We shouldn't have done a Level Three spell," Dee mutters. All she wanted to do was scrub cauldrons and *occasionally* text Sebastian in peace.

"Oh, *man*." Eugene winces. "And I thought being grounded for a week was bad. You two are going to be grounded *forever*."

"If we're lucky," Dee says in a mopey voice. "I'll probably never see Sebastian again. Not to mention daylight."

Bella shakes her head in disbelief. "That's who you're thinking about right now? Really? With everything going on?"

"What?" Dee blushes. "I can't help it. He's so *cute.*"

The raven squawks to signal the end of homeroom, and instead of going to first period, Bella and Dee head straight to Principal Koffin's office to come clean. They take their time climbing the winding staircase, and when they finally arrive at the top, the door is open and the principal is sitting at her desk, writing furiously on a piece of paper. Resting on his perch behind her, Argus the crow lets out a squawk.

"Come in," the principal says without raising her head.

The twins both try to shove the other through the doorway first, and then end up stumbling in at the same time.

"Um, hi, Principal Koffin," Dee says, straightening and plastering a false smile onto her face. "How are you today?"

"Out with it, Donna," the principal says, still not looking at the girls. "I have a nine thirty meeting."

"You *might* want to cancel it," Bella says, almost as an aside. Principal Koffin snaps her head up.

"What's happened now?" The principal puts down her pen and stands. "Another poltergeist?"

"No, no," Dee says, although if their theory is correct, there very well *could* be one lurking somewhere. "But we do think we know what's causing the poltergeists. And the sprite gremlins, and the hydra, and—"

"We accidentally knocked down the veil of protection," Bella blurts out. "At least, we think we did."

The twins brace themselves for outrage, but instead Principal Koffin goes very still. She stands there for a moment like a looming tower over the twins, her face unreadable as she processes what has just been said. Then, slowly, she sits back down. She places her hands on the desk in front of her, crosses her manicured talons, and says, "Tell me everything."

So they do. They tell her about the love potion, all the matchmaking schemes, and the vice principal's makeover. Dee even fesses up to breaking into Principal Koffin's office, though Bella thinks they probably could've left that part out.

When they finish speaking, Principal Koffin doesn't say anything. She stays silent for so long, in fact, that Bella and Dee swap a wary glance.

Finally she looks back at Argus, still and silent on his perch. She says one word: "Belinda." And the bird takes off out the door.

"This is very serious," the principal says, turning back to the girls. "You meddled in affairs that were not your own, with a potion that was much too advanced for you to carry out correctly, and have now managed to undo the work of magic that is centuries old and extremely powerful. Have I missed anything?"

"The fact that we're really sorry?" Dee tries.

"But I don't understand." Bella crosses her arms. "If it's so old and powerful, how did we mess it up with one little spell?"

The principal looks down her nose at Bella. "I once told you both that you have a great power inside you. I still believe this is true. But if you don't have the patience to learn how to control it, then believe me. *It* will control *you*."

In a flash Professor Belinda beams into the center of the room with Argus on her arm. She looks around warily. Leading the hunt against the dark monsters has left her even more exhausted than Principal Koffin.

"Girls? Yvette? What's going on?"

Principal Koffin stands up at her desk. "Belinda, summon all of Peculiar's witches to the flyball field at once. Let them know it's urgent."

Professor Belinda blinks, like she isn't sure she heard correctly. "*All* the witches in Peculiar? Even the students?"

Principal Koffin nods. "The spell we need will require an immense amount of magic." She walks over to the nearest window and pushes it open. "We're going to need all the help we can get."

The principal climbs out the window, spreads her wings wide, and soars away into the cloudy gray sky.

CHAPTER 10

A storm is brewing above Peculiar, and the chilly, gusty air nips at the noses of Bella, Dee, and all the other witches who gather on the flyball field. There must be at least a hundred of them, Bella observes, some of whom she recognizes from town but didn't even know were witches until now.

"Is that the librarian?" Bella asks Dee, pointing at an elderly woman across the crowd.

"Watch where you point!" Dee pushes her finger down. "You never know what kind of magic might slip out." Then she spots their neighbor and waves. "Hi, Mrs. Cromwell!"

"Don't *worry*," Bella, says zipping her puffy jacket up to her chin. "I have complete control."

Dee frowns just as a crack of thunder booms from the sky like a warning. She looks up, and that's when she notices Crypta and Jeanie walking toward them. Dee tries to turn away like she didn't see, but it's too late.

"Maleficents," Crypta says by way of greeting. "I'm surprised to see you here."

"Every witch in town is here," Bella says. "Where else would we be?"

Crypta shrugs. "Off playing with your dorky friends somewhere. My mother says this is important witch business." She looks to her left, through the crowd, to where

Gretchen Cauldronson appears to be deep in conversation with Principal Koffin and Professor Belinda.

Bella curls her hands into fists by her sides. Dee can sense the angry sparks building up inside her sister and gently touches her arm. "What was it you said about being in control?"

Crypta smirks. By now she's well aware that Bella's magic flares with her temper. "So," Crypta says, changing the subject now that she's gotten under Bella's skin. "Do you know what happened to the veil?"

Bella and Dee look at each other. Gretchen Cauldronson warned them what would happen to their family if they caused one more magical mishap in Peculiar. Crypta was the last person they wanted knowing the truth.

The twins shake their heads.

"No idea," Dee says. "Why would we?"

"Doesn't your mom know?" Bella adds. "Since she knows *everything*?"

Next to Crypta, Jeanie smiles into her chest

like she's trying not to laugh. Crypta shoots her a dirty look.

"No." Crypta says. "All she knows is that the veil is down. But I'll bet she's getting the rest of the story right now. She and Principal Koffin are as chummy as ogres."

Bella's pulse quickens. Would Principal Koffin really tell Gretchen that Bella and Dee were responsible for destroying the veil, knowing it would likely get them expelled from Peculiar?

Thunder roars in the sky again, and this time Dee feels a drop of rain hit her nose.

"Gather round!" commands Principal Koffin, her voice amplified by Professor Belinda's magic. She flaps her wings to hover above the center of the crowd, and everyone stops talking to look up.

"Thank you all for coming. I know you're wondering why I've called you here, so I won't waste any time on pleasantries."

"Does she ever?" Bella whispers to Dee as the rain starts to pick up.

"The veil of protection that has surrounded YIKESSS since its inception has fallen," the principal continues, the wind whipping at her clothes as murmurs run through the crowd. "Restoring it will take a great deal of strength—much more than any one witch is capable of. The only way we will succeed is if we work together. Do I have your support?"

The crowd claps and shouts out their agreement, and Principal Koffin returns to the ground. Professor Belinda, next to her in the center of the crowd, mounts her broom and takes the principal's place in the air.

"Form a circle and join hands," Professor Belinda calls out. "And we shall perform a binding spell to channel our magic into a new protective veil, one even more impenetrable than the last."

Professor Belinda stays still as the crowd of witches disperses to arrange themselves in a circle around her. When the shape is formed, Dee grabs Bella's right hand and Mrs. Crom-

392

well's left, while Bella, much to her chagrin, takes hold of Crypta's hand.

"Join me," Professor Belinda says. She raises an arm straight up in the air and shouts into the sky:

> *"We witches*
> *together as one*
> *call upon the moon and the sun.*
> *Grant us safety and protection,*
> *a veil that cannot be undone."*

She repeats herself, and gradually other witches start to echo the incantation. As the spell grows stronger, white sparks shoot from Professor Belinda's outstretched hand and into the sky, where they reach a peak and burst outward like shooting stars, then fall in an arc that encompasses all of YIKESSS and its surrounding grounds. Slowly, like weaving a sparkling web, the protective veil begins to reknit itself.

"I think it's working!" Bella says, marveling

at the shimmering threads of magic, radiant even through the heavy rain.

"It's beautiful," Dee adds, the sparks shining in her green eyes. "This must be how humans feel when they see fireworks."

"But better," Bella says. From their place at the top of the hill, she can see all the way to the welcome sign at the edge of town, just a tiny pink dot in an expanse of dark green grass. Then something in the sky catches her attention.

"Hey," she says to Dee, gesturing toward the shadowy figure with her chin. "Do you see that?"

Dee squints through the rain to get a better look. "It looks like . . ." She widens her eyes in surprise.

"A harpy," Bella finishes. She can only make out the birdlike woman's silhouette, but there's no mistaking the length of her body, or the expanse of her wings. Her long hair whips around her shoulders as she flutters in place just beyond the veil, watching them.

"I've never seen another harpy in Peculiar before," Dee says. "Or anywhere."

"It looks like Principal Koffin sees her too," Bella says. The twins turn to look at the principal standing in the middle of the circle, her gaze locked on the other harpy. Between the rain and the distance, it's hard to decipher the emotion on her face.

"Hello!" Crypta yanks on Bella's hand. "Sorry to interrupt your little chat, but some of us are trying to save the school!"

"Eat my warts, Crypta," Bella grumbles.

Dee shakes her head at her sister's remark. "No, she's right. We should concentrate." She leans over to Crypta and says, "Sorry." Bella rolls her eyes.

The twins get back to reciting the incantation, focusing on Professor Belinda, who's still leading the group from where she hovers on her broom in the center of the circle. Within a matter of minutes the last threads of magic are woven through the veil and the spell is finished. The witches stop chanting.

"We've done it!" Professor Belinda shouts, and the witches go wild, cheering and hugging and throwing their hats into the air. Amid all the excitement, Bella and Dee search the skies, trying to catch sight of the harpy again, but she's gone. Almost as if she were never there at all.

CHAPTER 11

With the spell complete and the protective veil successfully restored, Professor Belinda leads the soaking wet but cheerful group of witches to the cafeteria for some hot cocoa. On the way, Bella and Dee notice Principal Koffin break away from the group and fly off in the direction of her tower. Feeling remorseful and responsible for this whole mess, the twins decide to forgo the hot chocolate, which they aren't even sure they deserve, to follow her there.

They reach the top of the tower staircase, and the door to the principal's office swings all the way open, as if she were expecting them. They enter silently and sit down on the bench across from the principal's desk.

"Girls," the principal says, though she's standing at the back of the room, facing away from them. Before she can say any more, Dee stands up and clears her throat.

"Principal Koffin, we're so sorry for everything. We meddled where we shouldn't have and ended up putting the whole school in danger."

"I think you mean the entire supernatural community," the principal corrects her, still facing the wall. "The video of the flyball game was a PR nightmare for the Creepy Council. They've been scrambling all day to wipe the memory of every single person who has seen it.

And since it's gone 'viral,' as the humans say, that's been no easy task. Professor Belinda had to beam all the way to Bulgaria!"

Bella puts her head in her hands. "We're going to be expelled from YIKESSS, aren't we?"

Now the principal turns to look at the twins. "How did you get that idea?"

"The Creepy Council warned us that our family would be exiled if we caused any more trouble," Dee reminds her. When the principal doesn't immediately reply, she sits back down. "Aren't you going to tell Gretchen Cauldronson we were the ones who knocked down the veil?"

A look of understanding crosses over the principal's face. "I will not." Her gaze lifts from the twins and floats into the distance. "I'm afraid I don't much see the point in banishing children when they make mistakes. How can we ever expect them to learn if we do not teach them?"

Bella raises her head from her hands. Her face is red and splotchy from crying. "You mean, you protected us?"

The principal cracks the smallest of smiles. "That *is* my job." She looks back at the wall—or rather, at the small portrait of a man and three harpies that hangs there. "You girls told the truth even though it was difficult, because you knew I needed to understand. I suppose I must now do the same for you."

Dee furrows her brow. "What do you mean?"

The principal sits down at her desk. She takes a deep breath. "As you know, the veil of protection is essential for our safety here at YIKESSS. But it doesn't just exist to keep danger out. It also exists to keep me in."

Bella and Dee look at each other, confused.

"What do you—" Dee begins, but the principal holds up a hand to stop her.

"Long ago, in the years before I founded YIKESSS, my life was very different. I did not live in Peculiar, nor did I reside anywhere on the earthly plane at all. In fact, I lived in the Underworld, and I worked for Hades as a Bringer of Vengeance."

Bella tilts her head to the side. "Bringer of . . . what?"

"Who's Hades?" Dee adds.

Principal Koffin looks back at the portrait, but her face doesn't change. "Hades is the king of the Underworld. And I, along with my sisters, Estelle and Magdalene, was responsible for doling out whatever vengeance he brought forth."

"I knew it was you in the portrait!" Bella says. "You look great with your hair down."

"Shh!" Dee swats at Bella.

Principal Koffin remains unamused. "Anytime a monster broke the rules or disobeyed Hades, he would force us to punish them in terrible ways." She looks down at her hands and lowers her voice a little. "I'm not proud to say I carried out these punishments, without question, for many years. Creatures of the Underworld are wild and dangerous, just as Hades likes them to be. Most of the time, I even believed they deserved it." She lifts her head to look directly at the twins. "And then, one day, Hades ordered me to seek vengeance upon a child."

"No way." Bella leans forward in her seat. "A child who lived in the Underworld? What did they do?"

"And what was the punishment?" Dee says.

"Banishment," the principal replies. "And it does not matter what he did. No child ever deserves to be taken away from their loved ones. That's what I told Hades. I refused to send the child away from his family."

"And then what happened?" Dee asks eagerly.

"And then . . ." The principal's voice turns grave. "Hades sentenced me to imprisonment."

Dee covers her mouth with her hand.

"But you were doing the right thing," Bella says. "That's not fair!"

"I managed to escape the Underworld before Hades could get to me. He cannot set foot on earth, you see. Still, I crossed continents and oceans to separate myself from the entrance—a portal in the middle of the Black Sea. I decided to settle in Peculiar when I met a powerful witch who offered to help me by erecting a veil that would make all beneath it invisible and impenetrable. She cast the veil over an abandoned building, which I converted into a sanctuary for wayward monsters, and then, eventually, into a school. That's how YIKESSS was born."

"Wow," Dee marvels. "So you've been hiding here ever since?"

Principal Koffin nods. "That's right."

"But wait," Bella says. "If you can't leave, how did you chaperone the PPS fall dance?"

"The temporary veil that Professor Belinda cast over the public school," the principal explains. "It didn't have the same power or permanence as the YIKESSS veil, but it did the trick for just one night."

"*That's* why you said no to Vice Principal Archaic when he asked you to lunch," Bella says, understanding now. "You can't leave the veil. You have to stay hidden."

The principal nods again. "Hades has spies everywhere, and none better than my sisters. They looked for me for many years after I fled, and are still looking today. The gods are unforgiving that way."

Bella nudges Dee. "That's who we saw flying in the sky when the veil was being repaired!" She points at the portrait, to the sister on the far right.

"Magdalene, yes," Yvette says, a tinge of sadness in her voice. "My younger sister. She's the fastest of the three of us. Hades regularly sends her on scouting missions, but because of the veil, she's never been able to find me."

Dee looks down at her lap. "Until now."

"Because of us," Bella adds, equally glum. "We *really* screwed up."

The principal looks from Bella to Dee. "You did. But that doesn't mean all hope is lost. The veil has been restored and is stronger than ever." She pauses, giving the twins a chance to perk up a little. "Still, we will have to be extra vigilant now that Magdalene knows my location. When she returns to the Underworld, she will report her findings to Hades, and he will surely stop at nothing to take down the veil, and me with it."

Bella shakes her head in disbelief. "I can't believe your sisters would do that to you." She glances at Dee. Her sister is her best friend—her partner in crime. Dee would never betray her. It makes Bella sad that Principal Koffin can't say the same.

The principal looks down at her hands. "We have a complicated relationship. Hades has done many awful things, but he's also a father figure to us. He has provided for us, given us everything the Underworld has to offer. They don't understand why I would give all that up to save a single child."

She stands and walks back to the portrait. "This is the last picture I have of the three of us together. It was a gift from Hades, painted by Michelangelo on a visit to the Underworld.

It was the only thing I had time to grab before I fled." She looks at the twins. "This time of year is usually very hard for me. It's the anniversary of my exile." She moves to the front of her desk and leans against it. "Despite our differences, I still care for my sisters very much. I wish things could be different between us."

"So *that's* why you've been so cranky!" Bella realizes. The principal sends her a look of warning, and she backtracks. "Er—not *cranky*, really. Just a little less chipper than usual." She smiles innocently.

A wistful expression crosses the principal's face. "I am sorry for my misplaced anger. And furthermore, I want to thank the two of you. I know the broken veil put us all in danger, but because of it, I got to see my sister for the first time in more than three hundred years." She smiles at the twins.

"Um," Bella says. "You're welcome?"

"That's okay, Principal Koffin," Dee says. "If

I didn't see Bella for three hundred years, I'd probably be pretty upset too."

"Probably?" Bella says. "You know you'd be miserable without me."

Dee smiles at her sister. "I know."

"Oh!" Bella tries not to get her hopes up too high when she asks, "So now that the veil is back up, does this mean the Harvest Moon Feast is back on?"

The principal nods. "I suppose it does."

"And we aren't going to get into any trouble for telling the truth?" Dee asks. She stands up, hoping they can get out of there before Principal Koffin has any time to think about a punishment.

But the principal gives them a knowing look, stopping them in their tracks. "Not so fast." She looks back at Argus, who until now has been perched quietly with his four eyes closed. He opens his eyes, caws once, and flies to the closet in the back corner of the room. He disappears inside for a few moments, and when he returns, he carries a bucket in his talons, filled to the brim with sponges.

"No!" Dee jumps back in horror. "Expel me if you have to, but *please*, don't make me scrub any more cauldrons!"

Then, for the first time all week, Principal Koffin laughs. "These aren't for you," she says, as Argus flies past the twins and sets the bucket down by her feet. The sponges, glowing with magic, start spilling out and scrubbing the office floor on their own.

"*Phew*," Dee says, the color returning to her face.

"You'll be scrubbing cauldrons this week, though," Principal Koffin says casually, examining her talons. "*And* next. Let the punishment serve as a reminder that interfering in others' lives, when your opinions are neither warranted nor wanted, can lead to dangerous consequences."

Bella sighs. "Fine. I've already blown my

chances at getting on Horror Roll for the quarter, anyway."

"Our hands are going to turn into actual prunes," Dee says. She looks up at Principal Koffin. "But I guess that's our own fault. We took it too far this time."

"We should probably apologize to Vice Principal Archaic, too," Bella says. "I wonder if he's still in his office."

"I believe he is," Principal Koffin replies. "You can stop by on your way to get some hot cocoa."

Bella smiles. "You mean, we get to have some too?"

"With marshmallows and everything?" Dee adds.

"Of course," the principal replies. "You'd best be on your way before it gets cold."

The sisters leave the principal's office arm in arm, excited for hot cocoa and glad the worst is behind them. Principal Koffin watches them go with a melancholy expression on her face.

Argus caws and lands on her shoulder. He nuzzles the top of his head into her cheek.

"I know," she murmurs, stroking the bird's back. "I miss them too."

The principal turns away from the door, and it closes softly behind her.

CHAPTER 12

I n the middle of the night, Bella awakens to find a glowing marble of light hovering inches from her face.

"What the—" She sits up, shielding her eyes.

"It's me," Dee says softly, kneeling next to Bella's bed. She cups the tiny ball of light like precious porcelain in her hands. "I can't sleep."

Bella scoots over in bed and lifts the covers so Dee can get under them. "Did you have the nightmare about the giant spider again?"

Dee gets comfortable in Bella's bed while still carefully handling the light. If she loses focus for even a second, it will go out. "No," she says. "I just can't stop thinking about everything that's happened."

Bella turns onto her side so she's facing Dee. "You mean like how we accidentally knocked down a three-hundred-and-thirty-year-old magical veil with just one potion? Or how, because of us, the king of the Underworld knows where Principal Koffin has been hiding? *Or* how you tamed a room full of plants enchanted with chaos magic?"

Dee nods into the light. "You've been thinking about it too."

"Uh-huh." Bella pulls the comforter up to her chin. "How could I not?"

"Well, how did we do it?" Dee glances at Bella, and the ball of light flickers but doesn't go out. "I mean, we put everyone we know in danger, and we didn't even *mean* to."

"I know." Bella's eyes widen. "Imagine the kind of stuff we could do on purpose."

"That's my point," Dee says, and the light flickers again. "We've got power, Bella. *Real* power that neither of us knows how to control." She pauses a moment to refocus on the light, and its glow seems to strengthen. "It's scary, don't you think?"

Bella shakes her head. "Power doesn't scare me." She rolls onto her back and stares up at the ceiling with a smile growing on her face. "Just *think* about everything we'll be able to do once we master the craft. All the places we can go, and the humans we can influence. All the good we can do for supernaturalkind."

"And humankind," Dee adds, thinking, for a second, of Sebastian.

"Yeah," Bella says. "Them too. It's exciting to think about, isn't it?"

Dee smiles a little as she considers Bella's words. "I guess it's not all bad. We could spell every shelter cat into a loving home."

"Exactly," Bella says. "We can make the world a better place."

Dee's smile falters as she thinks about the veil again. "Or we could destroy the world." The ball of light starts to flicker more aggressively. "What if another one of our spells goes awry, and it's even worse than last time? What if we ruin everything?"

Bella's reply is immediate. "We won't."

"*Meow*," Cornelius cries across the room, from the foot of Dee's bed. The flickering light is disturbing his rest.

"But how can you be so sure?" Dee asks, still not convinced.

Suddenly the light goes out. The sisters lie, still and quiet, in the dark.

"Because we have each other," Bella says finally. "And all the magic in the world can't change that."

Dee finds Bella's hand under the blanket. Bella takes her sister's hand and squeezes back.

GLIMPSE THE
FUTURE

CHAPTER 1

In Peculiar, Pennsylvania, it is common knowledge among monsters and humans alike that the best place to get a milkshake any day of the week is Scary Good Shakes. The diner, located at 16 Main Street, has been operating since the 1980s, when a witch named Beatrice Wednesday bought the empty building a few blocks down from Ant and Ron's pharmacy and transformed it into the town's premiere destination for frozen desserts.

Nobody knows whether it's a spell that makes Beatrice's milkshakes so tasty or whether she simply has a way with a blender. In all her years running Scary Good Shakes, she has never shared her secret recipe, no matter how big the bribe or pleading the puppy-dog eyes may be. This bothers some people, especially her competitors, but it has never bothered Dee Maleficent. She thinks—she *knows*—that Beatrice makes the best strawberry shakes in the entire universe, and that's good enough for her.

It's a drizzly Saturday morning and Dee is seated in the back of her dads' van, daydreaming about one of Beatrice's strawberry milkshakes with hot fudge on top. She looks out the window, past the raindrops, where she can see a house with a sign posted in the front window that reads LET'S GO PPS PORCUPINES! Behind the house, in the distance, she sees YIKESSS up on the hill.

Principal Koffin's tower ascends into thick fog that, to Dee, looks a lot like whipped cream. A grumbling sound comes from her stomach.

"I'm *starving*," she says. "I might have to order two milkshakes when we get there."

"You're going to turn into a milkshake," Ron replies, smiling at his daughter through the rearview mirror. "How about some scrambled eggs too?"

"I still can't believe Scary Good Shakes serves breakfast now," Bella says, scrolling on her pink eyephone in the middle seat next to Dee. She shows her screen to Charlie, who's seated on her other side, and they both giggle.

"The perfect end to a totally wicked sleep-over!" Eugene remarks from the row of seats all the way in the back. He and Charlie spent the night at Bella and Dee's house, where they cooked homemade pizzas, coordinated and filmed an elaborate skit to post on Bella's WitchStitch account, and had a *Space Wars* movie marathon.

Eugene grips the headrest in front of him and bounces eagerly in his seat. "Man, I have no idea *what* I'm going to order. Do I go savory or sweet? Do I get a side of hash browns, bacon, or toast? Or do I get *french* toast?"

"You sure you're not a werewolf?" Ron jokes from behind the wheel, as Eugene certainly has the appetite of one.

"You can order as much food as you want, Eugene." Antony smiles at him from the passenger seat. He's wearing his human makeup. "I've heard the pancakes are delicious."

"Who knew Beatrice could make delicious pancakes, too?" Dee says, still looking out the window as they turn onto Main Street. She's thinking maybe she'll order some strawberry pancakes to go with her strawberry shake.

"Oh, I forgot to tell you: Beatrice retired," Ant says. "A new family owns Scary Good Shakes now."

Dee's shriek is so earsplitting that Ron slams on the brakes and yells, "WHAT HAPPENED?"

The driver in the car behind them honks their horn.

"Donna!" Ant's left arm is extended out to the side, a reflex to want to protect them all. "What have we said about overreacting when Pop is trying to concentrate?" He regains his composure and says to Ron, "Go, hon. That horn is giving me a headache."

"Overreacting?" Dee's face is a mix of shock and horror. "I'm never going to have another one of Beatrice's strawberry milkshakes *ever* again and you think I'm *overreacting*?"

"Yes," Bella says, not even bothering to glance up from her phone.

"Come on, Dee, you can't be that surprised," Eugene says. "The woman was ancient even when I was a baby."

"So what?" Dee says, and her tone comes out sharper than she intends it to. "That doesn't mean anything. Witches can live for a long time."

"Maybe she gave the new owners her secret recipe," Charlie says optimistically. "She knows how much her milkshakes mean to the town."

Dee says nothing. She crosses her arms and turns away.

The eye on Bella's phone closes, and she puts it down on her lap. "So who are the new owners, anyway?"

"The Nelson-Pans," Ron says. "A husband and wife with two kids. They moved to town a few weeks ago. Dad and I met them last week and told them about the PSBS. They're excited for the next meeting."

Ant and Ron have been members of the PSBS, or Peculiar Small Business Society, for nearly a decade. Any small business owner in town, human or monster, is invited to join.

"Are they witches like Beatrice?" Bella asks.

Ron and Ant exchange a wary glance.

"They're humans," Ant says. He turns to look directly at Bella. "But they're perfectly fine people, so you be nice. I mean it, Bella Boo."

"In case you haven't noticed, Dad, I'm not the one you need to worry about." Bella scoffs.

She gestures to Dee, who's still staring out the window. The gloomy weather now properly reflects her mood.

There's an empty space right in front of Scary Good Shakes, and Ron parallel parks the car into it. Dee gets out of the car and stands there for a moment, observing the place. From the outside, nothing has changed. The same bubblegum-pink paint coats the building's exterior, the same neon sign lights up the front window. The sight of it makes Dee's heart ache with longing. If only she had known when she got that strawberry shake after school on Monday that it would be her last! She would have savored it more.

"Jeepers creepers." Bella shakes her head, watching Dee sulk. She grabs her sister's arm and pulls her toward the door.

Inside, nearly every table is full, and the room swells with chatter and laughter. It's by far the busiest Bella and Dee have ever seen it. The decor remains largely unchanged except for one detail: The milkshake machine, which used to be on display behind the bar, has been removed. In its place is an open window that connects to the kitchen. The others in the group don't bat an eye, but Dee, of course, notices right away.

"Bella!" she whispers, tugging on her sister's sleeve. "Look, it's so horrible!"

But Bella isn't looking behind the bar. Her attention is fixed on a man sitting alone in a booth. He seems familiar.

"Is that Principal Pleasant?" Bella whispers to her friends.

Dee is half listening, still trying to locate the missing milkshake machine. "Who?"

"The PPS principal." Charlie peeks over Bella's shoulder, trying to get a better look without being too obvious. "I think it is. What's he doing all by himself?"

"Table for six?" the host cuts in, like she's in a hurry. The group follows her down the aisle toward a U-shaped booth at the back of the room. As they pass by Principal Pleasant's booth, he looks up from the big piece of paper he's reading—a map?—and locks eyes with Bella. After a split second of surprise, he smiles wide, putting his large, too-white teeth on full display. The sight is just as unsettling as she remembers.

"Ah, Bella Maleficent," he says cheerfully, quickly flipping over the piece of paper—a little *too* quickly, Bella and Dee both notice. "I told you we'd meet again!"

"Principal Pleasant," Bella says, and it comes out almost like a question. She doesn't remember ever telling him her name. "Nice to see you." Only Dee hears the sprinkle of suspicion in her sister's voice.

"Yes, great to see you all." The principal extends his smile to the rest of the group, making an extra effort to nod at Ron and Antony. "By the way, I'll be in to pick up that prescription later today. My apologies for letting it sit so long. I've been swamped with work."

"Not a problem," Ron says. "Just a reminder that we do have a maximum thirty-day hold policy."

"Understood." The principal nods once. Then he smiles at the kids again. Up this close, Bella notices the stubble on his jaw, the red veins that line the whites of his eyes. "Well, enjoy your breakfast. The banana pancakes are simply to die for."

Bella and Dee smile warily back. There's nothing on the principal's table but the mysterious paper and a nearly empty coffee cup.

The group walks to the back, where their host, a teenage girl, waits by the booth, looking irritated. They settle in and she hurriedly passes out the menus, then walks away without a word. Eugene watches her go with a smitten smile on his face.

"Wow," he says, leaning forward and resting his chin in his hands. "Who is *that*?"

Bella follows his gaze and then furrows her brow. "You mean Miss Miserable? Oh yeah, she seems like a real cup of witch's brew."

"Look, Dee," Charlie says, pointing to the top right corner of the menu. "They still have strawberry milkshakes, plus a bunch of other different flavors."

Dee, slouched into the back of the booth, doesn't smile. "They're not Beatrice's milk-shakes."

"All right, that's enough sulking," Ant says to Dee across the table. "Don't knock it until you try it, as the humans say." He opens the menu, then closes it just as quickly. "You know what, I don't even need the menu. I'm going to see what all the fuss is about with these pancakes. Gretchen was absolutely raving about them at the Creepy Council meeting last night."

The grumpy hostess-slash-waitress appears again. When she speaks, she has about as much enthusiasm as somebody going in for a root canal. "Are you ready to order?"

"No," Bella says, like it's obvious. "We've barely had time to look at the menu."

"What do you recommend?" Ron asks, while Ant shoots Bella a warning look for her snappy attitude. "We've heard great things about the pancakes."

"Yep" is all the waitress says. A moment of awkward silence ensues.

"Well, okay, then." Ron claps his hands together, breaking the tension. "Hands up if you want the pancakes."

Everyone puts their hands in the air except for Charlie, who asks for an order of scrambled eggs and bacon. Then Eugene says, "I'll have that too, plus the pancakes, and home fries, *and* a vanilla shake." The waitress scribbles down their orders on her notepad.

"Dee." Bella nudges her sister. "Don't you want a strawberry shake?"

Dee shrugs. "I guess so." She doesn't look up from her lap.

Bella rolls her eyes. She turns to the waitress and says, "Make that two."

The waitress finishes jotting down their

order, collects the menus, and then moves behind the bar to hang the order slip above the window that connects to the kitchen. Eugene, once again, follows her every move with his eyes.

"Hey, look," he says, pointing at the window.

Bella groans. "We get it. You think she's creepy."

"Not that," he says, though he doesn't meet Bella's eye. "There's a kid working in the kitchen."

Eugene's friends scoot toward him and crane their necks to get a better look. It's true: a boy is standing over the griddle with a spatula in his hand, flipping pancakes.

"*He's* the one making the pancakes everybody is obsessed with?" Bella says, skeptical.

"He looks like the waitress," Dee observes, noticing that they share the same round face and swoopy jet-black hair. "Maybe they're brother and sister."

"Mrs. Nelson-Pan mentioned that the kids

help out, the same way the two of you help out at the pharmacy," Ron says. He and Ant are still seated on the other side of the booth, all their attention now focused on the Saturday morning crossword, which they solve together every weekend.

As they wait for their food, the group discusses the big PPS basketball game coming up this Friday. Dee and Eugene want to go—Dee, because Sebastian invited her, and Eugene, because his proximity to the human world via his parents' taxidermy business has always kept him interested in human sports. Bella and Charlie do *not* want to go. They understand basketball about as well as they understand humans, which is to say, they don't get it at all.

While the four friends debate, they all continue to steal glances of the boy in the kitchen as he cooks. He appears to be about their age, and yet his pancakes are the talk of the whole town. What's his secret? At one point, he puts the spatula down and leans in close to the batter.

"What's he doing now?" Charlie says, drawing everyone's attention to the boy again. With their perceptive vampire vision, Charlie can see the pancake batter bubbling furiously on the griddle.

"Maybe it's part of the process," Eugene guesses. "He's gotta be doing something special to make them taste so good, right?"

Suddenly the boy stands upright and hurries out of the kitchen. He runs out from behind the bar and swerves through the crowd to the other side of the diner, where the waitress is carrying a tray of food and milkshakes. At the same time, a little kid tries to move around the waitress by ducking under the tray, but he doesn't quite go low enough. The kid's hat knocks into the edge of the tray, sending it flying out of her hands. But just before it crashes to the floor, the boy from the kitchen drops to the ground and slides on his knees to catch the tray in his arms.

Bella's eyes widen while Dee gasps. Not only did the boy manage to prevent sure disaster, but not even a single drop of syrup was spilled in the process.

The boy stands up and hands the tray back to the waitress. For once she doesn't look annoyed, only a little dazed. "Thanks, bro," she says.

And then, just as quickly as he arrived, he turns on his heel and heads back to the kitchen. Bella and Dee watch him take his post in front of the griddle and resume flipping pancakes like nothing at all has happened.

"Okay." Bella looks around the diner, still packed with crowds and buzzing with chatter. "Did anybody else see that?" She looks at her dads, who still have their eyes cast down over the newspaper.

"Uh, *yeah*. That was wild," Eugene says. "Some parkour moves, if you ask me."

"How did he know the tray was going to fall?" Dee asks. For the first time since they arrived at Scary Good Shakes, she isn't thinking about Beatrice's retirement.

The waitress appears at the end of the booth. Apparently, the tray of food that almost crashed to the floor belongs to them. She passes out the pancakes, the milkshakes, Eugene's breakfast of champions, and finally, Charlie's scrambled eggs with bacon.

Dee immediately takes a sip of her milkshake. Her eyes light up. "It tastes just like Beatrice's recipe!"

"Shocker," Bella says, her voice flat. "Dee, this place is still known for their milkshakes. They're not just going to taste disgusting all of a sudden."

"Yum," Charlie says, looking at their plate of food. They smile so big their fangs poke out. "Nothing quite like a perfectly scrambled egg."

Eugene raises an eyebrow at Charlie. "What about dragon plasma?"

Charlie frowns. "What, you think I can't enjoy human food?" They pick up their fork to take a bite. "Open your mind, Eugene. I contain multitudes."

"NO!"

An arm appears out of nowhere and swats the fork out of Charlie's hand. Bella, Dee, Charlie, and Eugene all look up in surprise. It's the boy from the kitchen.

"Sorry," he says, reaching for Charlie's plate. "But you don't want to eat that. The eggs were cooked in garlic butter. I, uh, think—well, do you maybe have an allergy to garlic?"

"*What?*" Charlie instinctively leans away from the plate as the boy takes it off the table. "Wow, thanks. I'm super allergic."

"Yeah, I—" the boy starts, but then stops himself. "It's no problem."

"Henry," a voice calls out from kitchen. The boy looks at the window behind the bar, where a dark-haired woman is watching him. "Your pancakes are going to burn!"

"Coming, Mom!" the boy replies. He turns

back to Charlie. "I'll bring you a fresh batch of eggs in just a minute."

He takes off through the crowd again, and all Bella, Dee, Charlie, and Eugene can do is watch him go, feeling more confused than ever.

CHAPTER 2

The rest of the weekend passes uneventfully, so when Bella and Dee get to school on Monday morning, they're still thinking about what happened with the boy at Scary Good Shakes.

"I just don't understand it." Bella zaps open her locker. "How did he know Charlie couldn't eat garlic? They didn't tell the waitress. Do you think the human knows they're a vampire somehow?" Both girls know that would be nearly impossible, though—humans never notice what is sitting right under their noses, including the community of supernatural creatures hiding in plain sight.

Dee removes her notebook from her locker and shrugs. "Maybe Beatrice had something to do with it. She knew all about Charlie's dietary restrictions." She bends over and unzips her book bag to put the notebook inside. Cornelius pokes his furry black head out, meowing excitedly.

"Cornelius!" Dee hurries to hide her book bag in her locker, looking around to make sure nobody else has spotted the cat. "We talked about this! Familiars aren't allowed at school. You'll get us in trouble."

Cornelius widens his big yellow eyes into a pleading sort of pout, and Dee softens. She can never resist that face. "Okay, I guess you can stay. But you have to be *really* quiet."

Cornelius meows his agreement, then ducks back down inside the bag.

Bella shakes her head. "You let him get away with everything." She takes out the books she needs for her morning classes and then zaps her locker closed.

"He'll be good," Dee says, assuring herself just as much as Bella. "But to be on the safe side, let's try to stay away from—"

"Principal Koffin!" Bella says, standing up straight.

"Exactly." Dee hoists her book bag on her back, leaving a little opening at the top for Cornelius, and then shuts her locker the human way. "I don't want to scrub any more cauldrons."

"Bella, Donna," says a familiar stern voice. Dee spins around and comes face-to-torso with Yvette Koffin, the seven-foot-tall harpy principal of YIKESSS. Standing next to her is a goblin woman neither sister has ever seen before.

"Oh, hi, Principal Koffin!" Dee takes a step backward and puts a hand over her shoulder, trying to telepathically communicate to Cornelius that he'd better not move a muscle. "How was your weekend?"

The principal stares at Dee a moment before responding. Though her face gives nothing away, the twins wonder if she already suspects they're hiding something.

"Restful," she says finally. "Thank you for asking." She gestures to the goblin woman standing next to her. "I'd like to introduce you to an old friend of mine, Kathleen Krumplebottom."

Kathleen smiles, revealing sharp teeth—a fashionable trend among mature goblins—and nods a greeting. She's dressed in a fancy suit and has voluminous purple hair. Dee admires the row of gold hoops that line her pointy goblin ears.

"Kathleen is a clairvoyant who has come to YIKESSS to discuss the ins and outs of her psychic abilities in an assembly this afternoon."

Bella's whole face lights up. She's never met a clairvoyant before.

Though anyone in the supernatural community can practice the art of divination, which is using tools such as herbs and cards to predict the future, natural psychic abilities are a rare phenomenon. They can appear in any monster, at any age, without any kind of warning, and tend to present themselves differently in everyone they inhabit. As a result, clairvoyance is the least-understood power in the supernatural community. There is simply no rhyme or reason for why future sight chooses some monsters and not others.

"No way! A real psychic?" Bella lowers her voice, trying to contain her enthusiasm. "Can you tell me if I'm going to be the next Bloody Mary?"

Kathleen shares a private, knowing glance with Principal Koffin, and then says, "Clairvoyance is rarely so specific, I'm afraid. Sight decides when it wants to reveal itself to us, not the other way around."

"Oh." Bella's excitement deflates. "Well, that's not very useful."

"Bella," Principal Koffin warns. "Do try to be polite to our guest."

A look of amusement washes over Kathleen's face. "It's all right, Yvette. Such is the life of a clairvoyant. We spend our days looking for ways to be useful until we drive ourselves mad with all the things we can't change!" She laughs a little maniacally, and then quickly gets serious. "Sadly, some of us don't recover as well as others."

Bella and Dee look at each other warily. Neither twin likes the sound of that.

"I'll go into more detail at the assembly this afternoon," Kathleen says. She glances at Principal Koffin and then leans in closer to Dee. "And keep an eye on your feline around Professor Belinda's raven, hmm? Quite vengeful birds, ravens. One swat and your familiar will have an enemy for life!"

Dee looks up at Principal Koffin, who's now frowning down at her, and smiles innocently. She can feel Cornelius shifting his weight in her book bag.

"I have no idea *what* she's talking about."

Bella and Dee are in the greenhouse, tending to their shrieking sunflowers for Botany class, when the ravens squawk to signal the end of seventh period. Usually the twins would head back to the witch wing for Divination, their final class of the day, but instead they make their way east, to the auditorium where the clairvoyance assembly is being held.

The auditorium and the greenhouse are on opposite ends of the school, so when the twins finally arrive, they look around and discover most of the seats have already been filled.

"I wanted a spot in front," Bella grumbles. She notices Crypta Cauldronson in the front row, right in the center, and glowers.

"Bella, Dee, over here!"

The twins turn their heads to the left, toward the sound of Eugene's voice. He and Charlie saved them two seats in the middle of the auditorium. Dee smiles at her friends and waves. Bella smiles too. At least they won't be stuck in the back.

They scoot through the row, past several classmates, and sit down—Bella next to Eugene, and Dee on the end. Right away they can tell Eugene is nearly bursting with anticipation.

"How wicked is this?" he says to the twins. "We get to meet a goblin psychic!"

Charlie leans around Eugene to look at Bella and Dee. "My mom told me about Kathleen before. She runs a school for psychics, and she works with Creepy Councils all over the world to let them know when trouble is brewing."

"Wow." Bella tucks her hair behind her ear, looking around for Kathleen. "I have *so* many questions."

"Me too." Eugene holds up a notepad and pen from his lap. "Don't worry, I'm going to write down everything. I don't want to forget a word."

"Eugene, I'm impressed," Dee says, leaning over to unzip her book bag. "I don't think I've ever seen you take notes before."

"Well, it's not every day you meet a goblin who decides not to be trickster for a living." He opens his notepad, where the words *Kathleen Krumplebottom, Clairvoyant (and goblin!!!)* are scribbled at the top of the page. "Speaking of, I think I've almost worked out all the kinks in the Tootmaster 6000. Want to help me take it for a test run after school on Wednesday?"

"Can't," Bella says. "I have scream team practice, and then we have to go to something with our dads."

"At a *human's* house," Dee adds, excited.

"Oh." Eugene looks down at his lap. "That's okay, maybe—"

"ACHOO." Charlie sneezes into their arm. "ACHOO. Sorry. I don't know where those came from."

On the floor, Cornelius peeks his head out of Dee's book bag. *"Meow."*

Charlie frowns down at the cat. They reach into the front pocket of their bag and pull out a small bottle of allergy medicine.

"Shh!" Dee looks at Cornelius and holds a finger up to her mouth. "Principal Koffin has ears like a hawk."

The chatter throughout the room starts to die down, and the four friends look up to see Principal Koffin and Kathleen walking to the center of the stage. Bella sits up a little straighter, eager for the assembly to begin. Dee gives Cornelius one more warning look.

"Good afternoon, students," Principal Koffin begins. Her voice is so naturally commanding that she doesn't need to turn on the microphone in front of her. "Today we have a very special visitor here with us, my good friend Kathleen Krumplebottom. Kathleen is a professor and the founder of SEE, the School for Extrasensory Excellence, up in Maine. SEE is a school for studying and harnessing psychic abilities. As a clairvoyant herself, she has graciously agreed to tell you everything you might want to know about her powers."

Bella's hand shoots up in the air. Principal Koffin sees it right away and says, "Hold your questions until the end, please. There will be plenty of time." Bella looks around, realizes she's the only one with her hand up, and then grudgingly lowers it.

"Now, you may be thinking, why must we have an assembly about clairvoyance when we have a whole unit dedicated to it in Divination class next semester? And the answer is simple. I want you to learn about psychic powers from someone who knows them firsthand. As it happens, many of you will probably never meet another clairvoyant in your lifetime." Here she pauses, as a wave of murmurs spreads across the room.

"Clairvoyance is extremely rare," the principal continues. "It's something one is born with, not something that can be taught. And though it can be studied to the best of our abilities, nothing about innate psychic powers can be said with one hundred percent certainty." The principal takes a step back, gesturing for Kathleen to step in front of the microphone. "Kathleen, if you'd like to begin."

Kathleen steps forward and takes a few seconds to lower the microphone to her height. Then she taps it with one long green finger, and the echo booms throughout the auditorium.

"Thank you, Yvette," she says, smiling at her friend. "And hello, YIKESSS! As your principal implied, natural psychic powers are hard to study because there are so many different variables involved. To put it plainly, that means no two clairvoyants are exactly alike in their abilities."

Kathleen takes the microphone off the stand and begins walking back and forth across the stage.

"Some of us experience visions as flashes that burst into our consciousness. Others see visions through objects. And still others can only see the future when the circumstances are right—say, on Wednesdays at noon, and *only* when it's raining. The frequency with which we experience these visions is different as well. Some of us get dozens of visions a day. Others, only one or two a month. And this, too, can change over time. That's why it takes some clairvoyants *years* to realize they have psychic powers at all."

Bella glances at Eugene, who is furiously scribbling in his notebook. He wasn't kidding when he said he didn't want to miss a single word. Bella zaps his pen with a writing spell, and it begins copying Kathleen's lecture on its own. Eugene looks up at Bella, surprised. He gives her a grateful smile.

"You might think it's swell to be psychic— and sometimes it is. You're on your way out the door, about to forget your keys, and then *bam!*" Kathleen yells into the microphone, making several students, including Dee and Charlie, jump out of their seats. "You have a vision of yourself locked out of your house. Now you can grab your keys and avoid a crisis."

"I could've used that one last week," Eugene whispers.

When Kathleen speaks again, her voice is much more somber. "Other times, though, visions of the future can be a real burden. Unwanted and unclear visions are common— more common, in fact, than clear, wanted visions—and often leave their hosts feeling conflicted about how to proceed, which can lead to severe mental strain."

Bella's hand shoots up in the air again. Principal Koffin, who has been hovering at the side of the stage, takes a step forward, presumably to silence Bella, but Kathleen holds out an arm to stop her.

"Yes, Bella Maleficent?"

Bella stands up, unfazed by the fact that every head in the room is now turned in her direction. "What kinds of unwanted visions?"

Kathleen nods, and Bella sits back down. "Every kind you can imagine. Disaster, destruction, fear—even death."

Murmurs sweep across the room again.

"The most important lesson a clairvoyant needs to learn is also the hardest, and it's that no matter how hard they try, they can't control everything. In fact, they can't control *anything*, apart from themselves. As clairvoyants, it's not our job to solve all the world's problems, no matter how badly we may want to. Those who realize this are the ones who will be able to harness their powers successfully. Those who don't, well . . ."

Kathleen stops walking and lets her gaze linger across the crowd. When she's sure she has everyone's attention, she says, "They will make an enemy of their own minds. Some will meet a *terrible* fate."

Without missing a beat, Bella raises her hand again. Dee winces, wishing her sister would stop drawing attention to them and the cat they've smuggled in.

Bella stands up. "Like what *kind* of terrible fate?"

Kathleen hesitates a moment before answering. She looks at Principal Koffin, whose face, as it often does, reveals no emotion. Then she looks at Bella again.

"When I was a young goblin coming to terms with my psychic powers, there weren't many resources available to me. All I had was a friend: a witch named Nina. A vision brought us together, funnily enough. She was clairvoyant too, although unlike me, whose visions come through my thoughts, Nina saw the future in puddles of water.

"I was always just trying to survive, but Nina wanted to help people. Whenever the sight showed either of us something bad, Nina *needed* to fix it. She dedicated years of her life to trying to change the future for the better, and I followed her wherever she went, because I thought it was what I was supposed to do. And then, gradually, I noticed a change in her.

She wasn't sleeping. She became irritable and started to get bad headaches. If she wasn't on a mission to track down a vision, she was staring at puddles of water, waiting for a vision to come. Her obsession with helping other people live better lives made her forget that she had one of her own. Eventually, it made her forget herself completely." She paused. "And it made her forget me."

Bella lets out a small gasp. She looks at Dee, trying to imagine how it would feel to be forgotten by her best friend. Just the idea shrouds Bella's curiosity in a dark cloak of dread. She feels her heartbeat quicken with fear and faces forward, trying to shake off the awful feeling. It's no use thinking about such things. Bella knows her sister would never leave her behind.

In the front row, Crypta Cauldronson raises her hand. "What happened to Nina?"

A distant look passes over Kathleen's face. "Nina passed away, I'm afraid. She interpreted a vision incorrectly, and the cost was her life."

Every student in the room is silent as Kathleen's words sink in. Even Eugene, once giddy with excitement, is now slouched in his seat with a disturbed look on his face.

"I'm not telling you this to scare you," Kathleen says, injecting some energy back into her voice. "Nina's story is a warning, yes, but more importantly, it's a lesson. Clairvoyance is a gift that can be used to help people, but if we're not careful, it can—and *will*—consume us."

She puts the microphone back in its stand and then claps her hands together.

"Now." She smiles. "Who else has questions?"

CHAPTER 3

Over the next couple of days, Kathleen's words weigh heavily on the twins' minds. Bella is frustrated—for all the supernatural community's many advancements, how is it possible there's still so much they don't know about clairvoyants? Surely, she thinks, someone could be doing more research to help the cause.

Dee, meanwhile, is worried—how many clair-voyants must there be, walking around with-out a clue as to what their visions of the future really are? She can't help but think about how confused and alone they must feel.

"We're lucky," Dee says to Bella in their room on Wednesday evening. She sits on her bed with Cornelius curled in her lap, stroking his fur as she speaks. "We've known about our powers since we were babies. We never had to worry about figuring things out on our own because we've always had Dad, Pop, and each other."

"I know." Bella brushes her hair in front of the vanity. "I feel bad for Kathleen. I mean, losing the one person who really understands what you're going through? That must be awful."

"I bet she feels really sad," Dee says, her voice somber. If Bella ever forgot about her the way Nina forgot about Kathleen, well—it goes without saying that Dee would be devastated.

Bella looks at Dee's reflection in the mirror. Her thoughts are an echo of her sister's. "That's never going to happen to us, right?"

Dee blinks in surprise. "Duh. I'd be completely lost without you." From her lap, Cornelius meows in agreement.

Bella gives her sister a small smile, reassured for the moment. "Me too." She puts down the hairbrush and turns to face Dee. "Do you think there are any clairvoyants at YIKESSS?"

Dee shrugs. "If there are, Principal Koffin probably knows about them." She pauses, considering her words. "At least, I really hope so."

"Girls." Ant pokes his head into their room. He's wearing his human makeup. "Ready to go to the meeting?"

Bella stands up. She's still wearing her scream team uniform from practice after school, wanting to show it off to all the humans. "Ready."

Dee tries to lift Cornelius from her lap. He lets out a forlorn meow and wraps his paws around her left leg.

"Sorry, buddy, but you know you can't come," she says. "We'll only be gone a little while."

"I know what will cheer him up," Bella says. She points at a toy mouse in the corner of the room, on top of Cornelius's toy basket, and zaps it with purple sparks. The mouse rises in the air, begins to squeak, and starts moving around the room, dragging a pink tail in its wake. Cornelius's yellow eyes widen. He leaps out of Dee's lap and begins chasing the mouse.

Dee smiles, satisfied. He's so stinkin' cute.

The first thing Bella and Dee notice when they walk into the human living room half an hour later is the color white. White couches, white walls, black-and-white photographs in white frames on a mantel that is coated in white paint.

"I guess it's better than beige," Dee says, taking off her sneakers by the doorway, as she was instructed to do by her dads, so she doesn't track mud on the white carpet.

"White, beige, it's all the same to me," Bella

says. "Boring human decor." She waits until the humans aren't looking and then zaps her boots off her feet and against the wall, next to several other pairs of shoes.

"Antony, Ron, we're so happy you made it," says the woman who answered the door. She has a blond bob and wears white jeans with a gray cardigan. "And you brought your girls!"

Once a month, the PSBS gathers to discuss and strategize how small business owners can work together to best serve their community. This month the group encouraged members to bring their kids and spouses. Bella and Dee have never been to a meeting before, thanks to their unpredictable magic, but since they've been exhibiting a bit more control lately, Ant and Ron decided to test their restraint and bring them along. And the twins were determined to make their dads proud.

"This is Bella and Donna," Ant says, gesturing to each daughter. "Girls, this is Amy Groff. She owns the Happy Hair Salon downtown."

"Hi," the twins say in unison. They look past Amy and see a group of adults—mostly humans—spread out on the couches and chairs that occupy the living room. A vampire who lives one street over from Bella and Dee, and who runs the library, stands in the corner with the least light and nods a familiar greeting in their direction.

"Oh, I just love your little cheerleading uniform," Amy says, and smiles down at Bella. "My Avery cheers too, at PPS. I'm sure you'll have so much to talk about. She's in the kitchen with the other kids."

Bella glances down the hall, toward the kitchen, and frowns.

"Go ahead, girls," Ron said, giving Bella a knowing smile. "Unless you'd rather discuss budget allocations with us."

"Hmm." Bella tilts her head. "Can I think about it?"

"Come on," Dee says, grabbing her sister's arm and pulling her down the hallway.

In the kitchen, Bella and Dee find white cabinets, white countertops, and three other kids seated around the dining table—shockingly not white, but a light oak—munching on an array of snacks. There's a blond girl who looks to be about their age seated in the middle, talking to a kid across from her who can't be more than six years old.

". . . have *got* to stop playing with dolls," she says. "Cool kids don't play with dolls."

"But I love my dolls," the kid replies.

"Well, then you're not going to be cool. Sorry, I don't make the rules."

The kid considers this for a moment, and then shrugs. "My dolls think I'm cool." They pick up a Cheeto from the glass bowl in front of them and pop it in their mouth.

At the end of the table, with all his focus on a handheld video game, a boy with swoopy black hair and a round face slouches into his chair. It only takes Bella and Dee a moment to realize where they've seen him before.

"Hey!" Bella says, and everyone but the boy looks up. "You're the kid from Scary Good Shakes!"

Now he does look up, a confused crease between his brows. When he sees Bella and Dee, something like recognition appears on his face. Then a *bleep-bloop* noise sounds from his video game. He looks back down at his screen and groans. "Shoot. I died."

Bella hurries to take the seat next to the boy. "Okay, you *have* to tell me how you knew Charlie was allergic to garlic. It's been bothering me for days. They hadn't mentioned anything about it in the restaurant, so . . . what's the deal? How did you know?"

"Charlie?" the boy says, looking back down at his game instead of meeting her eyes. "Oh, your friend? I didn't know. I just knew they didn't order it, that's all."

Bella purses her lips, dissatisfied with his answer. And now everyone's eyes are on the girls.

Pushing past her sister's rudeness, Dee says,

"Hi, I'm Dee," adding a little wave for good measure. "And this is my sister, Bella. Our dads own Ant & Ron's. You know, the pharmacy on Main Street?"

"I'm Avery," says the blond girl. "This is Henry and Sam." She locks her eyes on Bella's scream team uniform. "Oh. You two go to YIKESSS?"

Dee nods, trying not to feel bothered by Avery's judgmental tone. She takes the empty seat next to her sister, in front of a veggie platter.

"What's YIKESSS?" asks Sam, mouth full of Cheetos.

"A school for weirdos," Avery replies, as casually as she might have said *a school*, period.

Bella scowls at her. "Excuse me?"

"No offense." Avery picks up a tortilla chip and dips it into some salsa. "That's what my mom says." She puts the chip into her mouth and chews it loudly.

"None taken," Dee says with a genuine smile. "There's nothing wrong with being weird."

"Avery says I'm weird because I play with dolls," Sam tells them, studying the orange Cheeto dust on their fingers. "Maybe I should go to YIKESSS."

"Maybe you should," Dee replies. "I'll put in a good word for you."

Henry looks up from his video game. "Is it true you have to take tests with your feet?"

Dee scrunches up her nose. "What?"

"That's what the kids at PPS say," Henry tells them. "They say a *lot* of wild things about YIKESSS."

Bella rolls her eyes. "That's just a rumor. Some jealous hu—I mean, person probably made it up because they applied and got rejected." She looks across the table. "Hey, Avery, how many times have *you* applied to YIKESSS?"

"Me, apply to YIKESSS?" Avery says, forcing out a laugh. "What a joke. I'd never want to go there in a million years."

"Really?" Henry says. "Then why did you

just send in an application for spring semester?" Henry glances at Bella and Dee with a knowing smile on his face. "Her mom even slid a hundred-dollar bill into the envelope. Not that it's going to make a difference."

Dee covers her mouth with her hands, trying to stifle her laughter.

Avery's jaw drops. "How do *you* know that?"

The boy shrugs. "Just do."

Bella smirks into her lap. It's clear to her now that Avery is no friend of Henry's. For a human, he isn't so bad, after all.

"Whatever, Henry," Avery says. "I've tried to be nice to you since you're the new kid in school, but you know what? You're just as weird as them." She juts her chin out toward Bella and Dee.

"Welcome to the weirdo club!" Dee says to Henry, making him laugh. "We have lots of fun."

"And we have *way* better snacks," Bella says, frowning at the piece of celery in her hand and tossing it back on the table.

"Can I be in the club?" Sam asks. "I'll bring my dolls!"

Avery narrows her eyes at Bella. "I saw you at the fall dance, you know. You had that weird outfit and were dancing with those other two freaks." She eats another chip dipped in salsa. With a full mouth, she says, "I was embarrassed just watching you."

Bella stands up, her hands turning to fists at her sides. "Call my friends freaks one more time."

Dee freezes, glancing from Bella to Avery and back again. She can feel a spark of magic in the air.

"Bella," Dee says, her voice a warning and a salve. It occurs to her, again, how white and pristine everything around them is. How breakable. "Just relax."

"You and your friends . . . ," Avery starts.

"Bella," Dee cuts in, her heart pounding. She can feel the aura of angry magic getting stronger.

Avery doesn't break eye contact with Bella. ". . . are *freaks*."

Dee stands up, ready to jump across the table to snuff out the sparks if she has to. She can't let Bella's magic explode in front of all these humans. Gretchen Cauldronson wouldn't think twice about having their family exiled for much less serious offenses. And the girls can't let their dads down now, after Ant and Ron are finally starting to trust them.

Before Dee can do anything drastic, though, Henry gently touches Bella's wrist with his hand. Bella looks down at him.

Slowly, subtly, he shakes his head. *No.*

The anger drains from Bella's face, confusion taking its place.

"She's not worth it," he says. "Trust me."

Just as quickly as Bella's sparks ignited, they fizzle out. She sits down in her chair, and Dee exhales a breath she didn't realize she was holding.

Avery leans back in her seat, a look of satisfaction on her face. "That's what I thought," she says, and Dee frowns. Avery's arrogance is exactly the kind of stereotype that makes Bella so distrustful of humans.

Henry is frowning too. "You know, Avery, I'd rather be a weirdo with freaks for friends than a bully with no friends."

Dee smiles even though her heart is still racing. Henry stood up for them even though he didn't have to—even though he barely knows them. She decides, right then and there, that she wants to be his friend.

"Ooh!" Sam says, pointing a Cheeto at Avery. "You just got burned."

Bella is still looking curiously at Henry. "Dee," she says, and her gaze shifts to her sister. "I need to talk to you."

Dee follows Bella out of the kitchen and back into the hallway, where the guest bathroom is located. They hurry inside and lock the door behind them.

"Did you see that?" Bella says, eyes sparkling with an idea.

"Yeah," Dee replies, a little disgruntled. "You were two seconds away from casting in front of humans and getting us exiled out of Peculiar." She sits down on the toilet lid and studies the blue shower curtain as her heart rate returns to normal.

"But that didn't happen," Bella says. She hoists herself onto the edge of the counter and sits down, facing Dee. "Because Henry stopped me just in time. It was like he *knew* I was about to cast."

Dee considers this. "I don't think so. Maybe he just thought you were going to dump the bowl of salsa on her or something."

Bella shakes her head—though part of her wishes she would have thought of that in the moment. "First the waitress with the tray, then Charlie with the garlic, and now this. It's all too convenient that Henry always happens to intervene at the right time."

Dee raises her eyebrows. "What are you getting at?"

Bella lowers her voice. "Remember what Kathleen Krumplebottom said during the assembly on Monday? Clairvoyance can appear in anyone. I assumed she meant anyone *supernatural*, but what if humans can get psychic powers too? What if Henry can see the future?"

Dee's eyes widen as Bella's suspicions sink in. "He *did* say that thing about Avery's mom trying to bribe her way into YIKESSS—and how it wouldn't make a difference. *We* know that, since humans will never be allowed to attend YIKESSS, but how could he?"

"Exactly." Bella smiles and shakes her head in disbelief. "Principal Koffin said most of us wouldn't meet another clairvoyant in our lifetimes, and we've already met two in one week. How creepy is that?"

"Let's not get ahead of ourselves," Dee says. "We still don't know for sure that he actually has psychic powers. Either way, that kind of revelation could turn his life upside down."

"Yeah," Bella agrees. "We should know for

sure before we confront him. Otherwise, it wouldn't be just his life that gets turned upside down." She's thinking of the Creepy Council's cardinal rule: don't tell the humans about the supernatural community. Breaking that rule, of course, is punishable by exile, which means asking Henry outright whether he's psychic is out of the question.

"And I don't want to scare him away," Dee says. She picks up a section of green hair and starts anxiously picking at the ends. "I like him."

"Me too," Bella says. "It was really creepy, the way he stood up for us." In her experience, no human has *ever* done that before.

Dee looks up at her sister. "So how do we find out the truth?"

"First," Bella says, "we need a second opinion."

CHAPTER 4

During lunch the next day, Bella and Dee tell Eugene and Charlie about their theory.

"A human psychic?" Eugene takes a big bite of his hamburger. With a full mouth, he says, "I've never heard of that before."

"Well, if he's got psychic powers, he's not technically human, is he?" Charlie points out, looking at their friends behind dark sunglasses. The group is sitting at their usual table by the big window, and the early afternoon sunshine is pouring in. "He's supernatural."

"I knew there was something I liked about him." Bella grins, munching on a carrot from her dad's garden.

Dee nudges her sister. "You liked him when you thought he was just a regular human. And he still *might* be." She looks at Eugene and Charlie. "We don't have any real evidence yet."

"Then we need to get some, right?" Eugene says, taking another bite of his burger. "I mean, we can't just meddle in his life based on an assumption. The last time we tried that, it didn't exactly go so well." He gives Bella and Dee an accusatory look.

Bella frowns in his direction. She knows he's referring to the time they assumed Principal Koffin needed some love in her life—they ended up almost destroying the school. Also, she wishes he'd chew with his mouth closed.

"I get your point," she says. "But it's not like we can just ask him if he's clairvoyant. If we're wrong, we could get in some serious trouble. And he has no idea supernatural creatures even exist. Imagine telling him he might *be* one."

"Plus, we're still on thin ice with Principal Koffin," Dee reminds them. "She already helped us restore the veil. She's not going to want to clean up another mess."

Charlie winces. "I can't get into any more trouble." They pick up their water bottle full of plasma and take a sip. "My stomach hurts just thinking about it."

"And anyway," Bella adds, "if he *is* psychic, he probably doesn't even know it."

"You think?" Eugene says. "It seems like he's getting visions a lot."

Bella shrugs. "Kathleen said it takes some clairvoyants years to figure out they have powers. He doesn't have any monsters in his life to guide him—he probably doesn't understand what's happening."

Eugene picks up a french fry and starts twirling it between his fingers. "A supernatural living among humans, not knowing he's a supernatural." He looks at his friends. "That's pretty huge."

"*If* that's the case," Dee says, her forehead creased with concern, "we have to help him! It must be scary not knowing what he really is."

The group is quiet as they consider this. They've all grown up in the supernatural community, which means they've been aware of their powers—and the responsibility that goes along with them—their entire lives. By not knowing what he's capable of, Henry could unwittingly get himself into some real danger.

"Okay," Bella says. "So without meddling in his life, or doing anything that might accidentally expose the supernatural community, how can we find out for sure if he's psychic?"

"Find out if *who* is psychic?"

The group looks up to find Crypta Cauldronson standing at the end of the table, holding a lunch tray in her hands. Her shiny brown hair has been braided into two buns on the sides of her head.

"No one," Eugene says quickly. He shoves a handful of fries into his mouth.

Crypta narrows her eyes. "I just heard you talking about somebody you think is psychic."

"Psychic? She didn't say *psychic*," Charlie says, forcing laughter. "We said *sidekick*. Didn't we?"

Dee nods, faking laughter alongside Charlie. But Crypta doesn't move. Instead she locks eyes with Bella.

"Tell me."

"Honestly, Crypta," Bella says, resting her elbow on the table and putting her chin in her hand. "Why would we tell you anything?"

"Because if you tell me what you know," she says, "I'll tell you what I know."

This catches all four friends by surprise. They swap uncertain glances. Does Crypta *actually* know something, or is she just pretending to know so the friends will reveal their suspicions?

The last thing they want is for Crypta to find out about Henry and go running to her mom, Gretchen, with the news.

Finally Dee looks at Bella and shrugs as if to say, *why not?* As much as she hates to admit it, Bella sees her sister's point. They were hitting a dead end, anyway.

"Fine," Bella says. "But you can't tell your mom. Promise?"

Crypta smiles, pleased. "Cross my heart and hope to fly." She places her lunch tray on the table and sits down next to Charlie.

"Okay," Bella says. "Yes, we think we *might* know someone who *maybe* has psychic powers, but we're pretty sure he doesn't know."

"Why not?" Crypta picks up her spoon and plunges it into her yogurt. "Wasn't he at the assembly?"

Bella hesitates. She looks at Dee for help.

"He's a human," Dee says. Crypta widens her eyes. "And he's new to town. We just met him a few days ago at Scary Good Shakes."

"That makes sense," Crypta says, nodding.

Charlie furrows their brow. "It does?"

"Yeah." Crypta looks around to make sure nobody is lingering close by. Dee spots Jeanie in the distance, sitting at her usual table in the center of the cafeteria, an empty seat next to her. She's watching Crypta with a confused look on her face.

"My mom told me that Kathleen Krumple-bottom didn't *just* come to YIKESSS to see her old friend Yvette," Crypta says. "She came because she had a vision that there was a clair-voyant in Peculiar who needed her help."

"*What?*" Bella raises her eyebrows.

"But if Kathleen already knows about Hen—" Dee starts, and then backtracks. "About the boy, why didn't she contact him herself?"

"She doesn't know who it is," Crypta explains. "That's why she held the surprise assembly. She hoped it would help the psychic realize their abilities and come forward."

"A good plan in theory," Eugene says.

"Except that the psychic in question wasn't at the assembly."

Crypta nods. "Kathleen told my mom that the vision wasn't clear. All she saw was dark hair, the Peculiar town sign"—she looks at Bella and Dee—"and you two."

Bella grimaces. Dee sinks down in her seat.

"Typical," Charlie says, shaking their head. "Just typical."

"My mom told me to keep my ears open," Crypta says with a shrug. "She said if I overheard anything about who it could be, I should tell her right away. Otherwise, something bad might happen."

"Something bad?" Dee bites her lip, worried. She wonders if maybe they *should* tell Gretchen, after all. But then what would happen to Henry?

Crypta nods. "That's what she said." She eats a spoonful of yogurt, not seeming very worried about her mom's ominous threat. "As soon as they find the psychic, Principal Koffin and Kathleen want to send them away for training immediately, before they can do any damage to themselves or the town."

"Send him away?" Dee says, her concern growing. She doesn't want Henry to get sent away—he just got here. She's hardly even had a chance to get to know him.

"But you're *not* going to tell your mom yet," Bella says, her eyes pointed like daggers in Crypta's direction. "Because we don't want to screw with Henry's life until we know for sure that he's the one. And because you promised. Right?"

Crypta looks at Bella. She sticks out her pinky finger, and yellow sparks shoot from the tip. "I promise."

Bella holds out her pinky and conjures her own yellow sparks. The two girls' magic connects and intertwines, forming a magical pinky promise. If the promise is broken, the witch who goes against their word grows a long Pinocchio nose that can't be zapped away for twenty-four hours.

Once the promise is sealed, Crypta scoots her chair out from the table and stands up. "Keep me updated, 'kay?" She picks up her lunch tray. "And try not to make a total mess of things. If you do, I'm going to pretend I didn't know a thing."

She walks away, and Eugene shakes his head. "Maleficent, what are you thinking? You just made a deal with the devil."

"Worse," Charlie says. "With Crypta."

"I'm *thinking* that our hunch is right, and Henry has psychic powers." Bella looks around at her friends. "Who's up for a late-night stake-out at Scary Good Shakes?"

"You know me," Eugene says. "When mischief calls, I always answer."

"I'd prefer to let it go to voice mail," Charlie says. "But I'll come too."

They all look at Dee. Despite her worry about what could go wrong, she thinks it might be worse for Henry if they do nothing. It's one of their more noble efforts, as far as schemes go. Plus, there will surely be strawberry milkshakes involved.

"Okay." She nods. "I'm in."

CHAPTER 5

After checking in with their dads, Bella and
Dee meet Charlie and Eugene at Scary Good
Shakes at seven thirty, half an hour before closing time. It's not very busy—only a few tables
are occupied—and a sign by the host station
tells them to seat themselves. They decide on
the booth with the best view of the kitchen.

"There he is," Dee whispers. She can only see the back of him, but there's no mistaking his messy black hair as he stands in front of the griddle, flipping pancakes. "Try to act natural."

"Hi there!" A cheery middle-aged woman appears with a stack of laminated menu booklets and passes them out. It's Henry's mom. Bella and Dee recognize her from the kitchen on Saturday and the small business owners meeting yesterday. "Can I start you off with something to drink?"

Dee doesn't hesitate. "A strawberry milkshake, please."

The others in the group give their milkshake orders, and then Bella says, "Can we also get a stack of pancakes for the table?"

"A big stack," Eugene says, though he just came from dinner with his parents. "The bigger, the better."

Bella raises her brow. "Your stomach is a bottomless grave."

"Hey." He shrugs. "You're buying, I'm eating."

When the woman takes their order to the kitchen, the friends prop the menus up and use them to create a barrier to talk behind.

"So, what are we looking for, exactly?" Charlie asks, careful to keep their voice down.

"Evidence," Eugene says.

Charlie's mouth forms a straight line. "Thanks, Count Obvious. I meant what *kind*? Do we just wait until he has a vision?"

"Let's think about this," Dee says. "The last time we were here, he was flipping pancakes one minute and catching that falling tray the next. Same for when he stopped Charlie from eating the garlic."

Bella picks up a section of hair and starts twirling it around her finger, thinking back to Monday's assembly. "Kathleen said visions of the future aren't always in the mind. Sometimes they appear externally, in other objects."

"Like her friend seeing the future in puddles of water," Eugene says.

Bella nods. She peeks over the top of her

menu at Henry, who's still standing over the griddle in the kitchen. "I wonder if his visions are connected to the diner somehow."

Charlie reaches into their bag and pulls out a small leather book. There are no words written on the front. "I checked this out from the library after school. There were no textbooks on clairvoyance, but I did find this diary." They open it up to the first page. "It belonged to a vampire who lived in the early 1900s. From what I've read so far, it seems like they kept a log of every vision they ever had."

"Gnarly," Eugene says. "I can barely remember to write down my homework."

"The vampire's visions were activated by heat," Charlie continues. "You know when it's hot outside, and you see the little squiggles coming off the pavement? That triggered their visions. So did stoves, ovens, steam from hot baths—"

"Shh!" Bella snaps.

Henry's mom appears with a tray carrying

four milkshakes. "Now, what's going on here?" She gestures to the menus with a giggle. "Having a top secret meeting?"

"Oh, just doing some homework." Dee grins as her strawberry shake gets placed in front of her. "Thanks so much!"

The woman looks at Bella and Dee. "You two are Antony and Ron's girls, right?" Dee nods, and the woman smiles wide. "Oh, they're just the best. They've been so welcoming to us as we've gotten settled in." She finishes handing out the milkshakes and says, "I'll let you get back to it. That homework isn't going to do itself!"

"Not yet, anyway," Bella mutters. She's pretty sure her dads have that spell locked away in the Cabinet of Doom, the filing cabinet in Ant and Ron's study that is strictly off-limits to the twins.

When the woman is safely out of earshot, Bella leans behind the menus and whispers, "So what's your point, Charlie? You think Henry's visions are activated by heat too?"

"Not just heat," Charlie says, taking one long slurp of their vanilla shake. "*Pancakes* and heat."

Dee widens her eyes. "You mean, like, he sees the future in pancake batter?" She smiles. "That's awesome."

Charlie nods excitedly. "My theory is, the pancake batter hits the griddle and starts to bubble up, and that's what triggers the visions."

"That's a pretty specific way to see the future," Eugene says skeptically. His milkshake glass is already half-empty. "Maybe too much of a reach?"

Bella tilts her head, considering. "Kathleen *did* say no two clairvoyants have the same psychic powers. That means some powers would have to be pretty specific. Right?"

"Right," Charlie agrees. "Plus, it might not be the only way he gets visions. Just the most reliable way."

"Okay, okay. I see your points," Eugene says. "But how do we prove it?"

"Hey."

All four friends jump in their seats and look up over the menus. Henry is standing at the end of the table, holding a plateful of pancakes and looking at them curiously. "What are you doing?"

"Nothing," Dee says quickly, then takes a long sip of her milkshake. "Mm, tasty!"

Bella shoots her sister a look, then hurries to knock down the menus now that their cover is blown. "How did you know we were here?" she asks him. "Did you . . . have a feeling?"

"Uh." He raises an eyebrow. "No? My mom told me." He looks around the table, and his gaze rests on Eugene. "You okay? You look kind of green."

"Thanks!" Eugene smiles. "I've been getting a lot of sun lately."

Henry puts the plate of pancakes in the center of the table. He didn't skimp on the stack—there have to be a couple dozen pancakes there. "Here you go. I have to say, I think this is a first.

487

Nobody has ever ordered a stack of pancakes for the table before."

"We really love pancakes," Dee says. She scoots farther into the booth. "Can you take a break and sit with us?"

Henry glances around the diner. At this point it's almost closing time. There are two other tables still occupied, but both look like they're ready to pay the check.

"Okay, sure," he says. "I can sit for a few minutes." He takes a seat at the end of the table next to Dee.

"You're Henry, right?" Eugene says, piling pancakes on his plate. Henry nods. "I'm Eugene, and this is Charlie."

Charlie smiles and waves over their milkshake. "I use 'they, them' pronouns, by the way."

"Cool." Henry smiles back. "It's nice to meet you both."

"Hey, Henry." Eugene lowers his voice. "Where's that waitress who was here on Saturday?"

Bella rolls her eyes.

"My sister?" Henry makes a face. "Who knows. She hates working at the diner. She's still pretty mad at my parents for moving us here." He hesitates. "And me, for being the reason we had to move."

Bella leans in eagerly. Gathering evidence in favor of Henry's psychic powers just might be easier than they thought.

"Where did you move from?" Dee takes a big sip of her milkshake. She grimaces. "Ow, brain freeze."

"Just outside Philadelphia." Henry leans back in the booth and puts his hands in his sweatshirt pockets. "My parents used to run a restaurant in the city."

"Is that how you learned to cook so young?" Bella asks.

"Yeah," Henry says. "Food has always been a big part of our family. My mom's Korean, and my dad is from the South, and they loved incorporating food from both their families into the menu. I'd hang out in the kitchen after school and help them come up with cool new recipes."

"Oh, *man*," Eugene says, chewing on a pancake doused in syrup. "These pancakes are *delicious*. Seriously." He swallows and takes another big bite. "They're so good, it's like magic."

Bella bites the inside of her cheek to keep from laughing at the irony. Then it dawns on her: maybe magic really *is* the secret ingredient.

"People back home used to say that too," Henry says, smiling down bashfully into his lap. "My pancakes were the most popular thing on the menu."

"I'm not surprised." Eugene finishes the pancake in three bites, then moves onto the next one.

"But if the restaurant back home was doing so well," Bella says, a curious crease forming between her eyebrows, "why'd they move here and buy Scary Good Shakes?"

The smile fades from Henry's face. "I was sort of having a not-great time in school. The other kids, they . . . you know. They didn't get me." He shrugs.

"What?" The expression on Dee's face is one of disbelief. "But you're awesome."

Henry looks at Dee. "They didn't think so. And things only got worse after I started spending all my free time at the restaurant."

"What do you mean?" Bella asks, leaning forward. "Worse how?"

Henry seems uncertain. "I don't really know how to explain it. It was like . . . like I couldn't ever pay attention. Teachers and other kids would try to talk to me, and my mind was always somewhere else. The only place I could ever *really* feel calm was cooking in the kitchen."

Bella and Dee share a glance.

"My parents thought maybe it was stress related," Henry says. "That's why they moved us to Peculiar—for a fresh start."

"And has it been?" Charlie asks, finishing their pancake. "A fresh start?"

Henry runs a hand through his messy black hair. "Honestly? It's just more of the same. I'm still having trouble focusing, and the kids at school are . . ." Here Henry looks at Bella and Dee. "Well, you both met Avery Groff."

"Unfortunately," Bella scoffs.

Henry sighs. "I have to make it work here. I already put my family through so much with the move and making them give up the restaurant. I don't want to give them any more to worry about."

Dee frowns. She feels sorry for Henry. If he really is a clairvoyant, no number of fresh starts will fix his problems with concentration and feeling like an outsider. In fact, according to Kathleen's lecture, if he doesn't learn how to manage his visions properly, all this will seem like nothing compared to the bad stuff that could happen down the road.

Then Dee remembers Crypta's warning. When Principal Koffin and Kathleen find the clairvoyant, they're going to send whoever they are away for training. That means Henry's fresh start in Peculiar would be over before it even began.

Dee looks at her sister and knows they are both thinking the same thing. They have to help Henry. But how can they do it without uprooting his life *again*?

"Well, things will be different now," Dee says, giving Henry an encouraging smile. "Because you have us."

"Yeah. Consider this your official fresh start," Bella adds, raising her milkshake in the air. "Welcome to Club Weirdo."

"Club Weirdo?" Eugene says, though his mouth is so full of pancakes you can hardly make out his words. "That sounds wicked. I want in."

"You already *are* in." Bella nudges him. "We all are."

"To Club Weirdo," Charlie says, raising their fork in the air and clinking it against Bella's milkshake. The others follow their lead.

"Thanks," Henry says after they all clink. He looks down. "Honestly, I've never had a real group of friends before. I don't really know what it's like." He looks up and around the table. "Do you have sleepovers?"

"Oh, *do* we," Eugene says. "Last weekend we had a pizza-making contest and a movie marathon." He raises his brow at Henry. "Do you like *Space Wars*?"

Henry shrugs. "Sci-fi is okay. But what I really like"—he reaches into his pocket and pulls out a deck of cards—"is magic."

Dee's jaw drops. Does Henry know more about the supernatural community than he's letting on?

"Magic?" Bella says, just as shocked as Dee. "You can do magic?"

In one fluid motion, he fans the cards out and places them in front of Dee. "Pick a card."

Dee looks around warily at her friends before choosing the card right in the middle. She has no idea what to expect.

"You can look at it," Henry says. "But don't tell me what it is. Once you've memorized it, put it back in the deck."

Dee looks at her card—the two of hearts—and shows it to Bella, who's peering over her shoulder. Then Dee puts the card back in the deck.

All four friends watch, fascinated, as Henry thoroughly shuffles the deck. His movements are quick and precise, indicating to the twins that this is something he's done many times before. Finally he stops shuffling. He places the pile of cards down in front of Dee and pulls the first one off the top.

"Is *this* your card?" He flips the card over onto the table, revealing the two of hearts. Dee gasps in delight.

"Wow!" Dee claps her hands together. "That was amazing!"

Bella is a little more skeptical. "How did you know that?"

Henry smiles into his lap. "It's nothing. Just a little magic trick."

Bella's mouth widens in surprise. "Why didn't you tell us you know divination?"

Henry gives her a strange look.

"A magic *trick*, Maleficent," Eugene says. "Some humans—I mean, *people*—like to pretend to do magic. They're called magicians." He looks eagerly around the table. "One time, I saw one pull a rabbit out of a hat."

Bella scrunches up her nose. "What's so magical about a rabbit in a hat?"

Henry gathers the cards and puts them back in his pocket. "I'm not a magician or anything," he explains. "I can only do a few card tricks. But I do think magic is super cool." He sighs. "I wish it was real."

Bella, Dee, Charlie, and Eugene all look at each other. Nobody says a word.

CHAPTER 6

The next morning is fraught with indecision as Bella, Dee, and their friends go back and forth over what to do about Henry. While last night's stakeout gave them some clarity—namely, that Henry is probably psychic—it didn't make their decision about what to do next any easier. If Henry does have psychic powers, and they say nothing to Principal Koffin about their suspicions, they could be putting him in danger. But if they tell her, Henry will have to leave Peculiar, and he can kiss his fresh start—and their newfound friendship—goodbye. And that's assuming their theory is true. If Henry isn't actually psychic and Principal Koffin finds out they were meddling unnecessarily in her business again, they will probably get in big trouble. The girls are still on thin ice after what happened last time, when they almost destroyed the school, exposed the supernatural community, and got their principal taken away to the Underworld. Bella and Dee don't want to make a mistake like that again.

As Bella and Dee are on their way to lunch, still arguing about what to do, they're intercepted by Argus the four-eyed crow, holding a letter between his talons. It's addressed to Bella and Dee, written in Principal Koffin's telltale cursive handwriting. Bella takes it from Argus and rips it open as the bird flies away.

"Principal Koffin wants us to stop by her office for tea," Bella says, her eyes skimming the words. "Right now."

"Now?" Dee's eyes go wide with worry. "You don't think the birds heard us talking about Henry, do you?"

"I'm not sure." Bella lowers her voice and looks around. They tried to be discreet in their conversations, but the campus birds are like Principal Koffin's spies, always on the lookout for fresh gossip to bring her.

They turn around and head back in the direction they came from, making their way to Principal Koffin's tower office. When they get to the entrance at the bottom of the stairs, Bella says, "Remember, keep as quiet as a corpse. Don't say anything about Henry unless Principal Koffin brings him up first."

Dee nods in agreement.

They take their time moving up the winding staircase, not making a sound until they get to the top and use the brass knocker to announce their arrival. The door swings open on its own.

"Come in, girls," Principal Koffin says. She's not seated at her desk, where they usually find her, but in an antique chair in the corner of the room, next to a small, circular table. On the table are three teacups sitting atop matching saucers, decorated with a delicate floral pattern. The girls can see the steam rising from the hot tea.

"Take a seat," the principal says. Argus, resting on his perch, watches the twins' every step as they cross the room and sit down on the bench by Principal Koffin's desk.

"Would you like some green tea?" the principal asks. "I find it a divine way to relax when I'm feeling tense."

"Tense?" Bella laughs nervously. "We're not tense."

"Definitely not," Dee says, picking at her cuticles.

The principal tilts her head an inch to the

left. "I never said you were." She pauses. "So, no tea, then?"

Bella, who hates tea, looks at Dee. Normally Dee wouldn't hesitate to say yes, but today she's afraid her hands will shake if she tries to hold on to the cup and saucer.

"Um, okay," Dee says. As usual, her desire not to be perceived as rude trumps her fear. "I'll take some."

Principal Koffin stands up and brings her a cup. As Dee take the tea, she silently begs her hands to remain still. They don't obey. She quickly puts the cup and saucer down on the bench next to her.

"I'm glad you were both able to see me today," the principal says, returning to her seat. Her face, usually so stoic and composed, shows a trace of worry. This doesn't help Bella's and Dee's nerves at all. "I haven't had a chance to check in with you since the restoration of the veil."

Surprise crosses Bella's face. "The veil?" She

looks at Dee, who shares her confusion. Neither of them expected that.

Principal Koffin nods. "I've been worried about how you two have been getting on. What happened was quite . . . intense. Certainly a lot for two young witches to handle." She pauses to take a sip of tea. "I just want to make sure you're both doing all right."

"Oh." Bella exhales a sigh of relief. "No worries, Principal Koffin. We're doing just fine." She smiles. "Is that all?"

Principal Koffin turns her gaze to Dee, who's looking out the window, letting her tea get cold. Even though it's not the incident with the veil that's got her worried, Dee can't quite get behind her sister's assurance that everything is fine. She prefers looking out the window to meeting the principal's eye.

Principal Koffin stirs her spoon in her teacup. "You know, if something is bothering you—not just today, but anytime—I want you to feel comfortable confiding in me." She puts the spoon down on the table. "My door is open whenever you want to talk."

Dee turns away from the window. She picks up her tea and takes a sip. Her hands are no longer shaking, but she can still feel her heart beating quickly in her chest.

"Donna." The principal is watching her. "Is something on your mind?"

"No, not at all," Bella answers for her. "She's just upset because she messed up a charm in Spell Casting today. Right, Dee?" She makes a pleading face in her sister's direction and mouths the word "corpse."

Dee looks at Argus the crow, whose all-knowing eyes seem to bore right through her. She sighs. "It's just . . . We thought we were doing the right thing when we brewed that love potion. We wanted to help you, and we ended up making everything worse."

Principal Koffin nods, encouraging Dee to continue. Bella bites her lip, unsure what's about to come out of her sister's mouth.

"I guess I've been wondering. If you think someone you care about is in trouble, how do you know when it's your place to help them and when you should stay out of it?"

Dee takes another sip of her tea, now lukewarm. Bella sits back in her seat. It was a good question, she has to admit.

For a few moments Principal Koffin doesn't reply, just picks up her spoon and swirls it through the liquid in her cup again. "There's no right answer to your question, I'm afraid. What it really comes down to is intuition."

Bella raises her brow. "What do you mean, intuition?"

"Your gut feeling about the situation," the principal explains. "You have to weigh all the factors and decide for yourself if getting involved is going to make things better or worse."

Bella crosses her arms. She and her sister have been doing that all day and are still no closer to coming up with a decision.

"But what if your intuition is wrong?" Dee presses. "I mean, how can you ever really trust yourself to know the decision you're making is the right one?"

"You can't." Principal Koffin sips her tea. "The only thing you can know for sure is that your intentions are pure. Whether you choose to help or not, whatever happens as a result of your decision is out of your hands."

Bella shakes her head. "That's not good enough. What if you do nothing, and something bad happens? Or someone gets hurt?"

Principal Koffin takes one final sip of her tea and puts the cup down on the table. "Even if things don't go the way you want them to, you can find solace in the knowledge that you did what you thought was best."

Dee looks down at her feet. "It's frustrating," she says, "having all this power and still feeling so helpless."

Principal Koffin smiles sadly. "In time, it will get easier to trust yourself. You still have so much to learn—about your powers *and* yourselves. And as you grow in your abilities, so, too, will your confidence grow."

Suddenly Argus caws and flaps his wings on his perch, making Dee jump and spill some tea on her uniform skirt.

"Ah," the principal says. "That will be my twelve thirty lunch meeting with Vice Principal Archaic."

Bella perks up. "*Lunch* with Vice Principal Archaic? Ooh la la."

The look Principal Koffin gives Bella next could curl even Bloody Mary's toes.

The twins leave the principal's office feeling possibly even more conflicted than when they arrived.

"Maybe we should have told her about Henry," Dee says, walking behind Bella down the winding staircase.

"And get him sent away right when he's starting to feel like he belongs?" Bella says. "No way. Club Weirdo sticks together."

"I don't want Henry to leave either," Dee says. "But what if it's the best thing for him? *We* don't know anything about clairvoyance."

"Speak for yourself," Bella says. "You know I'm a fast reader."

Dee feels a buzz in her blazer pocket. She pulls out her eyephone, waits for the eye to open, and looks at the screen. "It's a group text from Henry. He's inviting us to the diner after hours tonight to try a new pancake recipe."

Bella unzips the front pouch of her book bag and takes out her eyephone. She immediately fires off a response in the new group chat, aptly named *Club Weirdo*: YES! Just have to make sure it's ok with our dads

Dee purses her lips, thinking of Sebastian. "But we were thinking about going to the PPS basketball game tonight."

"*You* were thinking that," Bella says. "I was thinking of faking my own disappearance."

Bella's and Dee's phones buzz with more incoming messages.

Eugene: A new recipe? OMG!!

Eugene: Henry, u should try pancakes with slugtruffles. Would totally enhance the flavor

Charlie immediately texts Eugene in a separate chat with just Bella and Dee, one they made after the first day of school, called *The Ghouls*.

Charlie: NO, EUGENE!

Charlie: Humans don't have slugtruffles

Eugene: Oh my b

Bella and Dee both laugh. Their phones buzz again. It's Eugene, back in the Club Weirdo chat:

Eugene: Nvm

Eugene: They're European

Eugene: Got any strawberries?

⤳∾• CHAPTER 7 •∿⤺

When Bella, Dee, Charlie, and Eugene get to Scary Good Shakes, it's half past eight in the evening, and the new moon is high in the sky. The front door is locked, and it's freezing outside, so Bella knocks aggressively on the glass until she sees Henry's familiar swoop of dark hair coming out of the kitchen, moving toward them. As soon as he gets close enough that she can see his face, Bella frowns.

"Something's wrong. Henry doesn't look too good."

Dee, Eugene, and Charlie all shove Bella out of the way to get a better look. She's right: Henry seems paler than usual, and he's got a grimace on his face like he's in pain. He unlocks the door and gives them all a weak smile. "Hey."

The four friends file into the diner one by one. "I'm happy you're all here," Henry says, and then locks the door behind them. Bella and Dee both notice the way he keeps his eyes down, away from the lights.

"Are you all right?" Bella asks without missing a beat. "You look terrible."

"Not *terrible*," Dee corrects her sister, unzipping her green coat. "Just a little sick, maybe."

"Oh." Henry runs a hand through his hair. "I'm fine. My head just hurts a little." He winces. "Or a lot."

"You have a headache?" Bella says, taking off her hat and looking meaningfully at Dee. They learned during Kathleen's assembly that headaches are a symptom of uncontrolled psychic abilities.

"I get them sometimes," Henry says, squinting at the ground. "It's no big deal."

The friends all look at each other. Nobody seems very convinced.

"Maybe you should sit down." Dee puts her coat on a table by the door and takes a step toward him. "We can get you some water."

Henry seems to hesitate. "Okay. I'll sit for just a minute. I don't want the pancakes to get cold." Dee heads to the kitchen for a glass of water while Henry sits down in the nearest booth and slumps forward, resting his head in his arms. When he speaks again, his voice is muffled. "Sorry about this. I'm probably just dehydrated from standing over the griddle for so long."

"Don't be sorry," Eugene says, sliding into

the booth across from him. "Do you get head-aches a lot?"

Henry lifts his head a little, propping his chin in his hand. "I used to get them only once in a while. But lately, they seem to be coming more and more."

"That's awful," Bella says. She puts her jacket and beanie on the same table as Dee's coat, and then sits down next to Henry. "Have you been to a healer?"

"She means a doctor," Charlie corrects her, sliding in next to Eugene. Bella waves away the mistake with a flick of her wrist.

Dee returns from the kitchen with a glass of water and places it on the table in front of Henry, then sits down next to Bella. Henry smiles gratefully as he picks up the glass—a movement that appears to cause him even more pain.

"Yeah," he says, and takes a sip of water. "Like three different ones. They run their tests, tell me everything looks normal, and then give me medicine and send me on my way." He pauses to take another sip. "It doesn't help, though. Nothing does. The headaches come out of nowhere and then . . ." He trails off. He blinks a couple of times and sits up straighter. "It's gone. Huh."

"Just like that?" Dee says. She notices that Henry already looks more energized. Some of the color is returning to his cheeks. "Your headache is gone?"

Henry nods. "It's strange. And it only started a couple of minutes before you got here."

"The same thing happened to the *character* in this *book* I read," Charlie says, raising their brow suggestively at their friends. Of course, Bella and Dee both know what *book* Charlie is referring to—the diary of the vampire with psychic powers they picked up from the library. "They got these headaches that would be really intense for a few minutes, and then they'd disappear like nothing ever happened."

"Yeah, that's exactly what it's like," Henry says. "What's the book called? Maybe I'll read it."

"Oh, um . . ." Charlie glances around. "It's called *Diary*. But you can't read it. It's . . ." Their gaze settles on Eugene. "It's European! I read it when I was on vacation with my mom in Italy."

"Oh, okay," Henry says. He turns his head toward the kitchen, and Eugene gives Charlie a subtle thumbs-up. "Wait here. I'll go get the pancakes from the kitchen."

Dee and Bella stand up to let Henry slide out of the booth, and then they sit back down. As soon as he's out of earshot, Bella says, "So I think it's safe to say that Henry is clairvoyant. Right?"

"Definitely," Charlie replies, their voice low. Next to them, Eugene nods in agreement.

"He said his headache started right before we got here," Dee reminds the others. "That was probably when he was cooking the pancake batter." She puts her elbows on the table. "I wonder what kind of vision he had."

"Poor guy." Eugene's ears droop a little. "He just wants to cook his pancakes and do his magic tricks in peace."

"Maybe he still can," Bella says. "He can live a normal life if he learns how to control his visions."

"Who's ready for some cookie dough crunch cakes?" Henry says, returning from the kitchen with two plates stacked full of pancakes. He sets them down in the middle of the table. "Pancakes with chunks of cookie dough and potato chips baked inside, and then drizzled in fudge. I hope they're still hot."

Eugene's ears perk up again, and his eyes nearly bulge out of their sockets in excitement. "Oh, hex yeah. Let me at 'em." He starts shoveling pancakes onto his plate.

"These pancakes are my way of saying thank you," Henry says, looking around the table. "You've all been so nice to me. My whole life, other kids have made me feel like an outsider, but you never made me feel that way. Right away you accepted me for who I am, and I can't tell you how much that means to me."

"Of course we did," Bella says. "We're all

weirdos here. It's so much more exciting than being normal and boring. Don't you think?"

"Yeah." Henry grins. "I do now."

"I'll eat to that," Eugene says with a full mouth.

Dee smiles, but her heart isn't in it. She's too worried about Henry—about the secret they're keeping from him—to feel very hungry.

The pancakes are delicious, and fortunately, Henry doesn't get another headache during the meal. Together, the five friends have no trouble clearing both plates—thanks in large part to Eugene—and even make themselves a round of milkshakes for dessert (strawberry for Dee, of course). After some serious urging by Eugene to put cookie dough crunch cakes on the menu, plus another one of Henry's card trick demonstrations, to the twins' delight, Bella, Dee, Charlie, and Eugene are ready to head back home. They put on their coats, hug Henry goodbye, thank him once more for the pancakes, and tell him they'll see him soon.

They wait until they leave the diner and are halfway down the block before anyone dares to speak.

"It's official. We have to tell Principal Koffin," Dee says, crossing her arms as she walks. The temperature has dropped even more since they were last outside, and a light snow has begun to fall. "Even if it means Henry has to leave Peculiar for training. It's the only way to help him."

"Maybe he doesn't have to go away," Bella says, her voice hopeful. She squints at her friends through the snowflakes. "Charlie, what did the vampire in the diary do to get rid of their headaches?"

"They tried a lot of different things," Charlie says. "But it seems like the only thing that really worked was not giving in to their visions. The more they let their clairvoyance control their life, the worse the headaches got."

Bella nods. It's just like what Kathleen said during the assembly. "Well, Henry can't control his visions if he doesn't even know what they are." She looks around at her friends. "Some-body has to tell him he's clairvoyant."

"Not me," Charlie says immediately. "Con-frontation gives me hives."

"It shouldn't be any of us," Dee insists. "It should be Principal Koffin."

Eugene doesn't look convinced. "I don't know. Wouldn't it be less scary if the news came from one of his friends, instead of, you know, a seven-foot-tall harpy?"

Dee shakes her head. "She's been around for hundreds of years and has probably met every kind of supernatural creature there is. She'll know how to handle it better than us."

They get to the end of the street and stop at the crosswalk, waiting for the walk signal to light up. The bus back to Eerie Estates is on the next block.

Bella sighs. "Dee's right. We should tell her." All three friends turn to look at Bella, shocked. This might be the first time she has ever agreed to get an adult involved in a crisis.

"What?" she snaps at them. "I want what's best for Henry too. Even if it means he has to go away. Jeepers creepers, can't a witch learn from her mistakes?"

"Totally," Eugene says. "I just wasn't sure if *you* could."

Bella snorts. She holds her hand out flat, palm facing the sky, and conjures a snowball in a burst of white sparks. Before Eugene has time to react, she throws it at him, and it hits him in the chest.

"Hey, no fair!" Eugene dusts himself off. "You can't bring magic to a snowball fight."

"Oh yeah?" Bella smirks, conjuring another snowball. "Watch me!"

She throws this one at him too, but he ducks just in time. The snowball whizzes past Eugene and collides with someone else, who until that moment has been lurking just out of sight.

Dee recognizes him first. She wonders how long he's been listening.

"Henry?"

Bella, Eugene, and Charlie freeze as they all

watch Henry step out of the shadows and into the dim light of a streetlamp. He has Bella's hat in his hand and a stunned expression on his face.

"How—how did you just do that with the snow?" Henry says, his eyes darting between them all. "And what do you mean I'm 'clairvoyant'?"

"Whoops," Eugene says. "Guess the cat's out of the cauldron."

"And you two—" He points at the twins. "Witches and supernatural creatures? What are you *talking* about?"

Dee takes a step toward him. "We can explain everything."

But Henry takes a step back, the shock on his face giving way to anger. "You've been lying to me this whole time." He takes a few more steps back. "I told you things I've never told anyone. I thought we were friends."

"We are friends!" Bella says. "Just *wait*. The feelings you've been having, the headaches you've been getting—there's a reason for all of it. We just wanted to make sure it was true before we—"

"No!" Henry drops Bella's hat on the snowy concrete and puts his hands over his ears. "I don't want to hear any more! I—*agh*." Henry leans over, his hands moving to his temples. He's getting another psychic headache.

"Henry, I know you're scared, but come with us," Charlie says. "We're on your side."

Henry shakes his head. "I'm not going anywhere with you." He takes a few more steps back. "You want to send me away!"

"We don't!" Dee says. "We want to help you!"

"No!"

Henry turns around and starts running in the opposite direction.

"Henry," Dee calls out. "Wait!"

"We try to do the right thing and it totally backfires," Bella mutters. "What else is new?" She picks up her hat, dusts off the snow, and pulls it down over her head.

"Well, what are we waiting for?" She looks back at her friends. "Let's go get him."

— CHAPTER 8 —

A ll four friends take off down Main Street.
Bella, Dee, and Eugene run after Henry on
foot, while Charlie transforms into a bat and
flies high up in the sky.

"Can you see him?" Bella yells up to Charlie,
pumping her legs as fast as she can.

"Uh-huh," Bat Charlie replies. "He made a

left on Strange Street and cut through the play-ground. It looks like he's heading right for the PPS gym."

"Oh no." Dee groans. As much as she wanted to go to the PPS basketball game tonight, it's probably the worst possible place for Henry to have a meltdown about supernatural beings. All those humans packed into one room! Not to mention the fact that Sebastian will be there—how is she supposed to be funny and charming in the middle of such a huge crisis?

"We have to run faster if we want to reach him before he gets inside!" Bella says. She and Dee pick up their pace while Eugene huffs and puffs behind them.

"If I had known we were going to be run-ning," he says, "I wouldn't have eaten so many pancakes!"

"If *I* had known," Dee replies, "I wouldn't have left my broom at home."

They follow Henry's path down Strange Street, across the playground, and through the field that PPS uses for football practice. When they arrive at the edge of the gymnasium parking lot, they find Henry hunched over in the middle of a row of cars, trying to catch his breath.

"Henry!" Bella calls out, and he turns his head toward the sound of her voice. At the same time, Bat Charlie appears behind Bella and transforms back into their mortal form.

"AH!" Henry sees the transformation and takes off running toward the gymnasium doors. Dee frowns at Charlie, while Bella turns around and gives them her best Bloody Mary glare.

"I'm sorry, I'm sorry! Jeez," Charlie says, covering their eyes with their hands. "Stop looking at me like that."

The group hurries to catch up to Henry, but he's too far away. By the time they get to the middle of the parking lot, where he *was*, Henry is swinging open the gymnasium doors and disappearing inside. Bella, knowing they could lose him in the crowd, stops running, braces herself, and then, using all the concentration she can muster, beams to the doorway, leaving Dee, Charlie, and Eugene behind in the parking lot.

"Whoa," Eugene says. "Now *that* was wicked."

Dee says nothing, but an uneasy expression crosses her face. Beaming, or zapping oneself from one location to another, is an advanced form of witch travel. Only Level 5 witches are allowed to practice it at YIKESSS, and even then, they're taught to proceed with extreme caution. Inexperienced beaming is very dangerous. If Bella isn't careful, she could wind up beaming to someplace she never meant to go, or worse, get herself stuck in the In-Between—a dimension for lost witches. But Bella, as usual, is impatient to unlock the full scope of her powers. When Dee has tried to discourage her, it's only made Bella more firm in her resolve to be the youngest witch ever to master beaming.

Bella stands in the doorway, propping the door open with her foot and keeping an eye on

Henry. "He's going under the bleachers," she calls out to her friends.

When Dee, Charlie, and Eugene catch up to Bella, she says, "We should split up. Dee, Eugene, you two go around to the other side. I'll stay over here with Charlie. We can try to corner Henry under the bleachers."

"You got it, boss," Eugene says with a salute.

Dee scrunches up her nose. "What makes her the boss?"

"I'm the oldest," Bella says, like it's simple. "Now hurry!"

Bella and Charlie move toward the home-team bleachers, where Henry went, and Dee and Eugene walk under the away-team bleachers to cross the gym unseen. It's not a hard thing to do—commotion fills the room. It's a rivalry basketball game, so the stands are packed. Both teams have cheerleading squads pumping up the crowds from the sidelines, each one fighting to be the loudest and most school-spirited. Bella recognizes Avery Groff in the middle of the PPS squad and sneers in her direction.

Under the bleachers, Bella and Charlie spot Henry right away. He's sitting on the ground, probably hoping he can remain there without being spotted until the game ends. When he sees Bella and Charlie, he stands up.

"Henry, please don't run away!" Bella says, as the crowd above erupts into cheers and applause. The PPS Porcupines must have scored. "I know it's a lot to take in, but you have to trust us."

"Club Weirdo has to stick together!" Charlie adds.

"Trust you?" Anger and betrayal are still written all over Henry's face. "Why would I trust you with anything *ever* again?"

Because we know what you're really going through, Bella wants to say. *Because we care about you.* But before she gets the chance, Henry turns in the opposite direction and runs away from them again. Fortunately, Dee and Eugene appear at the other end of the bleachers just in time, blocking Henry's path.

"Please, Henry." Dee struggles to keep her voice calm over the swell of the crowd above them. "Just wait a minute."

Henry stops in his tracks, looking back and forth between the friends, frantically trying to map out his next move. When it becomes clear that he's not going to be able to get past them, Bella and Dee each let out an exhale. Their plan worked: the chase is over.

And then Henry jumps up, grabbing onto the bleachers above him and hoisting himself up through the space between the bench and the walkway.

"No!" Dee screams, but her voice gets drowned out by the cheers that sound from the crowd above them. Another basket for the Porcupines, and the chase is on again.

Bella follows Henry's lead and climbs up through the bleachers right where she stands. Dee, who knows she's much too clumsy to carry

528

out such a maneuver, runs out from under the bleachers and climbs on in front—the old-fashioned way. Charlie and Eugene do the same, but on the other side.

Bella pulls herself through the bleachers and stands upright, startling the two humans on either side of her. She scans the crowd for Henry and finds him running down the middle aisle. "Dee!" She points at Henry, and her sister spots him. Dee hurries to meet him at the bottom of the stairs. When Henry sees her, though, he turns around and starts running up the aisle.

Dee takes off after him, knowing he'll get to the top and have nowhere to go. She motions for Charlie and Eugene to blockade the other aisles, so Henry has no choice but to run into one of them when he comes back down.

On the floor, the cheerleaders signal the crowd to start doing the wave. The people around Dee stand up and raise their arms, and the wave ripples across the bleachers. Henry, seeing this as an opportunity for escape, ducks into a row and follows the wave all the way down to the next aisle. By the time Dee realizes where he's gone, the crowd is sitting again, making it harder for her to move past them.

"Excuse me," she says, hurrying in front of people as fast as she can, trying her best not to trip over anyone's feet. "Sorry, sorry. I'm—oh! Sorry for stepping on your popcorn. Excuse me."

"Dee?" says a voice she'd know anywhere. Hearing it makes the bats in her stomach flutter their wings.

She looks up. Sebastian is sitting in the row behind the one she's currently shuffling through, wearing his PPS Porcupines hat. She stops moving and smiles. "Hi, Sebastian."

"I'm happy you made it," he says, scooting to the left. "I wasn't sure if you were coming, but I saved you a seat just in case."

"Really, you did?" She feels her cheeks heat up and hopes he can't tell. "That's so nice."

"Henry!" Dee hears Bella say.

Dee turns her head to find Henry two aisles

over, running down the stairs past Charlie. Eugene tries to block his path at the bottom of the aisle, but Henry spins around, faking Eugene out and narrowly slipping by him. Henry jumps out of the stands and lands on the gym floor, then takes off again.

"Well?" Sebastian looks at Dee curiously. "Do you want to sit down? You can have some of my nachos."

For a moment, Dee thinks about saying yes. She looks back at Henry, who's running to the opposite side of the gym with Charlie and Eugene trailing behind him. What if he never stops running? If he doesn't want their help, they can't force it on him. Dee could throw in the towel right now, sit down, and have a great time with Sebastian.

She frowns. Even as she's thinking it, she knows it's a fantasy. She wouldn't be able to have a great time, with Sebastian or anyone, knowing her friend is hurting.

"I wish I could," Dee says. "But my friend is

in trouble, and I have to help him. That's why I'm here."

"Oh." Sebastian's smile falls just a little, and it nearly cracks Dee's heart in half. "That's all right. We can hang out another time. I hope your friend is okay."

Dee smiles gratefully. "Me too."

Another round of the wave comes, giving Dee a chance to move easily through the rest of the row and get to the next aisle. She sees Bella standing on the bottom step and hurries to get to her.

"I'm here!" Dee says. Bella doesn't reply. She's focusing intensely on the basketball game. "What are you—"

Dee sees sparks out of the corner of her eye and looks down at Bella's hands, which she holds close to her stomach. One hand is casting, and she's using the other like a shield to block her sparks from view. The crowd around them lets out a collective gasp as the ball slips out of a PPS player's hand and bounces to the other side of the court. Across the gym, the away-team bleachers erupt with whoos and cheers.

"—*doing?*" Dee finishes.

"Henry is over there, using the basketball team to hide from Charlie and Eugene," Bella explains. "I had to get the ball to the other side of the room so they could get to him."

As she speaks, Dee watches Charlie and Eugene cross the court, hurrying to catch up to Henry. Henry, of course, sees them coming. He runs down the court, in front of the away-team cheerleaders, and crosses back over to the home-team side. The away team gets control of the ball and brings it back to the center of the court, blocking Eugene and Charlie once again.

"Do it again!" Dee says to Bella, and Dee jumps down from the bleachers to try and stop Henry from running. Bella zaps the ball to the opposite side of the room again, causing another ripple of gasps through the crowd, giving the ball back to PPS and allowing Eugene and Charlie enough time to cross back over.

A referee blows the whistle at Eugene and Charlie. She points angrily at the sidelines, signaling for them to get off the court. A section of the away-team crowd starts booing them, while the PPS crowd, who must think they're a diversion intended to trip up the away team, cheers them on.

Dee comes face-to-face with Henry in front of the PPS cheerleaders, who are in the middle of constructing their pyramid. She notices, with some distain, that Avery is being hoisted to the top. When Henry sees Dee, he swerves to the right, about to cut in front of the pyramid, but rethinks his route when he sees Eugene and Charlie coming that way. He cuts behind the cheerleaders instead, and Eugene tries to intercept him, but Henry gets away just in time. Eugene trips over Charlie's foot and falls into the base of the pyramid, sending Avery and all the other cheerleaders crashing down into one big pile on the floor.

Eugene, who has experienced much harder falls than this one, jumps right back up and smooths down his shirt. "My bad!" he says to the cheerleaders, and then resumes chasing after Henry.

Eugene, Dee, and Charlie follow Henry off the basketball court and into what turns out to be the away team's locker room. The lights are dimmed, and the only sound is the distant chatter of the crowd coming from the gym. The room, thankfully, is empty.

Bella arrives a few moments after everyone else. When she gets there, she finds Dee, Eugene, and Charlie standing over Henry, who's sitting on a bench with his head in his hands. It seems they've finally tired him out.

"Fine," he says, refusing to meet any of their eyes. "Let's talk."

CHAPTER 9

A crackling fire glows beneath the mantel in the Maleficent living room, setting a serene scene for Henry as he sits on the couch between Bella and Dee. Eugene and Charlie sit across from them, sharing a blanket on the love seat in front of the window. Through the glass, they can see the snow as it drifts gently down from the sky and settles into an even layer of white on the ground.

"So witches are real," Henry says, staring into the fire.

"Yep," Dee responds, stroking Cornelius's back as he rests in her lap.

"And vampires, goblins, ghosts, unicorns— all the magical creatures we read about in fairy tales. Those are real?"

"Pretty much," Bella says, munching on a chocolate chip cookie.

"Not unicorns," Eugene says, reaching for the popcorn bowl on the coffee table. "At least, I don't *think* so. I've never seen one."

Ant emerges from the kitchen, carrying three mugs of hot chocolate. "Eugene, have you ever taken a trip to the forests of Indonesia?"

Eugene shakes his head as Ant puts the hot chocolates on the coffee table. Ron walks into the room behind him, carrying two more mugs and a bag of mini marshmallows.

"Then it makes sense that you've never seen

one," Ron says. "They're very shy, and they don't show up on camera."

Henry picks up one of the mugs. "I thought that was vampires."

Charlie sighs and shakes their head. "Henry, you've got a lot to learn."

Suddenly the gold-rimmed mirror hanging above the mantel glows blue around the edges.

"That must be Yvette," Ron says. The first thing the Maleficents did when they got back to the house was call Principal Koffin to update her on the night's events. Of course, she insisted on speaking to Henry immediately. Since she's under the protection of the veil to hide from Hades and her sisters, and therefore can't leave YIKESSS to come to the house, they all decided the magic mirror was the best way to get through to him.

Ron approaches the mirror so it can scan his face. A moment later his reflection is replaced with Principal Koffin, framed by a view of her office.

"A magic mirror?" Henry widens his eyes. "What, do you have, like, a cauldron in the kitchen too?"

"Actually"—Bella sprinkles marshmallows into her mug—"our cauldrons are in our room."

"We can show you if you want!" Dee adds.

Henry grimaces. "That's okay. Another time."

"Ah, hello, Mr. Maleficent," Yvette says to Ron, and then looks off to the side. "Kathleen, I've gotten through to them." Yvette scoots a little to the left. Kathleen Krumplebottom's voluminous purple hair and the tips of her green ears appear in the frame.

"Hello there!"

"A little higher, Kathleen," Ron says. "We can't see you."

Kathleen's hair disappears for a moment. They can hear some rustling, followed by the sound of furniture being dragged across the room.

"Mind the floors, please, Kathleen," Yvette

says to her. "I just had them waxed." Then the back of a chair appears in the frame, followed by Kathleen's face.

"Is that better?" She leans in close to the mirror. "I'm standing on a chair."

"Perfect," Ron says. He steps off to the side, and Kathleen smiles at everyone in the room. "Hello, kids! Is this our clairvoyant, here, in the middle?"

"His name is Henry," Bella says, a little defensively.

"Henry, of course," she says. "I'm Kathleen. It's so lovely to meet you. I've been looking everywhere for you, you know."

"You have?" Henry says. As much as he tries to hide it, the twins can see how scared he really is. "Why?"

"Because I have psychic abilities, just the same as you, and I had a vision that you needed some guidance."

Henry raises his brow. "You mean, you see the future in pancake batter too?"

Kathleen laughs. "No, no. My visions come to me a little differently. In fact, every clairvoyant has their own unique method of accessing their gift."

"Gift," Henry repeats with a snort. "Getting random visions of bad things that are going to happen isn't a gift." He looks down at the mug in his hands. "It's a curse."

"Oh, you poor dear," Kathleen says, her forehead creased with sympathy. "I know how frightened you must be. You didn't ask for this—of course you didn't—but what you will learn, in time, is that clairvoyance is not all bad. In fact, you're seeing good things too. *Helpful* things. You've just been so consumed by the bad that you haven't been paying attention."

"Really?" Henry looks up, still skeptical, but for the first time since he learned the truth about his powers, there's a little glimmer of hope in his eyes too. "But how do you know that? I can't think of a single time I saw something good."

"Because, my dear boy, I've been where you are. It might come as a surprise, but I haven't always been this cool, collected goblin you see before you." Kathleen shares a private, amused glance with Principal Koffin. "I was quite consumed by fear for many years—fear that something bad would happen, fear that I wouldn't be able to stop it, fear that I felt like it was my *responsibility* to stop it. Fear was all I could see!"

Henry nods. Kathleen's words seem to be resonating with him even more than Bella and Dee realized they would.

"Tell me," Kathleen says, "have you been getting headaches?"

"Yeah," Henry says. "Bad ones. They make me dizzy sometimes."

"That's what we call a psychic migraine," Kathleen says. "Very common among young clairvoyants especially, as they're the ones who have the least amount of control over their powers."

"So you mean, if I learn to control my . . . powers"—Henry makes a face like he's in disbelief at his own words—"the headaches will stop?"

"Indeed they will," Kathleen says. "The headaches happen because your subconscious wants to push your visions out of your mind. But visions, as you'll learn, cannot be forced away. No matter how hard you try."

Henry doesn't say anything, just looks down at the floor and lets his black hair fall over his eyes. It seems this bit of information is the hardest for him to hear.

"So the visions will never stop," he says. "I'm going to have to deal with this forever." It's a statement, not a question.

Kathleen doesn't respond right away, and a heavy silence hangs over the room. Finally, Principal Koffin is the one to speak up.

"Yes, you'll be psychic forever," she says. "The same way all of us in this room must deal with our supernatural traits, which will forever ostracize us from the rest of humanity. We can choose to give in to despair that we are different, or we can learn to live with our abilities as best we can. And then, one day, we might even come to find that we love them, because they make us who we are."

Bella and Dee swap a glance. They know Principal Koffin is speaking from experience, though they've never heard her talk like this before.

"I know it feels like you're carrying the weight of the world on your shoulders right now," the principal continues. "But it doesn't have to be that way. If you let us, we can help make the weight lighter. We can make you *happier*."

"It's true," Dee says. She rests a comforting hand on Henry's shoulder. "We're all here for you, and we'll do whatever we can to help you."

"But why?" Henry looks at her. "Why do you want to help me so badly?" She notices his dark eyes are welling with tears.

"Because you're one of us," Bella says simply. "Maybe you've been having such a hard time because you haven't had anyone who really understands what you're going through. But we do. And we're not going anywhere."

"We meant it before, when we said we were your friends," Charlie adds.

"You're in Club Weirdo now." Eugene puts down his mug of hot chocolate. "You don't have to feel alone ever again."

With that, Henry smiles, letting them know their words of assurance are stronger than all the uncertainty he was harboring inside. He's *not* alone, and things *can* get better. Finally he realizes it.

"Okay." He wipes a tear from his cheek and then looks at Principal Koffin and Kathleen. "So, what do I have to do now?"

CHAPTER 10

It's a cold Saturday afternoon in Peculiar, Pennsylvania, and Bella, Dee, Charlie, and Eugene are throwing Henry a going-away party next to the lake in Moonlight Park. Despite the frost that clings to the grass around them, and the layer of ice on the lake, the friends are soaking up the sun in T-shirts and shorts. A warm-weather spell hangs like a spotlight over their picnic blanket, turning the harsh winter wind into a salty ocean breeze. Thanks to the unpleasant chill in the air, they have the place to themselves and are free to relax away from the prying eyes of any curious humans.

"Now this is the kind of magic I could get used to," Henry says, closing his eyes and raising his face toward the sun.

"Me too." Eugene licks an orange Popsicle. "You witches are really starting to get the hang of your powers."

"Don't look at me." Bella's eyes are hidden behind a pair of heart-shaped sunglasses. "This one was all Dee. She's got a knack for nature spells." She licks her cherry Popsicle, which is the same shade of red as her sunglasses.

Dee blushes, smiling into her lap. "I wanted Henry's last day in town to be extra special."

At the reminder that Henry has to leave soon, everyone's sunny dispositions dim just a little.

One week has passed since the conversation about Henry's powers in the Maleficents' living room. Since then, a lot has changed. Kathleen explained that it would be best for Henry if he went with her to SEE for a little while. At SEE, he can learn to control his psychic powers and harness his full potential as a clairvoyant. And since Kathleen is the headmaster, she'll be able to watch over him and make sure he's okay—a condition that Bella and Dee absolutely *insisted* on.

"I'm really going to miss you all," Henry says, fiddling with a balloon string instead of meeting their eyes. "I know we only met a couple of weeks ago, but it feels like I've known you all my whole life."

"Oh!" Dee leans forward and throws her arms around Henry. "We're going to miss you so much!"

"The next few months are going to feel like *forever*," Bella whines.

"But we'll still talk all the time," Charlie says, applying a fresh layer of Sunscream to their face. "Now that you're a supernatural, you *have* to get an eyephone so we can all eyechat."

"Definitely," Henry says. "And you'll look after my parents while I'm gone, right? I know they'll worry."

For Henry, the hardest part of this whole process is not being able to tell his parents the truth about where he's going, or anything about his powers at all. But as Principal Koffin explained, letting humans in on their secret is a dangerous game. She says it will be better for everyone if Henry's parents think he was accepted, on full scholarship, into a prestigious culinary school up in Maine. Though Henry hates to lie to his parents, he knows it's better than the alternative—his family getting exiled from Peculiar for revealing the existence of supernatural beings. He already made them uproot their lives once.

"Of course we will," Dee says. "And our dads will too."

"You know we'll be at Scary Good Shakes,

like, every day," Eugene adds. "Though it won't be the same without your pancakes." His ears droop a little.

"By the way," Henry says to Eugene. "As of this morning, cookie dough crunch cakes are officially on the menu." He grins. "Consider it my going-away present."

"Really?" Eugene's ears perk right back up. "You're the best!"

"We have a going-away present for you, too," Bella tells Henry. She reaches behind her and reveals a small black box tied with sparkly silver ribbon.

"Wow." Henry takes the box. "You didn't have to." He unties the ribbon and opens the lid, and his whole face lights up.

"A deck of cards!" He pulls the deck out of the box. The cards are shiny and black, and at first they appear to be blank. When he picks the top one off the pile and examines it more closely, ink appears. It's a moving image of Dee with a crown on her head, zapping hearts into each corner with red sparks. Then she looks out of the card and waves at Henry.

"They're infused with magic," Bella says. "Forget kings, queens, jacks, and aces. Now you've got Bellas, Dees, Charlies, and Eugenes."

Henry puts the cards back in the box and hugs the whole thing to his chest. "This is really special," he says, and all four friends can hear the emotion in his voice. "Thank you so much."

A burst of blue sparks to their left catches the group by surprise. They turn their heads to find Kathleen standing there, holding the handlebars of a strange-looking silver bicycle with two seats.

"No way!" Bella widens her eyes in excitement. "A beam bike? Those are super rare."

"You didn't think we were going to walk all the way to SEE, did you?" Kathleen smiles. Beam bikes are transportation devices imbued with witch's magic so other supernatural creatures can beam from place to place. In order to get her hands on one, Kathleen would've had to pass a series of rigorous tests. "I'm sorry to break up the party, kids. But it's time for me to take Henry home so he can pack up his things and say goodbye to his family. Then we will be on our merry way!"

Dee's eyes immediately fill with tears. She waits for Henry to gather his belongings and hoist his bag onto his back. Then she hugs him again. "Text us when you get there."

"And don't leave out any details about your trip on the beam bike," Eugene adds, hugging Henry after Dee. "I've always wanted to ride one."

"We'll see you in the spring," Bella says, next in line for a hug. Her sunglasses hide her tears, but her sniffles give her away. "By then, I just know you're going to be the most powerful psy-chic *ever*."

Charlie is the last to hug Henry. "I'm so glad we met you," they say, squeezing tight. Henry holds on to Charlie the longest. When he finally lets go, he has a strange look on his face.

"I know it's sad to say goodbye," Kathleen says. "But it's only for a short while. And when you return, you'll be a happier, healthier version of yourself."

Henry still seems uncertain. He steps off the picnic blanket, moving toward Kathleen, then gets hit with the cold and starts to shiver. He stops walking and turns back to face his friends.

Dee frowns, sensing something isn't right. "What's wrong, Henry?"

Henry looks at Kathleen. "I'm not sure. . . ." He looks back at his friends. "I think . . . I think I just saw something."

"What do you mean?" Bella says. "A vision?"

"Fascinating," Kathleen says. "Your visions are already evolving."

"I saw a castle," Henry recalls. "And a banshee woman, running away from someone. It looked like she was afraid." He furrows his brow like he's trying to remember. "She was speaking Spanish, so I couldn't understand most of what she said. . . . There was just one word I could make out."

Here, Henry looks directly at Charlie. "She said your name."

Charlie's face goes blank with fear. "Mom?"

Henry nods.

"I'm sorry, Charlie," he says, a grave look on his face. "But I think your mom is in trouble."